NON SANZ DROICT.

William Shakespeare

The Tragedy of
OTHELLO
The Moor of Venice

Edited by Alvin Kernan

The Signet Classic Shakespeare
GENERAL EDITOR: SYLVAN BARNET

Revised and Updated Bibliography

A SIGNET CLASSIC
NEW AMERICAN LIBRARY
TIMES MIRROR
NEW YORK AND SCARBOROUGH, ONTARIO
THE NEW ENGLISH LIBRARY LIMITED, LONDON

SIGNET, SIGNET CLASSICS, MENTOR, PLUME AND MERIDIAN BOOKS
are published *in the United States* by
The New American Library, Inc.,
1633 Broadway, New York, New York 10019,
in Canada by The New American Library of Canada Limited,
81 Mack Avenue, Scarborough, M1L 1M8, Ontario,
in the United Kingdom by The New English Library Limited,
Barnard's Inn, Holborn, London, EC1N 2JR, England.

16   17   18   19   20   21   22   23   24

PRINTED IN THE UNITED STATES OF AMERICA

Contents

Shakespeare: Prefatory Remarks

Between the record of his baptism in Stratford on 26 April 1564 and the record of his burial in Stratford on 25 April 1616, some forty documents name Shakespeare, and many others name his parents, his children, and his grandchildren. More facts are known about William Shakespeare than about any other playwright of the period except Ben Jonson. The facts should, however, be distinguished from the legends. The latter, inevitably more engaging and better known, tell us that the Stratford boy killed a calf in high style, poached deer and rabbits, and was forced to flee to London, where he held horses outside a playhouse. These traditions are only traditions; they may be true, but no evidence supports them, and it is well to stick to the facts.

Mary Arden, the dramatist's mother, was the daughter of a substantial landowner; about 1557 she married John Shakespeare, who was a glovemaker and trader in various farm commodities. In 1557 John Shakespeare was a member of the Council (the governing body of Stratford), in 1558 a constable of the borough, in 1561 one of the two town chamberlains, in 1565 an alderman (entitling him to the appelation "Mr."), in 1568 high bailiff—the town's highest political office, equivalent to mayor. After 1577, for an unknown reason he drops out of local politics. The birthday of William Shakespeare, the eldest son of this locally prominent man, is unrecorded; but the Stratford parish register records that the infant was baptized on 26 April 1564. (It is quite possible that he was born on 23 April, but this date has probably been assigned by tradition because it is the date on which, fifty-two years later, he died.) The attendance records of the Stratford grammar school of the period are not extant, but it is reasonable to assume that the son of a local official attended the school and received substantial training in Latin. The masters of the school from Shakespeare's seventh to fifteenth years held Oxford degrees; the Elizabethan curriculum excluded mathematics and the natural sciences but taught a good deal of Latin rhetoric, logic, and literature. On 27 November 1582 a marriage license was issued to Shakespeare and Anne Hathaway, eight years his senior. The couple had a child in May, 1583. Perhaps the marriage was necessary, but perhaps the couple had earlier engaged in a formal "troth-plight," which would render their children legitimate even if no further ceremony were performed. In 1585 Anne Hathaway bore Shakespeare twins.

That Shakespeare was born is excellent; that he married and had children is pleasant; but that we know nothing about his departure from Stratford to London, or about the beginning of his theatrical career, is lamentable and must be admitted. We would gladly sacrifice details about his children's baptism for details about his earliest days on the stage. Perhaps the poaching episode is true (but it is first reported almost a century after Shakespeare's death), or perhaps he first left Stratford to be a schoolteacher, as another tradition holds; perhaps he was moved by

Such wind as scatters young men through the world,
To seek their fortunes further than at home
Where small experience grows.

In 1592, thanks to the cantankerousness of Robert Greene, a rival playwright and a pamphleteer, we have our first reference, a snarling one, to Shakespeare as an actor and playwright. Greene warns those of his own educated friends who wrote for the theater against an actor who has presumed to turn playwright:

> There is an upstart crow, beautified with our feathers, that with his *tiger's heart wrapped in a player's hide* supposes he is as well able to bombast out a blank verse as the best of you, and being an absolute Johannes-factotum is in his own conceit the only Shake-scene in a country.

The reference to the player, as well as the allusion to Aesop's crow (who strutted in borrowed plumage, as an actor struts in fine words not his own), makes it clear that by this date Shakespeare had both acted and written. That Shakespeare is meant is indicated not only by "Shake-scene" but by the parody of a line from one of Shakespeare's plays, *3 Henry VI*: "O, tiger's heart wrapped in a woman's hide." If Shakespeare in 1592 was prominent enough to be attacked by an envious dramatist, he probably had served an apprenticeship in the theater for at least a few years.

In any case, by 1592 Shakespeare had acted and written, and there are a number of subsequent references to him as an actor: documents indicate that in 1598 he is a "principal comedian," in 1603 a "principal tragedian," in 1608 he is one of the "men players." The profession of actor was not for a gentleman, and it occasionally drew the scorn of university men who resented writing speeches for persons less educated than themselves, but it was respectable enough: players, if prosperous, were in effect members of the bourgeoisie, and there is nothing to suggest that Stratford considered William Shakespeare less than a solid citizen. When, in 1596, the Shakespeares were granted a coat of arms, the grant was made to Shakespeare's father, but probably William Shakespeare (who next year bought the second-largest house in town) had arranged the matter on his own behalf. In subsequent transactions he is occasionally styled a gentleman.

Although in 1593 and 1594 Shakespeare published two narrative poems dedicated to the Earl of Southampton, *Venus and Adonis* and *The Rape of Lucrece*, and may well have written most or all of his sonnets in the middle nineties, Shakespeare's literary activity seems to have been almost entirely devoted to the theater. (It may be significant that the two narrative poems were written in years when the plague closed the theaters for several months.) In 1594 he was a charter member of a theatrical company called the Chamberlain's Men (which in 1603 changed its name to the King's Men); until he retired to Stratford (about 1611, apparently), he was with this remarkably stable company. From 1599 this company acted primarily at the Globe Theatre, in which Shakespeare held a one-tenth interest. Other Elizabethan dramatists are known to have acted, but no other is known also to have been entitled to a share in the profits of the playhouse.

Shakespeare's first eight published plays did not have his name on them, but this is not remarkable; the most popular play of the sixteenth century, Thomas Kyd's *The Spanish Tragedy,* went through many editions without naming Kyd, and Kyd's authorship is known only because a book on the profession of acting happens to quote (and attribute to Kyd) some lines on the interest of Roman emperors in the drama. What is remarkable is that after 1598 Shakespeare's name commonly appears on printed plays—some of which are not his. Another indication of his popularity comes from Francis Meres, author of *Palladis Tamia: Wit's Treasury* (1598): in this anthology of snippets accompanied by an essay on literature, many playwrights are mentioned, but Shakespeare's name occurs more often than any other, and Shakespeare is the only playwright whose plays are listed.

From his acting, playwriting, and share in a theater, Shakespeare seems to have made considerable money. He put it to work, making substantial investments in Stratford real estate. When he made his will (less than a month before he died), he sought to leave his property intact to his descendants. Of small bequests to relatives and to friends (including three actors, Richard Burbage, John Heminges, and Henry Condell), that to his wife of the second-best bed has provoked the most comment; perhaps it was the bed the couple had slept in, the best being reserved for visitors. In any case, had Shakespeare not excepted it, the bed would have gone (with the rest of his household possessions) to his daughter and her husband. On 25 April 1616 he was buried within the chancel of the church at Stratford. An unattractive monument to his memory, placed on a wall near the grave, says he died on 23 April. Over the grave itself are the lines, perhaps by Shakespeare, that (more than his literary fame) have kept his bones undisturbed in the crowded burial ground where old bones were often dislodged to make way for new:

> Good friend, for Jesus' sake forbear
> To dig the dust enclosèd here.
> Blessed be the man that spares these stones
> And cursed be he that moves my bones.

Thirty-seven plays, as well as some nondramatic poems, are held to constitute the Shakespeare canon. The dates of composition of most of the works are highly uncertain, but there is often evidence of a *terminus a quo* (starting point) and/or a *terminus ad quem* (terminal point) that provides a framework for intelligent guessing. For example, *Richard II* cannot be earlier than 1595, the publication date of some material to which it is indebted; *The Merchant of Venice* cannot be later than 1598, the year Francis Meres mentioned it. Sometimes arguments for a date hang on an alleged topical allusion, such as the lines about the unseasonable weather in *A Midsummer Night's Dream,* II.i.81–117, but such an allusion (if indeed it is an allusion) can be variously interpreted, and in any case there is always the possibility that a topical allusion was inserted during a revision, years after the composition of a play. Dates are often attributed on the basis of style, and although conjectures about style usually rest on other conjectures, sooner or later one must rely on one's literary sense. There is no real proof, for example, that *Othello* is not as early as *Romeo and Juliet,* but one feels *Othello* is later, and because the first record of its performance is 1604, one is glad enough to set its composition at that date and not push it back into Shakespeare's early years. The following chronology, then, is as much indebted to informed guesswork and sensitivity as it is to fact. The dates, necessarily imprecise, indicate something like a scholarly consensus.

PLAYS

1588–93	*The Comedy of Errors*
1588–94	*Love's Labor's Lost*
1590–91	*2 Henry VI*
1590–91	*3 Henry VI*
1591–92	*1 Henry VI*
1592–93	*Richard III*
1592–94	*Titus Andronicus*
1593–94	*The Taming of the Shrew*
1593–95	*The Two Gentlemen of Verona*
1594–96	*Romeo and Juliet*
1595	*Richard II*
1594–96	*A Midsummer Night's Dream*
1596–97	*King John*
1596–97	*The Merchant of Venice*
1597	*1 Henry IV*
1597–98	*2 Henry IV*
1598–1600	*Much Ado About Nothing*
1598–99	*Henry V*
1599	*Julius Caesar*
1599–1600	*As You Like It*
1599–1600	*Twelfth Night*
1600–01	*Hamlet*
1597–1601	*The Merry Wives of Windsor*
1601–02	*Troilus and Cressida*
1602–04	*All's Well That Ends Well*
1603–04	*Othello*
1604	*Measure for Measure*
1605–06	*King Lear*
1605–06	*Macbeth*
1606–07	*Antony and Cleopatra*
1605–08	*Timon of Athens*
1607–09	*Coriolanus*
1608–09	*Pericles*

1609–10   *Cymbeline*
1610–11   *The Winter's Tale*
1611–12   *The Tempest*
1612–13   *Henry VIII*

POEMS

1592   *Venus and Adonis*
1593–94   *The Rape of Lucrece*
1593–1600   *Sonnets*
1600–01   *The Phoenix and the Turtle*

Shakespeare's Theater

In Shakespeare's infancy, Elizabethan actors performed wherever they could—in great halls, at court, in the courtyards of inns. The innyards must have made rather unsatisfactory theaters: on some days they were unavailable because carters bringing goods to London used them as depots; when available, they had to be rented from the innkeeper; perhaps most important, London inns were subject to the Common Council of London, which was not well disposed toward theatricals. In 1574 the Common Council required that plays and playing places in London be licensed. It asserted that

> sundry great disorders and inconveniences have been found to ensue to this city by the inordinate haunting of great multitudes of people, specially youth, to plays, interludes, and shows, namely occasion of frays and quarrels, evil practices of incontinency in great inns having chambers and secret places adjoining to their open stages and galleries,

and ordered that innkeepers who wished licenses to hold performances put up a bond and make contributions to the poor.

The requirement that plays and innyard theaters be licensed, along with the other drawbacks of playing at inns, probably drove James Burbage (a carpenter-turned-actor) to rent in 1576 a plot of land northeast of the city walls and to build here—on property outside the jurisdiction of the city—England's first permanent construction designed for plays. He called it simply the Theatre. About all that is known of its construction is that it was wood. It soon had imitators, the most famous being the Globe (1599), built across the Thames (again outside the city's jurisdiction), out of timbers of the Theatre, which had been dismantled when Burbage's lease ran out.

There are three important sources of information about the structure of Elizabethan playhouses—drawings, a contract, and stage directions in plays. Of drawings, only the so-called De Witt drawing (*c.* 1596) of the Swan—really a friend's copy of De Witt's drawing—is of much significance. It shows a building of three tiers, with a stage jutting from a wall into the yard or center of the building. The tiers are roofed, and part of the stage is covered by a roof that projects from the rear and is supported at its front on two posts, but the groundlings, who paid a penny to stand in front of the stage, were exposed to the sky. (Performances in such a playhouse were held only in the daytime; artificial illumination was not used.) At the rear of the stage are two doors; above the stage is a gallery. The second major source of information, the contract for the Fortune, specifies that although the Globe is to be the model, the Fortune is to be square, eighty feet outside and fifty-five inside. The stage is to be forty-three feet broad, and is to extend into the middle of the yard (i.e., it is twenty-seven and a half feet deep). For patrons willing to pay more than the general admission charged of the groundlings, there were to be three galleries provided with seats. From the third chief source, stage directions, one learns that entrance to the stage was by doors, presumably spaced widely apart at the rear ("Enter one citizen at one door, and another at the other"), and that in addition to the platform stage there was occasionally some sort of curtained booth or alcove allowing for "discovery" scenes, and some sort of playing space "aloft" or "above" to represent (for example) the top of a city's walls or a room above the street. Doubtless each theater had its own peculiarities, but perhaps we can talk about a "typical" Elizabethan theater if we realize that no theater need exactly have fit the description, just as no father is the typical father with 3.7 children. This hypothetical theater is wooden, round or polygonal (in *Henry V* Shakespeare calls it a "wooden *O*"), capable of holding some eight hundred spectators standing in the yard around the projecting elevated stage and some fifteen hundred additional spectators seated in the three roofed galleries. The stage, protected by a "shadow" or "heavens" or roof, is entered by two doors; behind the doors is the "tiring house" (attiring house, i.e., dressing room), and above the doors is some sort of gallery that may sometimes hold spectators but that can be used (for example) as the bedroom from which Romeo—according to a stage direction in one text—"goeth down." Some evidence suggests that a throne can be lowered onto the platform stage, perhaps from the "shadow"; certainly characters can descend from the stage through a trap or traps into the cellar or "hell." Sometimes this space beneath the platform accommodates a sound-effects man or musician (in *Antony and Cleopatra* "music of the hautboys is under the stage") or an actor (in *Hamlet* the "Ghost cries under the stage"). Most characters simply walk on and off, but because there is no curtain in front of the platform, corpses will have to be carried off (Hamlet must lug Polonius' guts into the neighbor room) or will have to fall at the rear, where the curtain on the alcove or booth can be drawn to conceal them.

Such may have been the so-called "public theater." Another kind of theater, called the "private theater" because its much greater admission charge limited its audience to the wealthy or the prodigal, must be briefly mentioned. The private theater was basically a large room, entirely roofed, and therefore artificially illuminated, with a stage at one end. In 1576 one such theater was established in Blackfriars, a Dominican priory in London that had been suppressed in 1538 and confiscated by the Crown and thus was not under the city's jurisdiction. All the actors in the Blackfriars theater were boys about eight to thirteen years old (in the public theaters similar boys played female parts, but a boy Lady Macbeth played to a man Macbeth). This private theater had a precarious existence, and ceased operations in 1584. In 1596 James Burbage, who had already made theatrical history by building the Theatre, began to construct a second Blackfriars theater. He died in 1597, and for several years this second Blackfriars theater was used by a troupe of boys, but in 1608 two of Burbage's sons and five other actors (including Shakespeare) became joint operators of the theater, using it in the winter when the open-air Globe was unsuitable. Perhaps such a smaller theater, roofed, artificially illuminated, and with a tradition of a courtly audience, exerted an influence on Shakespeare's late plays.

Performances in the private theaters may well have had intermissions during which music was played, but in the public theaters the action was probably uninterrupted, flowing from scene to scene almost without a break. Actors would enter, speak, exit, and others would immediately enter and establish (if necessary) the new locale by a few properties and by words and gestures. Here are some samples of Shakespeare's scene painting:

> This is Illyria, lady.
>
> Well, this is the Forest of Arden.
>
> This castle hath a pleasant seat; the air
> Nimbly and sweetly recommends itself
> Unto our gentle senses.

On the other hand, it is a mistake to conceive of the Elizabethan stage as bare. Although Shakespeare's Chorus in *Henry V* calls the stage an "unworthy scaffold" and urges the spectators to "eke out our performance with your mind," there was considerable spectacle. The last act of *Macbeth*, for example, has five stage directions calling for "drum and colors," and another sort of appeal to the eye is indicated by the stage direction "Enter Macduff, with Macbeth's head." Some scenery and properties may have been substantial; doubtless a throne was used, and in one play of the period we encounter this direction: "Hector takes up a great piece of rock and casts at Ajax, who tears up a young tree by the roots and assails Hector." The matter is of some importance, and will be glanced at again in the next section.

The Texts of Shakespeare

Though eighteen of his plays were published during his lifetime, Shakespeare seems never to have supervised their publication. There is nothing unusual here; when a playwright sold a play to a theatrical company, he surrendered his ownership of it. Normally a company would not publish the play, because to publish it meant to allow competitors to acquire the piece. Some plays, however, did get published: apparently treacherous actors sometimes pieced together a play for a publisher, sometimes a company in need of money sold a play, and sometimes a company allowed a play to be published that no longer drew audiences. That Shakespeare did not concern himself with publication, then, is scarcely remarkable; of his contemporaries only Ben Jonson carefully supervised the publication of his own plays. In 1623, seven years after Shakespeare's death, John Heminges and Henry Condell (two senior members of Shakespeare's company, who had performed with him for about twenty years) collected his plays—published and unpublished—into a large volume, commonly called the First Folio. (A folio is a volume consisting of sheets that have been folded once, each sheet thus making two leaves, or four pages. The eighteen plays published during Shakespeare's lifetime had been issued one play per volume in small books called quartos. Each sheet in a quarto has been folded twice, making four leaves, or eight pages.) The First Folio contains thirty-six plays; a thirty-seventh, *Pericles*, though not in the Folio is regarded as canonical. Heminges and Condell suggest in an address "To the great variety of readers" that the republished plays are presented in better form than in the quartos: "Before you were abused with diverse stolen and surreptitious copies, maimed and deformed by the frauds and stealths of injurious impostors that exposed them; even those, are now offered to your view cured and perfect of their limbs, and all the rest absolute in their numbers, as he [i.e., Shakespeare] conceived them."

Whoever was assigned to prepare the texts for publication in the First Folio seems to have taken his job seriously and yet not to have performed it with uniform care. The sources of the texts seem to have been, in general, good unpublished copies or the best published copies. The first play in the collection, *The Tempest,* is divided into acts and scenes, has unusually full stage directions and descriptions of spectacle, and concludes with a list of the characters, but the editor was not able (or willing) to present all of the succeeding texts so fully dressed. Later texts occasionally show signs of carelessness: in one scene of *Much Ado About Nothing* the names of actors, instead of characters, appear as speech prefixes (presumably evidence that the printer's copy for this play was a prompt copy); proofreading throughout the Folio is spotty and apparently was done without reference to the printer's copy; the pagination of *Hamlet* jumps from 156 to 257.

A modern editor of Shakespeare must first select his copy; no problem if the play exists only in the Folio, but a considerable problem if the relationship between a quarto and the Folio—or an early quarto and a later one—is unclear. When an editor has chosen what seems to him to be the most authoritative text or texts for his copy, he has not done with making decisions. First of all, he must reckon with Elizabethan spelling. If he is not producing a facsimile, he probably modernizes it, but ought he to preserve the old form of words that apparently were pronounced quite unlike their modern forms—"lanthorn," "alabaster"? If he preserves these forms, is he really preserving Shakespeare's forms or perhaps those of a compositor in the printing house? What is one to do when one finds "lanthorn" and "lantern" in adjacent lines? (The editors of this series in general, but not invariably, assume that words should be spelled in their modern forms.) Elizabethan punctuation, too, presents problems. For example, in the First Folio, the only text for the play, Macbeth rejects his wife's idea that he can wash the blood from his hand:

> no: this my Hand will rather
> The multitudinous Seas incarnadine,
> Making the Greene one, Red.

Obviously an editor will remove the superfluous capitals, and he will probably alter the spelling to "incarnadine," but will he leave the comma before "red," letting Macbeth speak of the sea as "the green one," or will he (like most modern editors) remove the comma and thus have Macbeth say that his hand will make the ocean *uniformly* red?

An editor will sometimes have to change more than spelling or punctuation. Macbeth says to his wife:

> I dare do all that may become a man,
> Who dares no more, is none.

For two centuries editors have agreed that the second line is unsatisfactory, and have emended "no" to "do": "Who dares do more is none." But when in the same play Ross says that fearful persons

> floate vpon a wilde and violent Sea
> Each way, and moue,

need "move" be emended to "none," as it often is, on the hunch that the compositor misread the manuscript? The editors of the Signet Classic Shakespeare have restrained themselves from making abundant emendations. In their minds they hear Dr. Johnson on the dangers of emending: "I have adopted the Roman sentiment, that it is more honorable to save a citizen than to kill an enemy." Some departures (in addition to spelling, punctuation, and lineation) from the copy text have of course been made, but the original readings are listed in a note following the play, so that the reader can evaluate them for himself.

The editors of the Signet Classic Shakespeare, following tradition, have added line numbers and in many cases act and scene divisions as well as indications of locale at the beginning of scenes. The Folio divided most of the plays into acts and some into scenes. Early eighteenth-century editors increased the divisions. These divisions, which provide a convenient way of referring to passages in the plays, have been retained, but when not in the text chosen as the basis for the Signet Classic text they are enclosed in square brackets [ ] to indicate that they are editorial additions. Similarly, although no play of Shakespeare's published during his lifetime was equipped with indications of locale at the heads of scene divisions, locales have here been added in square brackets for the convenience of the reader, who lacks the information afforded to spectators by costumes, properties, and gestures. The spectator can tell at a glance he is in the throne room, but without an editorial indication the reader may be puzzled for a while. It should be mentioned, incidentally, that there are a few authentic stage directions—perhaps Shakespeare's, perhaps a prompter's—that suggest locales: for example, "Enter Brutus in his orchard," and "They go up into the Senate house." It is hoped that the bracketed additions provide the reader with the sort of help provided in these two authentic directions, but it is equally hoped that the reader will remember that the stage was not loaded with scenery.

No editor during the course of his work can fail to recollect some words Heminges and Condell prefixed to the Folio:

It had been a thing, we confess, worthy to have been wished, that the author himself had lived to have set forth and overseen his own writings. But since it hath been ordained otherwise, and he by death departed from that right, we pray you do not envy his friends the office of their care and pain to have collected and published them.

Nor can an editor, after he has done his best, forget Heminges' and Condell's final words: "And so we leave you to other of his friends, whom if you need can be your guides. If you need them not, you can lead yourselves, and others. And such readers we wish him."

SYLVAN BARNET
Tufts University

Introduction

When Shakespeare wrote *Othello,* about 1604, his knowledge of human nature and his ability to dramatize it in language and action were at their height. The play offers, even in its minor characters, a number of unusually full and profound studies of humanity: Brabantio, the sophisticated, civilized Venetian senator, unable to comprehend that his delicate daughter could love and marry a Moor, speaking excitedly of black magic and spells to account for what his mind cannot understand; Cassio, the gentleman-soldier, polished in manners and gracious in bearing, wildly drunk and revealing a deeply rooted pride in his ramblings about senior officers being saved before their juniors; Emilia, the sensible and conventional waiting woman, making small talk about love and suddenly remarking that though she believes adultery to be wrong, still if the price were high enough she would sell—and so, she believes, would most women. The vision of human nature which the play offers is one of ancient terrors and primal drives—fear of the unknown, pride, greed, lust—underlying smooth, civilized surfaces—the noble senator, the competent and well-mannered lieutenant, the conventional gentlewoman.

The contrast between surface manner and inner nature is even more pronounced in two of the major characters. "Honest Iago" conceals beneath his exterior of the plain soldier and blunt, practical man of the world a diabolism so intense as to defy rational explanation—it must be taken like lust or pride as simply a given part of human nature, an anti-life spirit which seeks the destruction of everything outside the self. Othello appears in the opening acts as the very personification of self-control, of the man with so secure a sense of his own worth that nothing can ruffle the consequent calmness of mind and manner. But the man who has roamed the wild and savage world unmoved by its terrors, who has not changed countenance when the cannon killed his brother standing beside him, this man is still capable of believing his wife a whore on the slightest of evidence and committing murders to revenge himself. In Desdemona alone do the heart and the hand go together: she is what she seems to be. Ironically, she alone is accused of pretending to be what she is not. Her very openness and honesty make her suspect in a world where few men are what they appear, and her chastity is inevitably brought into question in a world where every other major character is in some degree touched with sexual corruption.

Most criticism of *Othello* has concerned itself with exploring the depths of these characters and tracing the intricate, mysterious operations of their minds. I should like, however, to leave this work to the individual reader and to the critical essays printed at the back of this volume in order to discuss, briefly, what might be called the "gross mechanics" of the play, the larger patterns in which events and characters are arranged. These patterns are the context within which the individual characters are defined, just as the pattern of a sentence is the context which defines the exact meaning of the individual words within it.

Othello is probably the most neatly, the most formally constructed of Shakespeare's plays. Every character is, for example, balanced by another similar or contrasting character. Desdemona is balanced by her opposite, Iago; love and concern for others at one end of the scale, hatred and concern for self at the other. The true and loyal soldier Cassio balances the false and traitorous soldier Iago. These balances and contrasts throw into relief the essential qualities of the characters. Desdemona's love, for example, shows up a good deal more clearly in contrast to Iago's hate, and vice versa. The values of contrast are increased and the full range of human nature displayed by extending these simple contrasts into developing series. The essential purity of Desdemona stands in contrast to the more "practical" view of chastity held by Emilia, and her view in turn is illuminated by the workaday view of sensuality held by the courtesan Bianca, who treats love, ordinarily, as a commodity. Or, to take another example, Iago's success in fooling Othello is but the culmination of a series of such betrayals that includes the duping of Roderigo, Brabantio, and Cassio. Each duping is the explanatory image of the other, for in every case Iago's method and end are the same: he plays on and teases to life some hitherto controlled and concealed dark passion in his victim. In each case he seeks in some way the same end, the symbolic murder of Desdemona, the destruction in some form of the life principle of which she is the major embodiment.

These various contrasts and parallelisms ultimately blend into a larger, more general pattern that is the central movement of the play. We can begin to see this pattern in the "symbolic geography" of the play. Every play, or work of art, creates its own particular image of space and time, its own symbolic world. The outer limits of the world of *Othello* are defined by the Turks—the infidels, the unbelievers, the "general enemy" as the play calls them— who, just over the horizon, sail back and forth trying to confuse and trick the Christians in order to invade their dominions and destroy them. Out beyond the horizon, reported but unseen, are also those "anters vast and deserts idle" of which Othello speaks. Out there is a land of "rough quarries, rocks, and hills whose heads touch heaven" inhabited by "cannibals that each other eat" and monstrous forms of men "whose heads grow beneath their shoulders." On the edges of this land is the raging ocean with its "high seas, and howling winds," its "guttered rocks and congregated sands" hidden beneath the waters to "enclog the guiltless keel."

Within the circle formed by barbarism, monstrosity, sterility, and the brute power of nature lie the two Christian strongholds of Venice and Cyprus. Renaissance Venice was known for its wealth acquired by trade, its political cunning, and its courtesans; but Shakespeare, while reminding us of the tradition of the "supersubtle Venetian," makes Venice over into a form of *The City,* the ageless image of government, of reason, of law, and of social concord. Here, when Brabantio's strong passions and irrational fears threaten to create riot and injustice, his grievances are examined by a court of law, judged by reason, and the verdict enforced by civic power. Here, the clear mind of the Senate probes the actions of the Turks, penetrates through their pretenses to their true purposes, makes sense of the frantic and fearful contradictory messages which pour in from the fleet, and arranges the necessary defense. Act I, Scene iii—the Senate scene—focuses on the magnificent speeches of Othello and Desdemona as they declare their love and explain it, but the lovers are surrounded, guarded, by the assembled, ranked governors of Venice, who control passions that otherwise would have led to a bloody street brawl and bring justice out of what otherwise would have been riot. The solemn presence and ordering power of the Senate would be most powerfully realized in a stage production, where the senators would appear in their rich robes, with all their symbols of office, seated in ranks around several excited individuals expressing such primal passions as pride of race, fear of dark powers, and violent love. In a play where so much of the language is magnificent, rich, and of heroic proportions, simpler statements come to seem more forceful; and the meaning of *The City* is perhaps nowhere more completely realized than in Brabantio's brief, secure answer to the first fearful cries of theft and talk of copulating animals that Iago and Roderigo send up from the darkness below his window:

> What tell'st thou me of robbing? This is Venice;
> My house is not a grange.   (I.i.102–03)

Here then are the major reference points on a map of the world of *Othello*: out at the far edge are the Turks, barbarism, disorder, and amoral destructive powers; closer and more familiar is Venice, *The City,* order, law, and reason. Cyprus, standing on the frontier between barbarism and *The City,* is not the secure fortress of civilization that Venice is. It is rather an outpost, weakly defended and far out in the raging ocean, close to the "general enemy" and the immediate object of his attack. It is a "town of war yet wild" where the "people's hearts [are] brimful of fear." Here passions are more explosive and closer to the surface than in Venice, and here, instead of the ancient order and established government of *The City,* there is only one man to control violence and defend civilization—the Moor Othello, himself of savage origins and a converted Christian.

The movement of the play is from Venice to Cyprus, from *The City* to the outpost, from organized society to a condition much closer to raw nature, and from collective life to the life of the solitary individual. This movement is a characteristic pattern in Shakespeare's plays, both comedies and tragedies: in *A Midsummer Night's Dream* the lovers and players go from the civilized, daylight world of Athens to the irrational, magical wood outside Athens and the primal powers of life represented by the elves and fairies; Lear moves from his palace and secure identity to the savage world of the heath where all values and all identities come into question; and everyone in *The Tempest* is shipwrecked at some time on Prospero's magic island, where life seen from a new perspective assumes strange and fantastic shapes. At the other end of this journey there is always some kind of return to *The City,* to the palace, and to old relationships, but the nature of this return differs widely in Shakespeare's plays. In *Othello* the movement at the end of the play is back toward Venice, the Turk defeated; but Desdemona, Othello, Emilia, and Roderigo do not return. Their deaths are the price paid for the return.

This passage from Venice to Cyprus to fight the Turk and encounter the forces of barbarism is the geographical form of an action that occurs on the social and psychological levels as well. That is, there are social and mental conditions that correspond to Venice and Cyprus, and there are forces at work in society and in man that correspond to the Turks, the raging seas, and "cannibals that each other eat."

The exposure to danger, the breakdown and the ultimate reestablishment of society—the parallel on the social level to the action on the geographical level—is quickly traced. We have already noted that the Venetian Senate embodies order, reason, justice, and concord, the binding forces that hold *The City* together. In Venice the ancient laws and the established customs of society work to control violent men and violent passions to ensure the safety and well-being of the individual and the group. But there are anarchic forces at work in the city, which threaten traditional social forms and relationships, and all these forces center in Iago. His discontent with his own rank and his determination to displace Cassio endanger the orderly military hierarchy in which the junior serves his senior. He endangers marriage, the traditional form for ordering male and female relationships, by his own unfounded suspicions of his wife and by his efforts to destroy Othello's marriage by fanning to life the darker, anarchic passions of Brabantio and Roderigo. He tries to subvert the operation of law and justice by first stirring up Brabantio to gather his followers and seek revenge in the streets; and then when the two warlike forces are met, Iago begins a quarrel with Roderigo in hopes of starting a brawl. The nature of the antisocial forces that Iago represents are focused in the imagery of his advice to Roderigo on how to call out to her father the news of Desdemona's marriage. Call, he says,

> with like timorous [frightening] accent and dire yell
> As when, by night and negligence, the fire
> Is spied in populous cities.   (I.i.72–74)

Fire, panic, darkness, neglect of duty—these are the natural and human forces that destroy great cities and turn their citizens to mobs.

In Venice, Iago's attempts to create civic chaos are frustrated by Othello's calm management of himself and the orderly legal proceedings of the Senate. In Cyprus, however, society is less secure—even as the island is more exposed to the Turks—and Othello alone is responsible for finding truth and maintaining order. Here Iago's poison begins to work, and he succeeds at once in manufacturing the riot that he failed to create in Venice. Seen on stage, the fight on the watch between Cassio and Montano is chaos come again: two drunken officers, charged with the defense of the town, trying to kill each other like savage animals, a bedlam of voices and shouts, broken, disordered furniture, and above all this the discordant clamor of the "dreadful" alarm bell—used to signal attacks and fire. This success is but the prologue for other more serious disruptions of society and of the various human relationships that it fosters. The General is set against his officer, husband against wife, Christian against Christian, servant against master. Justice becomes a travesty of itself as Othello—using legal terms such as "It is the *cause*"—assumes the offices of accuser, judge, jury, and executioner of his wife. Manners disappear as the Moor strikes his wife publicly and treats her maid as a procuress. The brightly lighted Senate chamber is now replaced with a dark Cyprus street where Venetians cut one another down and men are murdered from behind. This anarchy finally gives way in the last scene, when Desdemona's faith is proven, to a restoration of order and an execution of justice on the two major criminals.

What we have followed so far is a movement expressed in geographical and social symbols from Venice to a Cyprus exposed to attack, from *The City* to barbarism, from Christendom to the domain of the Turks, from order to riot, from justice to wild revenge and murder, from truth to falsehood. It now remains to see just what this movement means on the level of the individual in the heart and mind of man. Of the three major characters, Desdemona, Othello, and Iago, the first and the last do not change their natures or their attitudes toward life during the course of the play. These two are polar opposites, the antitheses of each other. To speak in the most general terms, Desdemona expresses in her language and actions an innocent, unselfish love and concern for others. Othello

catches her very essence when he speaks of her miraculous
love, which transcended their differences in age, color,
beauty, and culture:

> She loved me for the dangers I had passed,
> And I loved her that she did pity them. (I.iii.166–67)

This love in its various forms finds expression not only in
her absolute commitment of herself to Othello, but in her
gentleness, her kindness to others, her innocent trust in all
men, her pleas for Cassio's restoration to Othello's favor;
and it endures even past death at her husband's hands, for
she comes back to life for a moment to answer Emilia's
question, "who hath done this deed?" with the unbeliev-
able words,

> Nobody—I myself. Farewell.
> Commend me to my kind lord. O, farewell!
> (V.ii.123–24)

Iago is her opposite in every way. Where she is open
and guileless, he is never what he seems to be; where she
thinks the best of everyone, he thinks the worst, usually
turning to imagery of animals and physical functions to
express his low opinion of human nature; where she seeks
to serve and love others, he uses others to further his own
dark aims and satisfy his hatred of mankind; where she
is emotional and idealistic, he is icily logical and cynical.
Desdemona and Iago are much more complicated than
this, but perhaps enough has been said to suggest the nature
of these two moral poles of the play. One is a life force that
strives for order, community, growth, and light. The other
is an anti-life force that seeks anarchy, death, and darkness.
One is the foundation of all that men have built in the
world, including *The City;* the other leads back toward
ancient chaos and barbarism.

Othello, like most men, is a combination of the forces
of love and hate, which are isolated in impossibly pure
states in Desdemona and Iago. His psychic voyage from

Venice to Cyprus is a passage of the soul and the will from the values of one of these characters to those of the other. This passage is charted by his acceptance and rejection of one or the other. He begins by refusing to have Iago as his lieutenant, choosing the more "theoretical" though less experienced Cassio. He marries Desdemona. Though he is not aware that he does so, he expresses the full meaning of this choice when he speaks of her in such suggestive terms as "my soul's joy" and refers to her even as he is about to kill her, as "Promethean heat," the vital fire that gives life to the world. Similarly, he comes to know that all that is valuable in life depends on her love, and in the magnificent speech beginning, "O now, forever/ Farewell the tranquil mind" (III.iii.344–45), he details the emptiness of all human activity if Desdemona be proved false. But Iago, taking advantage of latent "Iagolike" feelings and thoughts in Othello, persuades him that Desdemona is only common clay. Othello then gives himself over to Iago at the end of III.iii, where they kneel together to plan the revenge, and Othello says, "Now art thou my lieutenant." To which Iago responds with blood-chilling simplicity, "I am your own forever." The full meaning of this choice is expressed, again unconsciously, by Othello when he says of Desdemona,

> Perdition catch my soul
> But I do love thee! and when I love thee not,
> Chaos is come again. (III.iii.90–92)

The murder of Desdemona acts out the final destruction in Othello himself of all the ordering powers of love, of trust, of the bond between human beings.

Desdemona and Iago then represent two states of mind, two understandings of life, and Othello's movement from one to the other is the movement on the level of character and psychology from Venice to Cyprus, from *The City* to anarchy. His return to *The City* and the defeat of the Turk is effected, at the expense of his own life, when he learns *what* he has killed and executes himself as the only fitting judgment on his act. His willingness to speak of what he has done—in contrast to Iago's sullen silence—is a willingness to recognize the meaning of Desdemona's faith and chastity, to acknowledge that innocence and love do exist, and that therefore *The City* can stand, though his life is required to validate the truth and justice on which it is built.

Othello offers a variety of interrelated symbols that locate and define in historical, natural, social, moral, and human terms those qualities of being and universal forces that are forever at war in the universe and between which tragic man is always in movement. On one side there are Turks, cannibals, barbarism, monstrous deformities of nature, the brute force of the sea, riot, mobs, darkness, Iago, hatred, lust, concern for the self only, and cynicism. On the other side there are Venice, *The City,* law, senates, amity, hierarchy, Desdemona, love, concern for others, and innocent trust. As the characters of the play act and speak, they bring together, by means of parallelism and metaphor, the various forms of the different ways of life. There is, for example, a meaningful similarity in the underhanded way Iago works and the ruse by which the Turks try to fool the Venetians into thinking they are bound for Rhodes when their object is Cyprus. Or, there is again a flash of identification when we hear that the reefs and shoals that threaten ships are "ensteeped," that is, hidden under the surface of the sea, as Iago is hidden under the surface of his "honesty." But Shakespeare binds the various levels of being more closely together by the use of imagery that compares things on one level of action with things on another. For example, when Iago swears that his low judgment of all female virtue "is true, or else I am a Turk" (II.i.113), logic demands, since one woman, Desdemona, *is* true and chaste, that we account him "a Turk." He is thus identified with the unbelievers, the Ottoman Turks, and that Asiatic power, which for centuries threatened Christendom, is shown to have its social and psychological equivalent in Iago's particular attitude toward life. Similarly, when Othello sees the drunken brawl on the watchtower, he exclaims,

> Are we turned Turks, and to ourselves do that
> Which heaven hath forbid the Ottomites? (II.iii.169–70)

At the very time when the historical enemy has been defeated, his fleet providentially routed by the great storm, his characteristics—drunken loss of control, brawling over honor, disorder—begin to conquer the island only so recently and fortuitously saved. The conquest continues, and the defender of the island, Othello, convinced of Desdemona's guilt, compares his determination to revenge himself to "the Pontic Sea, / Whose icy current and compulsive course / Nev'r keeps retiring ebb" (III.iii.450–52). The comparison tells us that in his rage and hatred he has become one with the savage seas and the brute, amoral powers of nature that are displayed in the storm scene at the beginning of Act II. But most important is Othello's identification of himself at the end of the play as the "base Judean" who "threw a pearl away richer than all his tribe." The more familiar Quarto reading is "base Indian," but both words point toward the barbarian who fails to recognize value and beauty when he possesses it—the primitive savage who picks up a pearl and throws it away not knowing its worth; or the Jews (Judas may be specifically meant) who denied and crucified another great figure of love, thinking they were dealing with only a troublesome rabble-rouser. A few lines further on Othello proceeds to the final and absolute identification of himself with the infidel. He speaks of a "malignant and a turbaned Turk" who "beat a Venetian and traduced the state," and he then acknowledges that he is that Turk by stabbing himself, even as he once stabbed the other unbeliever. So he ends as both the Turk and the destroyer of the Turk, the infidel and the defender of the faith.

When Iago's schemes are at last exposed, Othello, finding it impossible for a moment to believe that a *man* could have contrived such evil, stares at Iago's feet and then says sadly, "but that's a fable." What he hopes to find when he looks down are the cloven hoofs of the devil, and had they been there he would have been an actor in a morality play, tempted beyond his strength, like many a man before him, by a supernatural power outside himself. In some ways I have schematized *Othello* as just such a morality play, offering an allegorical journey between heaven and hell on a stage filled with purely symbolic figures. This is the kind of abstraction of art toward which criticism inevitably moves, and in this case the allegorical framework is very solidly there. But Othello does not see the cloven hoofs when he looks down; he sees a pair of human feet at the end of a very human body; and he is forced to realize that far from living in some simplified, "fabulous" world where evil is a metaphysical power raiding human life from without, he dwells where evil is somehow inextricably woven with good into man himself. On his stage the good angel does not return to heaven when defeated, but is murdered, and her body remains on the bed, "cold, cold." He lives where good intentions, past services, psychic weaknesses, and an inability to see through evil cannot excuse an act, as they might in some simpler world where more perfect justice existed. In short, Othello is forced to recognize that he lives in a tragic world, and he pays the price for having been great enough to inhabit it.

Here is the essence of Shakespeare's art, an ability to create immediate, full, and total life as men actually live and experience it; and yet at the same time to arrange this reality so that it gives substance to and derives shape from a formal vision of all life that comprehends and reaches back from man and nature through society and history to cosmic powers that operate through all time and space. His plays are both allegorical and realistic at once; his characters both recognizable men and at the same time devils, demigods, and forces in nature. I have discussed only the more allegorical elements in *Othello,* the skeleton of ideas and formal patterns within which the characters must necessarily be understood. But it is equally true that the exact qualities of the abstract moral values and ideas, their full reality, exist only in the characters. It is necessary to know that Desdemona represents one particular human value, love or charity, in order to avoid making such mistakes as searching for some tragic flaw in her which would justify her death. But at the same time, if we would know what love and charity *are* in all their fullness, then our definition can only be the actions, the language, the emotions of the character Desdemona. She is Shakespeare's word for love. If we wish to know not just the obvious fact that men choose evil over good, but *why* they do so, then we must look both analytically and feelingly at all the evidence that the world offers for believing that Desdemona is false and at all the biases in Othello's mind that predispose him to believe such evidence. Othello's passage from Venice to Cyprus, from absolute love for Desdemona to extinguishing the light in her bedchamber, and to the execution of himself, these are Shakespeare's words for tragic man.

ALVIN KERNAN
Yale University

The Tragedy of
OTHELLO
The Moor of Venice

The Names of the Actors

Othello, the Moor
Brabantio, father to Desdemona
Cassio, an honorable lieutenant
Iago, a villain
Roderigo, a gulled gentleman
Duke of Venice
Senators
Montano, Governor of Cyprus
Gentlemen of Cyprus
Lodovico and Gratiano, two noble Venetians
Sailors
Clown
Desdemona, wife to Othello
Emilia, wife to Iago
Bianca, a courtesan
[Messenger, Herald, Officers, Gentlemen,
   Musicians, Attendants
      Scene: Venice and Cyprus]

The Tragedy of Othello

ACT I

Scene I. [*Venice. A street.*]

Enter Roderigo and Iago.

Roderigo. Tush! Never tell me? I take it much un-
kindly
That thou, Iago, who hast had my purse
As if the strings were thine, shouldst know of this.

Iago. 'Sblood,° ¹ but you'll not hear me! If ever I did
dream
Of such a matter, abhor me.

Roderigo.   Thou told'st me   5
Thou didst hold him in thy hate.

Iago.   Despise me
If I do not. Three great ones of the city,
In personal suit to make me his lieutenant,
Off-capped° to him; and, by the faith of man,
I know my price; I am worth no worse a place.   10
But he, as loving his own pride and purposes,
Evades them with a bombast circumstance,°

---

¹ The degree sign (°) indicates a footnote, which is keyed to the text by
the line number. Text references are printed in *italic* type; the annota-
tion follows in roman type. I.i.⁴ *'Sblood* by God's blood ⁹ *Off-capped*
doffed their caps—as a mark of respect ¹² *bombast circumstance*
stuffed, roundabout speech

Horribly stuffed with epithets of war;
Nonsuits° my mediators. For, "Certes," says he,
"I have already chose my officer." And what was
15   he?
Forsooth, a great arithmetician,°
One Michael Cassio, a Florentine,
(A fellow almost damned in a fair wife)°
That never set a squadron in the field,
20   Nor the division of a battle knows
More than a spinster; unless the bookish theoric,
Wherein the tonguèd° consuls can propose
As masterly as he. Mere prattle without practice
Is all his soldiership. But he, sir, had th' election;
25   And I, of whom his eyes had seen the proof
At Rhodes, at Cyprus, and on other grounds
Christian and heathen, must be belee'd and calmed
By debitor and creditor. This counter-caster,°
He, in good time, must his lieutenant be,
And I—God bless the mark!—his Moorship's an-
80   cient.°

Roderigo. By heaven, I rather would have been his
      hangman.

Iago. Why, there's no remedy. 'Tis the curse of service:
Preferment goes by letter and affection,°
And not by old gradation,° where each second
85   Stood heir to th' first. Now, sir, be judge yourself,
Whether I in any just term am affinèd°
To love the Moor.

Roderigo.   I would not follow him then.

---

14 *Nonsuits* rejects   16 *arithmetician* theorist (rather than practical)
18 *A . . . wife* (a much-disputed passage, which is probably best taken as
a general sneer at Cassio as a dandy and a ladies' man. But in the story
from which Shakespeare took his plot the counterpart of Cassio is
married, and it may be that at the beginning of the play Shakespeare
had decided to keep him married but later changed his mind)
22 *tonguèd* eloquent   28 *counter-caster* i.e., a bookkeeper who *casts*
(reckons up) figures on a *counter* (abacus)   30 *ancient* standard-bearer;
an underofficer   33 *letter and affection* recommendations (from men
of power) and personal preference   34 *old gradation* seniority
36 *affined* bound

Iago. O, sir, content you.
    I follow him to serve my turn upon him.
    We cannot all be masters, nor all masters   40
    Cannot be truly followed. You shall mark
    Many a duteous and knee-crooking° knave
    That, doting on his own obsequious bondage,
    Wears out his time, much like his master's ass,
    For naught but provender; and when he's old,
      cashiered.   45
    Whip me such honest knaves! Others there are
    Who, trimmed in forms and visages of duty,
    Keep yet their hearts attending on themselves,
    And, throwing but shows of service on their lords,
    Do well thrive by them, and when they have lined
      their coats,   50
    Do themselves homage. These fellows have some
      soul; *he puts on show of loyalty*
    And such a one do I profess myself. For, sir,
    It is as sure as you are Roderigo,
    Were I the Moor, I would not be Iago. *If he were moore, he would*
    In following him, I follow but myself. *not trust I.* 55
    Heaven is my judge, not I for love and duty,
    But seeming so, for my peculiar° end;
    For when my outward action doth demonstrate *he keeps*
    The native° act and figure of my heart *private. He*
    In complement extern,° 'tis not long after *hides* 60
    But I will wear my heart upon my sleeve *his true*
    For daws to peck at; I am not what I am. *motives.*

Roderigo. What a full fortune does the thick-lips owe°
    If he can carry't thus!

Iago.   Call up her father,
    Rouse him. Make after him, poison his delight,
    Proclaim him in the streets, incense her kinsmen,   65
    And though he in a fertile climate dwell,
    Plague him with flies; though that his joy be joy,

---

42 *knee-crooking* bowing   57 *peculiar* personal   59 *native* natural, innate
60 *complement extern* outward appearances   63 *owe* own

Yet throw such chances of vexation on't
70 As it may lose some color.

Roderigo. Here is her father's house. I'll call aloud.

Iago. Do, with like timorous° accent and dire yell
As when, by night and negligence, the fire
Is spied in populous cities.

Roderigo. What, ho, Brabantio! Signior Brabantio,
75   ho!

Iago. Awake! What, ho, Brabantio! Thieves! Thieves!
Look to your house, your daughter, and your bags!
Thieves! Thieves!

                Brabantio above° [at a window].

Brabantio. What is the reason of this terrible summons?
80 What is the matter there?

Roderigo. Signior, is all your family within?

Iago. Are your doors locked?

Brabantio.   Why, wherefore ask you
this?

Iago. Zounds, sir, y'are robbed! For shame. Put on
your gown!
Your heart is burst, you have lost half your soul.
85 Even now, now, very now, an old black ram
Is tupping your white ewe. Arise, arise!
Awake the snorting citizens with the bell,
Or else the devil will make a grandsire of you.
Arise, I say!

Brabantio.   What, have you lost your wits?

Roderigo. Most reverend signior, do you know my
90   voice?

Brabantio. Not I. What are you?

---

72 *timorous* frightening   **78** s.d. *above* (i.e., on the small upper stage
above and to the rear of the main platform stage, which resembled the
projecting upper story of an Elizabethan house)

Roderigo. My name is Roderigo.

Brabantio.   The worser welcome!
  I have charged thee not to haunt about my doors.
  In honest plainness thou hast heard me say
  My daughter is not for thee; and now, in madness,   95
  Being full of supper and distemp'ring draughts,°
  Upon malicious knavery dost thou come
  To start° my quiet.

Roderigo. Sir, sir, sir——

Brabantio.   But thou must needs be sure
  My spirits and my place° have in their power   100
  To make this bitter to thee.

Roderigo.   Patience, good sir.

Brabantio. What tell'st thou me of robbing? This is
    Venice;
  My house is not a grange.°

Roderigo.   Most grave Brabantio,
  In simple and pure soul I come to you.

Iago. Zounds, sir, you are one of those that will not   105
  serve God if the devil bid you. Because we come
  to do you service and you think we are ruffians,
  you'll have your daughter covered with a Barbary°
  horse, you'll have your nephews° neigh to you,
  you'll have coursers for cousins,° and gennets for   110
  germans.°

Brabantio. What profane wretch art thou?

Iago. I am one, sir, that comes to tell you your daughter
  and the Moor are making the beast with two backs.

Brabantio. Thou art a villain.

Iago.   You are—a senator.   115

Brabantio. This thou shalt answer. I know thee,
  Roderigo.

⁹⁶ *distemp'ring draughts* unsettling drinks   ⁹⁸ *start* disrupt   ¹⁰⁰ *place* rank, i.e., of senator   ¹⁰³ *grange* isolated house   ¹⁰⁸ *Barbary* Arabian, i.e., Moorish   ¹⁰⁹ *nephews* i.e., grandsons   ¹¹⁰ *cousins* relations ¹¹⁰⁻¹¹ *gennets for germans* Spanish horses for blood relatives

Roderigo. Sir, I will answer anything. But I beseech
    you,
If't be your pleasure and most wise consent,
As partly I find it is, that your fair daughter,
120 At this odd-even° and dull watch o' th' night,
Transported, with no worse nor better guard
But with a knave of common hire, a gondolier,
To the gross clasps of a lascivious Moor—
If this be known to you, and your allowance,
125 We then have done you bold and saucy wrongs;
But if you know not this, my manners tell me
We have your wrong rebuke. Do not believe
That from the sense of all civility°
I thus would play and trifle with your reverence.
130 Your daughter, if you have not given her leave,
I say again, hath made a gross revolt,
Tying her duty, beauty, wit, and fortunes
In an extravagant° and wheeling stranger
Of here and everywhere. Straight satisfy yourself.
135 If she be in her chamber, or your house,
Let loose on me the justice of the state
For thus deluding you.

Brabantio.   Strike on the tinder, ho!
Give me a taper! Call up all my people!
This accident° is not unlike my dream.
140 Belief of it oppresses me already.
Light, I say! Light!   *Exit [above].*

Iago.   Farewell, for I must leave you.
It seems not meet, nor wholesome to my place,
To be produced—as, if I stay, I shall—
Against the Moor. For I do know the State,
145 However this may gall him with some check,°
Cannot with safety cast° him; for he's embarked
With such loud reason to the Cyprus wars,

---

120 *odd-even* between night and morning   128 *sense of all civility* feeling of what is proper   133 *extravagant* vagrant, wandering (Othello is
not Venetian and thus may be considered a wandering soldier of fortune)   139 *accident* happening   145 *check* restraint   146 *cast* dismiss

Which even now stands in act,° that for their souls
Another of his fathom° they have none
To lead their business; in which regard,   150
Though I do hate him as I do hell-pains,
Yet, for necessity of present life,
I must show out a flag and sign of love,
Which is indeed but sign. That you shall surely find
    him,
Lead to the Sagittary° the raisèd search;   155
And there will I be with him. So farewell.   *Exit.*

*Enter Brabantio [in his nightgown], with Servants
            and torches.*

Brabantio. It is too true an evil. Gone she is;
    And what's to come of my despisèd time
    Is naught but bitterness. Now, Roderigo,
    Where didst thou see her?—O unhappy girl!—   160
    With the Moor, say'st thou?—Who would be a
        father?—
    How didst thou know 'twas she?—O, she deceives
        me
    Past thought!—What said she to you? Get moe°
        tapers!
    Raise all my kindred!—Are they married, think
        you?

Roderigo. Truly I think they are.   165

Brabantio. O heaven! How got she out? O treason of
        the blood!
    Fathers, from hence trust not your daughters' minds
    By what you see them act.° Is there not charms
    By which the property° of youth and maidhood
    May be abused? Have you not read, Roderigo,   170
    Of some such thing?

Roderigo.   Yes, sir, I have indeed.

Brabantio. Call up my brother.—O, would you had
        had her!—

---

¹⁴⁸ *stands in act* takes place ¹⁴⁹ *fathom* ability ¹⁵⁵ *Sagittary* (probably
the name of an inn) ¹⁶³ *moe* more ¹⁶⁸ *act* do ¹⁶⁹ *property* true
nature

Some one way, some another.—Do you know
Where we may apprehend her and the Moor?

175 *Roderigo.* I think I can discover him, if you please
To get good guard and go along with me.

Brabantio. Pray you lead on. At every house I'll call;
I may command at most.—Get weapons, ho!
And raise some special officers of might.—
180   On, good Roderigo; I will deserve your pains.°
                                        Exeunt.

Scene II. [*A street.*]

Enter Othello, Iago, Attendants with torches.

Iago. Though in the trade of war I have slain men,
Yet do I hold it very stuff° o' th' conscience
To do no contrived murder. I lack iniquity
Sometime to do me service. Nine or ten times
I had thought t' have yerked° him here, under the
5   ribs.

Othello. 'Tis better as it is.

Iago.   Nay, but he prated,
And spoke such scurvy and provoking terms
Against your honor, that with the little godliness
I have
I did full hard forbear him. But I pray you, sir,
10   Are you fast married? Be assured of this,
That the magnifico° is much beloved,
And hath in his effect a voice potential
As double as the Duke's.° He will divorce you,
Or put upon you what restraint or grievance

---

180 *deserve your pains* be worthy of (and reward) your efforts
I.ii.² *stuff* essence   ⁵ *yerked* stabbed   ¹¹ *magnifico* nobleman   ¹²⁻¹³ *hath
. . . Duke's* i.e., can be as effective as the Duke

The law, with all his might to enforce it on,   15
Will give him cable.°

Othello.   Let him do his spite.
My services which I have done the Signiory°
Shall out-tongue his complaints. 'Tis yet to know° —
Which when I know that boasting is an honor
I shall promulgate—I fetch my life and being   20
From men of royal siege;° and my demerits°
May speak unbonneted to as proud a fortune
As this that I have reached.° For know, Iago,
But that I love the gentle Desdemona,
I would not my unhousèd° free condition   25
Put into circumscription and confine
For the seas' worth. But look, what lights come
   yond?

   Enter Cassio, with [Officers and] torches.

Iago. Those are the raisèd father and his friends.
You were best go in.

Othello.   Not I. I must be found.
My parts, my title, and my perfect soul°   30
Shall manifest me rightly. Is it they?

Iago. By Janus, I think no.

Othello. The servants of the Duke? And my lieutenant?
The goodness of the night upon you, friends.
What is the news?

Cassio.   The Duke does greet you, general;   35
And he requires your haste-posthaste appearance
Even on the instant.

Othello.   What is the matter, think you?

Cassio. Something from Cyprus, as I may divine.
It is a business of some heat. The galleys

---

¹⁶ *cable* range, scope   ¹⁷ *Signiory* the rulers of Venice   ¹⁸ *yet to know* unknown as yet   ²¹ *siege* rank   ²¹ *demerits* deserts   ²²⁻²³ *May . . . reached,* i.e., are the equal of the family I have married into   ²⁵ *unhousèd* unconfined   ³⁰ *perfect soul* clear, unflawed conscience

40   Have sent a dozen sequent° messengers
       This very night at one another's heels,
       And many of the consuls, raised and met,
       Are at the Duke's already. You have been hotly
           called for.
       When, being not at your lodging to be found,
45   The Senate hath sent about three several° quests
       To search you out.

Othello.   'Tis well I am found by you.
       I will but spend a word here in the house,
       And go with you.   [*Exit.*]

Cassio.   Ancient, what makes he here?
Iago. Faith, he tonight hath boarded a land carack.°
50   If it prove lawful prize, he's made forever.

Cassio. I do not understand.

Iago.   He's married.

Cassio.   To who?
                 [*Enter Othello.*]

Iago. Marry,° to—Come, captain, will you go?

Othello.   Have with you.

Cassio. Here comes another troop to seek for you.

   Enter Brabantio, Roderigo, with Officers and torches.

Iago. It is Brabantio. General, be advised.
       He comes to bad intent.

55   *Othello.*   Holla! Stand there!

Roderigo. Signior, it is the Moor.

Brabantio.   Down with him, thief!
                        [*They draw swords.*]

Iago. You, Roderigo? Come, sir, I am for you.

Othello. Keep up your bright swords, for the dew will
       rust them.

---

40 *sequent* successive 45 *several* separate 49 *carack* treasure ship
52 *Marry* By Mary (an interjection)

Good signior, you shall more command with years
Than with your weapons.   60

Brabantio. O thou foul thief, where hast thou stowed
  my daughter?
Damned as thou art, thou hast enchanted her!
For I'll refer me to all things of sense,°
If she in chains of magic were not bound,
Whether a maid so tender, fair, and happy,   65
So opposite to marriage that she shunned
The wealthy, curlèd darlings of our nation,
Would ever have, t' incur a general mock,°
Run from her guardage to the sooty bosom
Of such a thing as thou—to fear, not to delight.   70
Judge me the world if 'tis not gross in sense°
That thou hast practiced ° on her with foul charms,
Abused her delicate youth with drugs or minerals
That weaken motion.° I'll have't disputed on;
'Tis probable, and palpable to thinking.   75
I therefore apprehend and do attach° thee
For an abuser of the world, a practicer
Of arts inhibited and out of warrant.°
Lay hold upon him. If he do resist,
Subdue him at his peril.

Othello.   Hold your hands,   80
Both you of my inclining and the rest.
Were it my cue to fight, I should have known it
Without a prompter. Whither will you that I go
To answer this your charge?

Brabantio.   To prison, till fit time
Of law and course of direct session   85
Call thee to answer.

Othello.   What if I do obey?
How may the Duke be therewith satisfied,
Whose messengers are here about my side

---

⁶³ *refer . . . sense* i.e., base (my argument) on all ordinary under-
standing of nature ⁶⁸ *general mock* public shame ⁷¹ *gross in sense*
obvious ⁷² *practiced* used tricks ⁷⁴ *motion* thought, i.e., reason
⁷⁶ *attach* arrest ⁷⁸ *inhibited . . . warrant* prohibited and illegal (black
magic)

Upon some present° business of the state
To bring me to him?

90 *Officer.*   'Tis true, most worthy signior.
The Duke's in council, and your noble self
I am sure is sent for.

Brabantio.   How? The Duke in council?
In this time of the night? Bring him away.
Mine's not an idle cause. The Duke himself,
95 Or any of my brothers° of the state,
Cannot but feel this wrong as 'twere their own;
For if such actions may have passage free,
Bondslaves and pagans shall our statesmen be.
                              Exeunt.

Scene III. [*A council chamber.*]

*Enter Duke, Senators, and Officers [set at a table,
with lights and Attendants].*

Duke. There's no composition° in this news
That gives them credit.°

First Senator.   Indeed, they are disproportioned.
My letters say a hundred and seven galleys.

Duke. And mine a hundred forty.

Second Senator.   And mine two hundred.
5 But though they jump° not on a just accompt° —
As in these cases where the aim° reports
'Tis oft with difference—yet do they all confirm
A Turkish fleet, and bearing up to Cyprus.

Duke. Nay, it is possible enough to judgment.°
10   I do not so secure me in the error,

---

89 *present* immediate   95 *brothers* i.e., the other senators   I.iii.[1] *composition* agreement   [2] *gives them credit* makes them believable   [5] *jump* agree   [5] *just accompt* exact counting   [6] *aim* approximation   [9] *to judgment* when carefully considered

But the main article I do approve
In fearful sense.°

Sailor. (*Within*) What, ho! What, ho! What, ho!

Enter Sailor.

Officer. A messenger from the galleys.

Duke.　　　　　　　　Now? What's the business?

Sailor. The Turkish preparation makes for Rhodes.
So was I bid report here to the State　　　　　　15
By Signior Angelo.

Duke. How say you by this change?

First Senator.　　　　　　This cannot be
By no assay of reason. 'Tis a pageant°
To keep us in false gaze.° When we consider
Th' importancy of Cyprus to the Turk,　　　　20
And let ourselves again but understand
That, as it more concerns the Turk than Rhodes,
So may he with more facile question° bear it,
For that it stands not in such warlike brace,°
But altogether lacks th' abilities　　　　　25
That Rhodes is dressed in. If we make thought of
　this,
We must not think the Turk is so unskillful
To leave that latest which concerns him first,
Neglecting an attempt of ease and gain
To wake and wage a danger profitless.　　　　30

Duke. Nay, in all confidence he's not for Rhodes.

Officer. Here is more news.

Enter a Messenger.

Messenger. The Ottomites, reverend and gracious,
Steering with due course toward the isle of Rhodes,
Have there injointed them with an after° fleet.　　35

10–12 *I do . . . sense* i.e., just because the numbers disagree in the reports,
I do not doubt that the principal information (that the Turkish fleet is
out) is fearfully true　18 *pageant* show, pretense　19 *in false gaze* looking the wrong way　23 *facile question* easy struggle　24 *warlike brace*
"military posture"　35 *after* following

First Senator. Ay, so I thought. How many, as you
 guess?

Messenger. Of thirty sail; and now they do restem
 Their backward course, bearing with frank ap-
 pearance
 Their purposes toward Cyprus. Signior Montano,
40 Your trusty and most valiant servitor,
 With his free duty° recommends° you thus,
 And prays you to believe him.

Duke. 'Tis certain then for Cyprus.
 Marcus Luccicos, is not he in town?

45 *First Senator.* He's now in Florence.

Duke. Write from us to him; post-posthaste dispatch.

First Senator. Here comes Brabantio and the valiant
 Moor.

 *Enter Brabantio, Othello, Cassio, Iago, Roderigo,
 and Officers.*

Duke. Valiant Othello, we must straight° employ you
 Against the general° enemy Ottoman.
 [*To Brabantio*] I did not see you. Welcome, gentle
50 signior.
 We lacked your counsel and your help tonight.

Brabantio. So did I yours. Good your grace, pardon
 me.
 Neither my place, nor aught I heard of business,
 Hath raised me from my bed; nor doth the general
 care
55 Take hold on me; for my particular grief
 Is of so floodgate and o'erbearing nature
 That it engluts and swallows other sorrows,
 And it is still itself.

Duke. Why, what's the matter?

Brabantio. My daughter! O, my daughter!

---

41 *free duty* unlimited respect 41 *recommends* informs 48 *straight* at
once 49 *general* universal

Senators.   Dead?

Brabantio.   Ay, to me.
  She is abused, stol'n from me, and corrupted   60
  By spells and medicines bought of mountebanks;
  For nature so prepost'rously to err,
  Being not deficient, blind, or lame of sense,
  Sans° witchcraft could not.

Duke. Whoe'er he be that in this foul proceeding   65
  Hath thus beguiled your daughter of herself,
  And you of her, the bloody book of law
  You shall yourself read in the bitter letter
  After your own sense; yea, though our proper° son
  Stood in your action.°

Brabantio.   Humbly I thank your Grace.   70
  Here is the man—this Moor, whom now, it seems,
  Your special mandate for the state affairs
  Hath hither brought.

All.   We are very sorry for't.

Duke. [*To Othello*] What in your own part can you
  say to this?

Brabantio. Nothing, but this is so.   75

Othello. Most potent, grave, and reverend signiors,
  My very noble and approved° good masters,
  That I have ta'en away this old man's daughter,
  It is most true; true I have married her.
  The very head and front° of my offending   80
  Hath this extent, no more. Rude am I in my speech,
  And little blessed with the soft phrase of peace,
  For since these arms of mine had seven years' pith°
  Till now some nine moons wasted,° they have used
  Their dearest° action in the tented field;   85
  And little of this great world can I speak

---

[64] *Sans* without   [69] *proper* own   [70] *Stood in your action* were the
accused in your suit   [77] *approved* tested, proven by past performance
[80] *head and front* extreme form (*front* = forehead)   [83] *pith* strength
[84] *wasted* past   [85] *dearest* most important

More than pertains to feats of broils and battle;
And therefore little shall I grace my cause
In speaking for myself. Yet, by your gracious
    patience,
90 I will a round° unvarnished tale deliver
Of my whole course of love—what drugs, what
    charms,
What conjuration, and what mighty magic,
For such proceeding I am charged withal,
I won his daughter—

Brabantio.   A maiden never bold,
95 Of spirit so still and quiet that her motion
Blushed at herself;° and she, in spite of nature,
Of years, of country, credit, everything,
To fall in love with what she feared to look on!
It is a judgment maimed and most imperfect
100 That will confess perfection so could err
Against all rules of nature, and must be driven
To find out practices of cunning hell
Why this should be. I therefore vouch again
That with some mixtures pow'rful o'er the blood,
105 Or with some dram, conjured to this effect,
He wrought upon her.

Duke.   To vouch this is no proof,
Without more wider and more overt test
Than these thin habits° and poor likelihoods
Of modern° seeming do prefer against him.

110 First Senator. But, Othello, speak.
Did you by indirect and forcèd courses
Subdue and poison this young maid's affections?
Or came it by request, and such fair question°
As soul to soul affordeth?

Othello.   I do beseech you,
115 Send for the lady to the Sagittary

---

⁹⁰ *round* blunt   ⁹⁵⁻⁹⁶ *her motion/Blushed at herself* i.e., she was so
modest that she blushed at every thought (and movement)   ¹⁰⁸ *habits*
clothing   ¹⁰⁹ *modern* trivial   ¹¹³ *question* discussion

And let her speak of me before her father.
If you do find me foul in her report,
The trust, the office, I do hold of you
Not only take away, but let your sentence
Even fall upon my life.

Duke.   Fetch Desdemona hither.   120

Othello. Ancient, conduct them; you best know the
    place.
          [*Exit Iago, with two or three Attendants.*]

And till she come, as truly as to heaven
I do confess the vices of my blood,
So justly to your grave ears I'll present
How I did thrive in this fair lady's love,   125
And she in mine.

Duke.   Say it, Othello.

Othello. Her father loved me; oft invited me;
    Still° questioned me the story of my life
    From year to year, the battle, sieges, fortune
    That I have passed.   130
    I ran it through, even from my boyish days
    To th' very moment that he bade me tell it.
    Wherein I spoke of most disastrous chances,
    Of moving accidents by flood and field,
    Of hairbreadth scapes i' th' imminent° deadly
        breach,   135
    Of being taken by the insolent foe
    And sold to slavery, of my redemption thence
    And portance° in my travel's history,
    Wherein of anters° vast and deserts idle,°
    Rough quarries, rocks, and hills whose heads touch
        heaven,   140
    It was my hint to speak. Such was my process.
    And of the Cannibals that each other eat,
    The Anthropophagi,° and men whose heads

---

128 *Still* regularly   135 *imminent* threatening   138 *portance* manner of
acting   139 *anters* caves   139 *idle* empty, sterile   143 *Anthropophagi*
man-eaters

Grew beneath their shoulders. These things to hear
145   Would Desdemona seriously incline;
But still the house affairs would draw her thence;
Which ever as she could with haste dispatch,
She'd come again, and with a greedy ear
Devour up my discourse. Which I observing,
150   Took once a pliant hour, and found good means
To draw from her a prayer of earnest heart
That I would all my pilgrimage dilate,°
Whereof by parcels she had something heard,
But not intentively.° I did consent,
155   And often did beguile her of her tears
When I did speak of some distressful stroke
That my youth suffered. My story being done,
She gave me for my pains a world of kisses.
She swore in faith 'twas strange, 'twas passing°
    strange;
160   'Twas pitiful, 'twas wondrous pitiful.
She wished she had not heard it; yet she wished
That heaven had made her such a man. She thanked
    me,
And bade me, if I had a friend that loved her,
I should but teach him how to tell my story,
165   And that would woo her. Upon this hint I spake.
She loved me for the dangers I had passed,
And I loved her that she did pity them.
This only is the witchcraft I have used.
Here comes the lady. Let her witness it.

Enter Desdemona, Iago, Attendants.

170   *Duke.* I think this tale would win my daughter too.
Good Brabantio, take up this mangled matter at the
    best.°
Men do their broken weapons rather use
Than their bare hands.

---

152 *dilate* relate in full   154 *intentively* at length and in sequence
159 *passing* surpassing   171 *Take . . . best* i.e., make the best of this
disaster

Brabantio.   I pray you hear her speak.
 If she confess that she was half the wooer,
 Destruction on my head if my bad blame   *175*
 Light on the man. Come hither, gentle mistress.
 Do you perceive in all this noble company
 Where most you owe obedience?

Desdemona.   My noble father,
 I do perceive here a divided duty.
 To you I am bound for life and education;   *180*
 My life and education both do learn me
 How to respect you. You are the lord of duty,
 I am hitherto your daughter. But here's my husband,
 And so much duty as my mother showed
 To you, preferring you before her father,   *185*
 So much I challenge° that I may profess
 Due to the Moor my lord.

Brabantio.   God be with you. I have done.
 Please it your Grace, on to the state affairs.
 I had rather to adopt a child than get° it.
 Come hither, Moor.   *190*
 I here do give thee that with all my heart
 Which, but thou hast already, with all my heart
 I would keep from thee. For your sake,° jewel,
 I am glad at soul I have no other child,
 For thy escape would teach me tyranny,   *195*
 To hang clogs on them. I have done, my lord.

Duke. Let me speak like yourself and lay a sentence°
 Which, as a grise° or step, may help these lovers.
 When remedies are past, the griefs are ended
 By seeing the worst, which late on hopes depended.° *200*
 To mourn a mischief that is past and gone
 Is the next° way to draw new mischief on.
 What cannot be preserved when fortune takes,

---

¹⁸⁶ *challenge* claim as right   ¹⁸⁹ *get* beget   ¹⁹³ *For your sake* because of you   ¹⁹⁷ *lay a sentence* provide a maxim   ¹⁹⁸ *grise* step   ²⁰⁰ *late on hopes depended* was supported by hope (of a better outcome) until lately   ²⁰² *next* closest, surest

Patience her injury a mock'ry makes.
The robbed that smiles, steals something from the
205   thief;
He robs himself that spends a bootless° grief.

Brabantio. So let the Turk of Cyprus us beguile:
We lose it not so long as we can smile.
He bears the sentence well that nothing bears
210   But the free comfort which from thence he hears;
But he bears both the sentence and the sorrow
That to pay grief must of poor patience borrow.
These sentences, to sugar, or to gall,
Being strong on both sides, are equivocal.
215   But words are words. I never yet did hear
That the bruisèd heart was piercèd° through the ear.
I humbly beseech you, proceed to th' affairs of state.

Duke. The Turk with a most mighty preparation makes
for Cyprus. Othello, the fortitude° of the place is
220   best known to you; and though we have there a
substitute° of most allowed sufficiency,° yet opinion, a more sovereign mistress of effects, throws a
more safer voice on you.° You must therefore be
content to slubber° the gloss of your new fortunes
225   with this more stubborn and boisterous° expedition.

Othello. The tyrant Custom, most grave senators,
Hath made the flinty and steel couch of war
My thrice-driven° bed of down. I do agnize°
A natural and prompt alacrity
230   I find in hardness and do undertake
This present wars against the Ottomites.

---

206 *bootless* valueless   216 *piercèd* (some editors emend to *pieced,* i.e.,
"healed." But *pierced* makes good sense: Brabantio is saying in effect
that his heart cannot be further hurt [pierced] by the indignity of the
useless, conventional advice the Duke offers him. *Pierced* can also
mean, however, "lanced" in the medical sense, and would then mean
"treated")   219 *fortitude* fortification   221 *substitute* viceroy   221 *most
allowed sufficiency* generally acknowledged capability   221–23 *opinion
. . . you* i.e., the general opinion, which finally controls affairs, is that
you would be the best man in this situation   224 *slubber* besmear
225 *stubborn and boisterous* rough and violent   228 *thrice-driven* i.e.,
softest   228 *agnize* know in myself

Most humbly, therefore, bending to your state,
I crave fit disposition for my wife,
Due reference of place, and exhibition,°
With such accommodation and besort   235
As levels with° her breeding.

Duke.   Why, at her father's.

Brabantio. I will not have it so.

Othello.   Nor I.

Desdemona.   Nor would I there reside,
To put my father in impatient thoughts
By being in his eye. Most gracious Duke,
To my unfolding° lend your prosperous° ear,   240
And let me find a charter° in your voice,
T' assist my simpleness.

Duke.   What would you, Desdemona?

Desdemona. That I love the Moor to live with him,
My downright violence, and storm of fortunes,
May trumpet to the world. My heart's subdued   245
Even to the very quality of my lord.°
I saw Othello's visage in his mind,
And to his honors and his valiant parts
Did I my soul and fortunes consecrate.
So that, dear lords, if I be left behind,   250
A moth of peace, and he go to the war,
The rites° for why I love him are bereft me,
And I a heavy interim shall support
By his dear absence. Let me go with him.

Othello. Let her have your voice.°   255
Vouch with me, heaven, I therefore beg it not
To please the palate of my appetite,
Nor to comply with heat° —the young affects°

---

²³⁴ *exhibition* grant of funds ²³⁶ *levels with* is suitable to ²⁴⁰ *unfolding* explanation ²⁴⁰ *prosperous* favoring ²⁴¹ *charter* permission ²⁴⁵⁻⁴⁶ *My . . . lord* i.e., I have become one in nature and being with the man I married (therefore, I too would go to the wars like a soldier) ²⁵² *rites* (may refer either to the marriage rites or to the rites, formalities, of war) ²⁵⁵ *voice* consent ²⁵⁸ *heat* lust ²⁵⁸ *affects* passions

In me defunct—and proper satisfaction;°
260 But to be free and bounteous to her mind;
And heaven defend° your good souls that you think
I will your serious and great business scant
When she is with me. No, when light-winged toys
Of feathered Cupid seel° with wanton° dullness
265 My speculative and officed instrument,°
That my disports corrupt and taint my business,
Let housewives make a skillet of my helm,
And all indign° and base adversities
Make head° against my estimation!° —

270 *Duke.* Be it as you shall privately determine,
Either for her stay or going. Th' affair cries haste,
And speed must answer it.

First Senator.   You must away tonight.

Othello. With all my heart.

Duke. At nine i' th' morning here we'll meet again.
275 Othello, leave some officer behind,
And he shall our commission bring to you,
And such things else of quality and respect
As doth import you.

Othello.   So please your grace, my ancient;
A man he is of honesty and trust.
280 To his conveyance I assign my wife,
With what else needful your good grace shall think
To be sent after me.

Duke.   Let it be so.
Good night to every one. [*To Brabantio*] And, noble
signior,
If virtue no delighted° beauty lack,
285 Your son-in-law is far more fair than black.

First Senator. Adieu, brave Moor. Use Desdemona
well.

²⁵⁹ *proper satisfaction* i.e., consummation of the marriage ²⁶¹ *defend*
forbid ²⁶⁴ *seel* sew up ²⁶⁴ *wanton* lascivious ²⁶⁵ *speculative . . .
instrument* i.e., sight (and, by extension, the mind) ²⁶⁸ *indign* unworthy ²⁶⁹ *Make head* form an army, i.e., attack ²⁶⁹ *estimation* rep-
utation ²⁶⁴ *delighted* delightful

Brabantio. Look to her, Moor, if thou hast eyes to see:
　She has deceived her father, and may thee.
　　　　　　　[*Exeunt Duke, Senators, Officers, &c.*]

Othello. My life upon her faith! Honest Iago,
　My Desdemona must I leave to thee.　　　　　　　*290*
　I prithee let thy wife attend on her,
　And bring them after in the best advantage.°
　Come, Desdemona. I have but an hour
　Of love, of wordly matter, and direction
　To spend with thee. We must obey the time.　　　*295*
　　　　　　　Exit [Moor with Desdemona].

Roderigo. Iago?

Iago. What say'st thou, noble heart?

Roderigo. What will I do, think'st thou?

Iago. Why, go to bed and sleep.

Roderigo. I will incontinently° drown myself.　　*300*

Iago. If thou dost, I shall never love thee after. Why,
　thou silly gentleman?

Roderigo. It is silliness to live when to live is torment;
　and then have we a prescription to die when death is
　our physician.　　　　　　　　　　　　　　　　　*305*

Iago. O villainous! I have looked upon the world for
　four times seven years, and since I could distinguish
　betwixt a benefit and an injury, I never found man
　that knew how to love himself. Ere I would say I
　would drown myself for the love of a guinea hen,　*310*
　I would change my humanity with a baboon.

Roderigo. What should I do? I confess it is my shame
　to be so fond, but it is not in my virtue° to amend it.

Iago. Virtue? A fig! 'Tis in ourselves that we are thus,
　or thus. Our bodies are our gardens, to the which　*315*
　our wills are gardeners; so that if we will plant
　nettles or sow lettuce, set hyssop and weed up thyme,

---

²⁹² *advantage* opportunity　　³⁰⁰ *incontinently* at once　　³¹³ *virtue* strength
(Roderigo is saying that his nature controls him)

supply it with one gender of herbs or distract° it
with many—either to have it sterile with idleness or
320   manured with industry—why, the power and corri-
gible° authority of this lies in our wills. If the bal-
ance of our lives had not one scale of reason to poise
another of sensuality, the blood and baseness of
our natures would conduct us to most prepost'rous
325   conclusions.° But we have reason to cool our raging
motions, our carnal stings or unbitted° lusts,
whereof I take this that you call love to be a sect
or scion.°

Roderigo. It cannot be.

330 *Iago.* It is merely a lust of the blood and a permission of
the will. Come, be a man! Drown thyself? Drown
cats and blind puppies! I have professed me thy
friend, and I confess me knit to thy deserving with
cables of perdurable toughness. I could never better
335   stead° thee than now. Put money in thy purse.
Follow thou the wars; defeat thy favor° with an
usurped° beard. I say, put money in thy purse.
It cannot be long that Desdemona should continue
her love to the Moor. Put money in thy purse. Nor
340   he his to her. It was a violent commencement in
her and thou shalt see an answerable° sequestra-
tion—put but money in thy purse. These Moors
are changeable in their wills—fill thy purse with
money. The food that to him now is as luscious as
345   locusts° shall be to him shortly as bitter as coloquintida.° She must change for youth; when she is
sated with his body, she will find the errors of her
choice. Therefore, put money in thy purse. If thou
wilt needs damn thyself, do it a more delicate way
350   than drowning. Make all the money thou canst. If

---

³¹⁸ *distract* vary ³²⁰⁻²¹ *corrigible* corrective ³²⁵ *conclusions* ends
³²⁶ *unbitted* i.e., uncontrolled ³²⁷⁻²⁸ *sect or scion* offshoot ³³⁵ *stead*
serve ³³⁶ *defeat thy favor* disguise your face ³³⁷ *usurped* assumed
³⁴¹ *answerable* similar ³⁴⁵ *locusts* (a sweet fruit) ³⁴⁵⁻⁴⁶ *coloquintida*
(a purgative derived from a bitter apple)

sanctimony° and a frail vow betwixt an erring°
barbarian and supersubtle Venetian be not too hard
for my wits, and all the tribe of hell, thou shalt enjoy
her. Therefore, make money. A pox of drowning
thyself, it is clean out of the way. Seek thou rather *355*
to be hanged in compassing° thy joy than to be
drowned and go without her.

Roderigo. Wilt thou be fast to my hopes, if I depend
on the issue?

Iago. Thou art sure of me. Go, make money. I have *360*
told thee often, and I retell thee again and again, I
hate the Moor. My cause is hearted;° thine hath no
less reason. Let us be conjunctive° in our revenge
against him. If thou canst cuckold him, thou dost
thyself a pleasure, me a sport. There are many *365*
events in the womb of time, which will be delivered.
Traverse, go, provide thy money! We will have more
of this tomorrow. Adieu.

Roderigo. Where shall we meet i' th' morning?

Iago. At my lodging.   *370*

Roderigo. I'll be with thee betimes.

Iago. Go to, farewell. Do you hear, Roderigo?

Roderigo. I'll sell all my land.   *Exit.*

Iago. Thus do I ever make my fool my purse;
For I mine own gained knowledge° should profane *375*
If I would time expend with such snipe
But for my sport and profit. I hate the Moor,
And it is thought abroad that 'twixt my sheets
H'as done my office. I know not if't be true,
But I, for mere suspicion in that kind,   *380*
Will do, as if for surety.° He holds me well;
The better shall my purpose work on him.

---

³⁵¹ *sanctimony* sacred bond (of marriage) ³⁵¹ *erring* wandering
³⁵⁶ *compassing* encompassing, achieving ³⁶² *hearted* deep-seated in the
heart ³⁶³ *conjunctive* joined ³⁷⁵ *gained knowledge* i.e., practical,
worldly wisdom ³⁸¹ *surety* certainty

Cassio's a proper° man. Let me see now:
To get his place, and to plume up my will°
In double knavery. How? How? Let's see.
After some time, to abuse Othello's ears
That he is too familiar with his wife.
He hath a person and a smooth dispose°
To be suspected—framed° to make women false.
The Moor is of a free and open nature
That thinks men honest that but seem to be so;
And will as tenderly be led by th' nose
As asses are.
I have't! It is engendered! Hell and night
Must bring this monstrous birth to the world's light.
                                             [*Exit.*]

---

³⁸³ *proper* handsome   ³⁸⁴ *plume up my will* (many explanations have been offered for this crucial line, which in Q1 reads "make up my will." The general sense is something like "to make more proud and gratify my ego")   ³⁸⁸ *dispose* manner   ³⁸⁹ *framed* designed

The Jungle Book

Mowgli is not like any other boy. When he was a baby he wandered deep into the jungle and was found there by a family of wolves. Now he is a member of the Wolf Pack and is the only "man-cub" in a forest filled with wild animals. In many exciting adventures, Mowgli proves his strength and skill to the beasts in the jungle and to the people in the nearby villages.

But not all the stories in THE JUNGLE BOOK are about Mowgli. You'll read about a mongoose named Rikki-tikki-tavi, a brave white seal named Kotick, and several other delightful animals created by the ever popular author, Rudyard Kipling.

THE JUNGLE BOOK

Rudyard Kipling

Troll

Contents

Mowgli's Brothers

Now Chil the Kite brings home the night
   That Mang the Bat sets free—
The herds are shut in byre and hut
   For loosed till dawn are we.
This is the hour of pride and power,
   Talon and tush and claw.
Oh, hear the call!—Good hunting all
   That keep the Jungle Law!
           Night Song in the Jungle

It was seven o'clock of a very warm evening in the Seeonee hills when Father Wolf woke up from his day's rest, scratched himself, yawned, and spread out his paws one after the other to get rid of the sleepy feeling in their tips. Mother Wolf lay with her big gray nose dropped across her four tumbling, squealing cubs, and the moon shone into the mouth of the cave where they all lived.

"Augrh!" said Father Wolf. "It is time to hunt again." He was going to spring downhill when a little shadow with a bushy tail crossed the threshold and whined: "Good luck go with you, O

Chief of the Wolves. And good luck and strong white teeth go with the noble children that they may never forget the hungry in this world."

It was the jackal—Tabaqui, the Dish-licker—and the wolves of India despise Tabaqui because he runs about making mischief, and telling tales, and eating rags and pieces of leather from the village rubbish heaps. But they are afraid of him too, because Tabaqui, more than anyone else in the jungle, is apt to go mad, and then he forgets that he was ever afraid of anyone, and runs through the forest biting everything in his way. Even the tiger runs and hides when little Tabaqui goes mad, for madness is the most disgraceful thing that can overtake a wild creature. We call it hydrophobia, but they call it *dewanee*—the madness—and run.

"Enter, then, and look," said Father Wolf stiffly, "but there is no food here."

"For a wolf, no," said Tabaqui, "but for so mean a person as myself a dry bone is a good feast. Who are we, the *Gidur-log* [the jackal people], to pick and choose?" He scuttled to the back of the cave, where he found the bone of a buck with some meat on it, and sat cracking the end merrily.

"All thanks for this good meal," he said, licking his lips. "How beautiful are the noble children! How large are their eyes! And so young too! Indeed, indeed, I might have remembered that the children of kings are men from the beginning."

Now, Tabaqui knew as well as anyone else that there is nothing so unlucky as to compliment children to their faces. It pleased him to see Mother and Father Wolf look uncomfortable.

Tabaqui sat still, rejoicing in the mischief that he had made, and then he said spitefully:

"Shere Khan, the Big One, has shifted his hunting grounds. He will hunt among these hills for the next moon, so he has told me."

Shere Khan was the tiger who lived near the Waingunga River, twenty miles away.

"He has no right!" Father Wolf began angrily— "By the Law of the Jungle he has no right to change his quarters without due warning. He will frighten every head of game within ten miles, and I—I have to kill for two, these days."

"His mother did not call him Lungri [the Lame One] for nothing," said Mother Wolf quietly. "He has been lame in one foot from his birth. That is why he has only killed cattle. Now the villagers of the Waingunga are angry with him, and he has come here to make *our* villagers angry. They will scour the jungle for him when he is far away, and we and our children must run when the grass is set alight. Indeed, we are very grateful to Shere Khan!"

"Shall I tell him of your gratitude?" said Tabaqui.

"Out!" snapped Father Wolf. "Out and hunt with thy master. Thou hast done harm enough for one night."

"I go," said Tabaqui quietly. "Ye can hear Shere Khan below in the thickets. I might have saved myself the message."

Father Wolf listened, and below in the valley that ran down to a little river he heard the dry, angry, snarly, singsong whine of a tiger who has caught nothing and does not care if all the jungle knows it.

"The fool!" said Father Wolf. "To begin a night's work with that noise! Does he think that our buck are like his fat Waingunga bullocks?"

"H'sh. It is neither bullock nor buck he hunts tonight," said Mother Wolf. "It is Man."

The whine had changed to a sort of humming purr that seemed to come from every quarter of the compass. It was the noise that bewilders woodcutters and gypsies sleeping in the open, and makes them run sometimes into the very mouth of the tiger.

"Man!" said Father Wolf, showing all his white teeth. "Faugh! Are there not enough beetles and frogs in the tanks that he must eat Man, and on our ground too!"

The Law of the Jungle, which never orders anything without a reason, forbids every beast to eat Man except when he is killing to show his children how to kill, and then he must hunt outside the hunting grounds of his pack or tribe. The real reason for this is that man-killing means, sooner or later, the arrival of white men on elephants, with guns, and hundreds of brown men with gongs and rockets and torches. Then everybody in the jungle suffers. The reason the beasts give among themselves is that Man is the weakest and most defenseless of all living things, and it is unsportsmanlike to touch him. They say too—and it is true—that man-eaters become mangy, and lose their teeth.

The purr grew louder, and ended in the full-throated "Aaarh!" of the tiger's charge.

Then there was a howl—an untigerish howl—from Shere Khan. "He has missed," said Mother Wolf. "What is it?"

Father Wolf ran out a few paces and heard Shere Khan muttering and mumbling savagely as he tumbled about in the scrub.

"The fool has had no more sense than to jump at a woodcutter's campfire, and has burned his feet," said Father Wolf with a grunt. "Tabaqui is with him."

"Something is coming uphill," said Mother Wolf, twitching one ear. "Get ready."

The bushes rustled a little in the thicket, and Father Wolf dropped with his haunches under him, ready for his leap. Then, if you had been watching, you would have seen the most wonderful thing in the world—the wolf checked in mid-spring. He made his bound before he saw what it was he was jumping at, and then he tried to stop himself. The result was that he shot up straight into the air for four or five feet, landing almost where he left ground.

"Man!" he snapped. "A man's cub. Look!"

Directly in front of him, holding on by a low branch, stood a naked brown baby who could just walk—as soft and as dimpled a little atom as ever came to a wolf's cave at night. He looked up into Father Wolf's face and laughed.

"Is that a man's cub?" said Mother Wolf. "I have never seen one. Bring it here."

A wolf accustomed to moving his own cubs can, if necessary, mouth an egg without breaking it, and though Father Wolf's jaws closed right on the child's back not a tooth even scratched the skin as he laid it down among the cubs.

"How little! How naked, and—how bold!" said Mother Wolf softly. The baby was pushing his way between the cubs to get close to the warm hide. "Ahai! He is taking his meal with the others. And so this is a man's cub. Now, was there ever a wolf that could boast of a man's cub among her children?"

"I have heard now and again of such a thing, but never in our Pack or in my time," said Father

Wolf. "He is altogether without hair, and I could kill him with a touch of my foot. But see, he looks up and is not afraid."

The moonlight was blocked out of the mouth of the cave, for Shere Khan's great square head and shoulders were thrust into the entrance. Tabaqui, behind him, was squeaking: "My lord, my lord, it went in here!"

"Shere Khan does us great honor," said Father Wolf, but his eyes were very angry. "What does Shere Khan need?"

"My quarry. A man's cub went this way," said Shere Khan. "Its parents have run off. Give it to me."

Shere Khan had jumped at a woodcutter's campfire, as Father Wolf had said, and was furious from the pain of his burned feet. But Father Wolf knew that the mouth of the cave was too narrow for a tiger to come in by. Even where he was, Shere Khan's shoulders and forepaws were cramped for want of room, as a man's would be if he tried to fight in a barrel.

"The Wolves are a free people," said Father Wolf. "They take orders from the Head of the Pack, and not from any striped cattle-killer. The man's cub is ours—to kill if we choose."

"Ye choose and ye do not choose! What talk is this of choosing? By the bull that I killed, am I to stand nosing into your dog's den for my fair dues?

It is I, Shere Khan, who speaks!"

The tiger's roar filled the cave with thunder. Mother Wolf shook herself clear of the cubs and sprang forward, her eyes, like two green moons in the darkness, facing the blazing eyes of Shere Khan.

"And it is I, Raksha [The Demon], who answers. The man's cub is mine, Lungri—mine to me! He shall not be killed. He shall live to run with the Pack and to hunt with the Pack; and in the end, look you, hunter of little naked cubs— frog-eater—fish-killer—he shall hunt *thee!* Now get hence, or by the Sambhur that I killed (*I* eat no starved cattle), back thou goest to thy mother, burned beast of the jungle, lamer than ever thou camest into the world! Go!"

Father Wolf looked on amazed. He had almost forgotten the days when he won Mother Wolf in fair fight from five other wolves, when she ran in the Pack and was not called The Demon for compliment's sake. Shere Khan might have faced Father Wolf, but he could not stand up against Mother Wolf, for he knew that where he was she had all the advantage of the ground, and would fight to the death. So he backed out of the cave mouth growling, and when he was clear he shouted:

"Each dog barks in his own yard! We will see what the Pack will say to this fostering of man-cubs. The cub is mine, and to my teeth he will come in the end, O bush-tailed thieves!"

Mother Wolf threw herself down panting among the cubs, and Father Wolf said to her gravely:

"Shere Khan speaks this much truth. The cub must be shown to the Pack. Wilt thou still keep him, Mother?"

"Keep him?" she gasped. "He came naked, by night, alone and very hungry; yet he was not afraid! Look, he has pushed one of my babes to one side already. And that lame butcher would have killed him and would have run off to the Waingunga while the villagers here hunted through all our lairs in revenge! Keep him? Assuredly I will keep him. Lie still, little frog. O thou Mowgli—for Mowgli the Frog I will call thee—the time will come when thou wilt hunt Shere Khan as he has hunted thee."

"But what will our Pack say?" said Father Wolf.

The Law of the Jungle lays down very clearly that any wolf may, when he marries, withdraw from the Pack he belongs to. But as soon as his cubs are old enough to stand on their feet he must bring them to the Pack Council, which is generally held once a month at full moon, in order that the other wolves may identify them. After that inspection the cubs are free to run where they please, and until they have killed their first buck no excuse is accepted if a grown wolf of the Pack kills one of them. The punishment is death where the murderer can be found; and if you think for a minute you will see that this must be so.

Father Wolf waited till his cubs could run a little, and then on the night of the Pack Meeting took them and Mowgli and Mother Wolf to the Council Rock—a hilltop covered with stones and boulders where a hundred wolves could hide. Akela, the great gray Lone Wolf, who led all the Pack by strength and cunning, lay out at full length on his rock, and below him sat forty or more wolves of every size and color, from badger-colored veterans who could handle a buck alone to young black three-year-olds who thought they could. The Lone Wolf had led them for a year now. He had fallen twice into a wolf trap in his youth, and once he had been beaten and left for dead; so he knew the manners and customs of men. There was very little talking at the Rock. The cubs tumbled over each other in the center of the circle where their mothers and fathers sat, and now and again a senior wolf would go quietly up to a cub, look at him carefully, and return to his place on noiseless feet. Sometimes a mother would push her cub far out into the moonlight to be sure that he had not been overlooked. Akela from his rock would cry: "Ye know the Law—ye know the Law. Look well, O Wolves!" And the anxious mothers would take up the call: "Look—look well, O Wolves!"

At last—and Mother Wolf's neck bristles lifted as the time came—Father Wolf pushed "Mowgli the Frog," as they called him, into the center, where he sat laughing and playing with some pebbles that glistened in the moonlight.

Akela never raised his head from his paws, but went on with the monotonous cry: "Look well!" A muffled roar came up from behind the rocks—the voice of Shere Khan crying: "The cub is mine. Give him to me. What have the Free People to do with a man's cub?" Akela never even twitched his ears. All he said was: "Look well, O Wolves! What have the Free People to do with the orders of any save the Free People? Look well!"

There was a chorus of deep growls, and a young wolf in his fourth year flung back Shere Khan's question to Akela: "What have the Free People to do with a man's cub?" Now, the Law of the Jungle lays down that if there is any dispute as to the right of a cub to be accepted by the Pack, he must be spoken for by at least two members of the Pack who are not his father and mother.

"Who speaks for this cub?" said Akela. "Among the Free People who speaks?" There was no answer and Mother Wolf got ready for what she knew would be her last fight, if things came to fighting.

Then the only other creature who is allowed at the Pack Council—Baloo, the sleepy brown bear who teaches the wolf cubs the Law of the Jungle: old Baloo, who can come and go where he pleases because he eats only nuts and roots and honey— rose upon his hind quarters and grunted.

"The man's cub—the man's cub?" he said. "*I* speak for the man's cub. There is no harm in a man's cub. I have no gift of words, but I speak the truth. Let him run with the Pack, and be entered with the others. I myself will teach him."

"We need yet another," said Akela. "Baloo has spoken, and he is our teacher for the young cubs. Who speaks besides Baloo?"

A black shadow dropped down into the circle. It was Bagheera the Black Panther, inky black all over, but with the panther markings showing up in certain lights like the pattern of watered silk.Everybody knew Bagheera, and nobody cared to cross his path; for he was as cunning as Tabaqui, as bold as the wild buffalo, and as reckless as the wounded elephant. But he had a voice as soft as wild honey dripping from a tree, and a skin softer than down.

"O Akela, and ye the Free People," he purred, "I have no right in your assembly, but the Law of the Jungle says that if there is a doubt which is not a killing matter in regard to a new cub, the life of that cub may be bought at a price. And the Law does not say who may or may not pay that price. Am I right?"

"Good! Good!" said the young wolves, who are always hungry. "Listen to Bagheera. The cub can be bought for a price. It is the Law."

"Knowing that I have no right to speak here, I ask your leave."

"Speak then," cried twenty voices.

"To kill a naked cub is shame. Besides, he may make better sport for you when he is grown. Baloo has spoken in his behalf. Now to Baloo's word I will add one bull, and a fat one, newly killed, not half a mile from here, if ye will accept the man's cub according to the Law. Is it difficult?"

There was a clamor of scores of voices, saying: "What matter? He will die in the winter rains. He will scorch in the sun. What harm can a naked frog do us? Let him run with the Pack. Where is the bull, Bagheera? Let him be accepted." And then came Akela's deep bay, crying: "Look well—look well, O Wolves!"

Mowgli was still deeply interested in the pebbles, and he did not notice when the wolves came and looked at him one by one. At last they all went down the hill for the dead bull, and only Akela, Bagheera, Baloo, and Mowgli's own wolves were left. Shere Khan roared still in the night, for he was very angry that Mowgli had not been handed over to him.

"Ay, roar well," said Bagheera, under his whiskers, "for the time will come when this naked thing will make thee roar to another tune, or I know nothing of man."

"It was well done," said Akela. "Men and their cubs are very wise. He may be a help in time."

"Truly, a help in time of need; for none can hope to lead the Pack forever," said Bagheera.

Akela said nothing. He was thinking of the time that comes to every leader of every pack when his strength goes from him and he gets feebler and feebler, till at last he is killed by the wolves and a new leader comes up—to be killed in his turn.

"Take him away," he said to Father Wolf, "and train him as befits one of the Free People."

And that is how Mowgli was entered into the Seeonee Wolf Pack for the price of a bull and on Baloo's good word.

Now you must be content to skip ten or eleven whole years, and only guess at all the wonderful life that Mowgli led among the wolves, because if it were written out it would fill ever so many books. He grew up with the cubs, though they, of course, were grown wolves almost before he was a child. And Father Wolf taught him his business, and the meaning of things in the jungle, till every rustle in the grass, every breath of the warm night air, every note of the owls above his head, every scratch of a bat's claws as it roosted for a while in a tree, and every splash of every little fish jumping in a pool meant just as much to him as the work of his office means to a business man.

When he was not learning he sat out in the sun and slept, and ate and went to sleep again. When he felt dirty or hot he swam in the forest pools; and when he wanted honey (Baloo told him that honey and nuts were just as pleasant to eat as raw meat) he climbed up for it, and that Bagheera showed him how to do. Bagheera would lie out on a branch and call, "Come along, Little Brother," and at first Mowgli would cling like the sloth, but afterward he would fling himself through the branches almost as boldly as the gray ape. He took his place at the Council Rock, too, when the Pack met, and there he discovered that if he stared hard at any wolf, the wolf would be forced to drop his eyes, and so he used to stare for fun.

At other times he would pick the long thorns out of the pads of his friends, for wolves suffer terribly from thorns and burs in their coats. He would go down the hillside into the cultivated lands by night, and look very curiously at the villagers in their huts, but he had a mistrust of men because Bagheera showed him a square box with a drop gate so cunningly hidden in the jungle that he nearly walked into it, and told him that it was a trap. He loved better than anything else to go with Bagheera into the dark warm heart of the forest, to sleep all through the drowsy day, and at night see how Bagheera did his killing. Bagheera killed right and left as he felt hungry, and so did Mowgli—with one exception. As soon as he was old enough to understand things, Bagheera told him that he must never touch cattle because he had been bought into the Pack at the price of a bull's life.

"All the jungle is thine," said Bagheera, "and thou canst kill everything that thou art enough to kill; but for the sake of the bull that bought thee thou must never kill or eat any cattle young or old. That is the Law of the Jungle."

Mowgli obeyed faithfully.

And he grew and grew strong as a boy must grow who does not know that he is learning any lessons, and who has nothing in the world to think of except things to eat.

Mother Wolf told him once or twice that Shere Khan was not a creature to be trusted, and that some day he must kill Shere Khan. But though a young wolf would have remembered that advice every hour, Mowgli forgot it because he was only a boy—though he would have called himself a wolf if he had been able to speak in any human tongue.

Shere Khan was always crossing his path in the jungle, for as Akela grew older and feebler the lame tiger had come to be great friends with the younger wolves of the Pack, who followed him for scraps, a thing Akela would never have allowed if he had dared to push his authority to the proper bounds. Then Shere Khan would flatter them and wonder that such fine young hunters were content to be led by a dying wolf and a man's cub. "They tell me," Shere Khan would say, "that at Council ye dare not look him between the eyes." And the young wolves would growl and bristle.

Bagheera, who had eyes and ears everywhere, knew something of this, and once or twice he told Mowgli in so many words that Shere Khan would kill him some day. Mowgli would laugh and answer: "I have the Pack and I have thee; and Baloo, though he is so lazy, might strike a blow or two for my sake. Why should I be afraid?"

It was one very warm day that a new notion came to Bagheera—born of something that he had heard. Perhaps Sahi the Porcupine had told him; but he said to Mowgli when they were deep in the jungle, as the boy lay with his head on Bagheera's beautiful black skin, "Little Brother, how often have I told thee that Shere Khan is thy enemy?"

"As many times as there are nuts on that palm," said Mowgli, who, naturally, could not count. "What of it? I am sleepy, Bagheera, and Shere Khan is all long tail and loud talk—like Mor the Peacock."

"But this is no time for sleeping. Baloo knows

it; I know it; the Pack know it; and even the foolish, foolish deer know. Tabaqui has told thee too."

"Ho! Ho!" said Mowgli. "Tabaqui came to me not long ago with some rude talk that I was a naked man's cub and not fit to dig pignuts. But I caught Tabaqui by the tail and swung him twice against a palm tree to teach him better manners."

"That was foolishness, for though Tabaqui is a mischief-maker, he would have told thee of something that concerned thee closely. Open those eyes, Little Brother. Shere Khan dare not kill thee in the jungle. But remember, Akela is very old, and soon the day comes when he cannot kill his buck, and then he will be leader no more. Many of the wolves that looked thee over when thou wast brought to the Council first are old too, and the young wolves believe, as Shere Khan has taught them, that a man-cub has no place with the Pack. In a little time thou wilt be a man."

"And what is a man that he should not run with his brothers?" said Mowgli. "I was born in the jungle. I have obeyed the Law of the Jungle, and there is no wolf of ours from whose paws I have not pulled a thorn. Surely they are my brothers!"

Bagheera stretched himself at full length and half shut his eyes. "Little Brother," said he, "feel under my jaw."

Mowgli put up his strong brown hand, and just

under Bagheera's silky chin, where the giant rolling muscles were all hid by the glossy hair, he came upon a little bald spot.

"There is no one in the jungle that knows that I, Bagheera, carry that mark—the mark of the collar; and yet, Little Brother, I was born among men, and it was among men that my mother died—in the cages of the king's palace at Oodeypore. It was because of this that I paid the price for thee at the Council when thou wast a little naked cub. Yes, I too was born among men. I had never seen the jungle. They fed me behind bars from an iron pan till one night I felt that I was Bagheera—the Panther—and no man's plaything, and I broke the silly lock with one blow of my paw and came away. And because I had learned the ways of men, I became more terrible in the jungle than Shere Khan. Is it not so?"

"Yes," said Mowgli, "all the jungle fear Bagheera—all except Mowgli."

"Oh, *thou* art a man's cub," said the Black Panther very tenderly. "And even as I returned to my jungle, so thou must go back to men at last—to the men who are thy brothers—if thou art not killed in the Council."

"But why—but why should any wish to kill me?" said Mowgli.

"Look at me," said Bagheera. And Mowgli looked at him steadily between the eyes. The big panther turned his head away in half a minute.

"That is why," he said, shifting his paw on the leaves. "Not even I can look thee between the eyes, and I was born among men, and I love thee, Little Brother. The others they hate thee because their eyes cannot meet thine; because thou art wise; because thou hast pulled out thorns from their feet—because thou art a man."

"I did not know these things," said Mowgli sullenly, and he frowned under his heavy black eyebrows.

"What is the Law of the Jungle? Strike first and then give tongue. By thy very carelessness they know that thou art a man. But be wise. It is in my heart that when Akela misses his next kill—and at each hunt it costs him more to pin the buck—the Pack will turn against him and against thee. They will hold a jungle Council at the Rock, and then— and then—I have it!" said Bagheera, leaping up. "Go thou down quickly to the men's huts in the valley, and take some of the Red Flower which they grow there, so that when the time comes thou mayest have even a stronger friend than I or Baloo or those of the Pack that love thee. Get the Red Flower."

By Red Flower Bagheera meant fire, only no creature in the jungle will call fire by its proper name. Every beast lives in deadly fear of it, and invents a hundred ways of describing it.

"The Red Flower?" said Mowgli. "That grows outside their huts in the twilight. I will get some."

"There speaks the man's cub," said Bagheera proudly. "Remember that it grows in little pots. Get one swiftly, and keep it by thee for time of need."

"Good!" said Mowgli. "I go. But art thou sure, O my Bagheera"—he slipped his arm around the splendid neck and looked deep into the big eyes—"art thou sure that all this is Shere Khan's doing?"

"By the Broken Lock that freed me, I am sure, Little Brother."

"Then, by the Bull that bought me, I will pay Shere Khan full tale for this, and it may be a little over," said Mowgli, and he bounded away.

"That is a man. That is all a man," said Bagheera to himself, lying down again. "Oh, Shere Khan, never was a blacker hunting than that frog hunt of thine ten years ago!"

Mowgli was far and far through the forest, running hard, and his heart was hot in him. He came to the cave as the evening mist rose, and drew breath, and looked down the valley. The cubs were out, but Mother Wolf, at the back of the cave, knew by his breathing that something was troubling her frog.

"What is it, Son?" she said.

"Some bat's chatter of Shere Khan," he called back. "I hunt among the plowed fields tonight," and he plunged downward through the bushes, to the stream at the bottom of the valley. There he checked, for he heard the yell of the Pack hunting, heard the bellow of a hunted Sambhur, and the snort as the buck turned at bay. Then there were wicked, bitter howls from the young wolves: "Akela! Akela! Let the Lone Wolf show his strength. Room for the leader of the Pack! Spring, Akela!"

The Lone Wolf must have sprung and missed his hold, for Mowgli heard the snap of his teeth and then a yelp as the Sambhur knocked him over with his forefoot.

He did not wait for anything more, but dashed on; and the yells grew fainter behind him as he ran into the croplands where the villagers lived.

"Bagheera spoke truth," he panted, as he nestled down in some cattle fodder by the window of a hut. "Tomorrow is one day both for Akela and for me."

Then he pressed his face close to the window and watched the fire on the hearth. He saw the husbandman's wife get up and feed it in the night with black lumps. And when the morning came and the mists were all white and cold, he saw the man's child pick up a wicker pot plastered inside with earth, fill it with lumps of red-hot charcoal, put it under his blanket, and go out to tend the cows in the byre.

"Is that all?" said Mowgli. "If a cub can do it, there is nothing to fear." So he strode round the corner and met the boy, took the pot from his hand, and disappeared into the mist while the boy howled with fear.

"They are very like me," said Mowgli, blowing into the pot as he had seen the woman do. "This thing will die if I do not give it things to eat"; and he dropped twigs and dried bark on the red stuff. Halfway up the hill he met Bagheera with the morning dew shining like moonstones on his coat.

"Akela has missed," said the Panther. "They would have killed him last night, but they needed thee also. They were looking for thee on the hill."

"I was among the plowed lands. I am ready. See!" Mowgli held up the fire pot.

"Good! Now, I have seen men thrust a dry branch into that stuff, and presently the Red Flower blossomed at the end of it. Art thou not afraid?"

"No. Why should I fear? I remember now—if it is not a dream—how, before I was a Wolf, I lay beside the Red Flower, and it was warm and pleasant."

All that day Mowgli sat in the cave tending his fire pot and dipping dry branches into it to see how they looked. He found a branch that satisfied him, and in the evening when Tabaqui came to the cave and told him rudely enough that he was wanted at the Council Rock, he laughed till Tabaqui ran away. Then Mowgli went to the Council, still laughing.

Akela the Lone Wolf lay by the side of his rock as a sign that the leadership of the Pack was open, and Shere Khan with his following of scrap-fed wolves walked to and fro openly being flattered. Bagheera lay close to Mowgli, and the fire pot was between Mowgli's knees. When they were all gathered together, Shere Khan began to speak—a thing he would never have dared to do when Akela was in his prime.

"He has no right," whispered Bagheera. "Say so. He is a dog's son. He will be frightened."

Mowgli sprang to his feet. "Free People," he cried, "does Shere Khan lead the Pack? What has a tiger to do with our leadership?"

"Seeing that the leadership is yet open, and being asked to speak—" Shere Khan began.

"By whom?" said Mowgli. "Are we *all* jackals, to fawn on this cattle butcher? The leadership of the Pack is with the Pack alone."

There were yells of "Silence, thou man's cub!" "Let him speak. He has kept our Law"; and at last the seniors of the Pack thundered: "Let the Dead Wolf speak." When a leader of the Pack has missed his kill, he is called the Dead Wolf as long as he lives, which is not long.

Akela raised his old head wearily:

"Free People, and ye too, jackals of Shere Khan, for twelve seasons I have led ye to and from the kill, and in all that time not one has been trapped or maimed. Now I have missed my kill. Ye know how that plot was made. Ye know how ye brought me up to an untried buck to make my weakness known. It was cleverly done. Your right is to kill me here on the Council Rock, now. Therefore, I ask, who comes to make an end of the Lone Wolf? For it is my right, by the Law of the Jungle, that ye come one by one."

There was a long hush, for no single wolf cared to fight Akela to the death. Then Shere Khan roared: "Bah! What have we to do with this toothless fool? He is doomed to die! It is the man-cub who has lived too long. Free People, he was my meat from the first. Give him to me. I am weary of this man-wolf folly. He has troubled the jungle for ten seasons. Give me the man-cub, or I will hunt here always, and not give you one bone. He is a man, a man's child, and from the marrow of my bones I hate him!"

Then more than half the Pack yelled: "A man! A man! What has a man to do with us? Let him go to his own place."

"And turn all the people of the villages against us?" clamored Shere Khan. "No, give him to me. He is a man, and none of us can look him between the eyes."

Akela lifted his head again and said, "He has

eaten our food. He has slept with us. He has driven game for us. He has broken no word of the Law of the Jungle."

"Also, I paid for him with a bull when he was accepted. The worth of a bull is little, but Bagheera's honor is something that he will perhaps fight for," said Bagheera in his gentlest voice.

"A bull paid ten years ago!" the Pack snarled. "What do we care for bones ten years old?"

"Or for a pledge?" said Bagheera, his white teeth bared under his lip. "Well are ye called the Free People!"

"No man's cub can run with the people of the jungle," howled Shere Khan. "Give him to me!"

"He is our brother in all but blood," Akela went on, "and ye would kill him here! In truth, I have lived too long. Some of ye are eaters of cattle, and of others I have heard that, under Shere Khan's teaching, ye go by dark night and snatch children from the villager's doorstep. Therefore I know ye to be cowards, and it is to cowards I speak. It is certain that I must die, and my life is of no worth, or I would offer that in the man-cub's place. But for the sake of the Honor of the Pack—a little matter that by being without a leader ye have forgotten—I promise that if ye let the man-cub go to his own place, I will not, when my time comes to die, bare one tooth against ye. I will die without fighting. That will at least save the Pack three lives. More I cannot do; but if ye will, I can save ye the shame that comes of killing a brother against whom there is no fault—a brother spoken for and bought into the Pack according to the Law of the Jungle."

"He is a man—a man—a man!" snarled the Pack. And most of the wolves began to gather round Shere Khan, whose tail was beginning to switch.

"Now the business is in thy hands," said Bagheera to Mowgli. *"We* can do no more except fight."

Mowgli stood upright—the fire pot in his hands. Then he stretched out his arms, and yawned in the face of the Council; but he was furious with rage and sorrow, for, wolflike, the wolves had never told him how they hated him. "Listen you!" he cried. "There is no need for this dog's jabber. Ye have told me so often tonight that I am a man (and indeed I would have been a wolf with you to my life's end) that I feel your words are true. So I do not call ye my brother anymore, but *sag* [dogs], as a man should. What ye will do, and what ye will not do, is not yours to say. That matter is with *me;* and that we may see the matter more plainly, I, the man, have brought here a little of the Red Flower which ye, dogs, fear."

He flung the fire pot on the ground, and some of

the red coals lit a tuft of dried moss that flared up, as all the Council drew back in terror before the leaping flames.

Mowgli thrust his dead branch into the fire till the twigs lit and crackled, and whirled it above his head among the cowering wolves.

"Thou art the master," said Bagheera in an undertone. "Save Akela from the death. He was ever thy friend."

Akela, the grim old wolf who had never asked for mercy in his life, gave one piteous look at Mowgli as the boy stood all naked, his long black hair tossing over his shoulders in the light of the blazing branch that made the shadows jump and quiver.

"Good!" said Mowgli, staring round slowly. "I see that ye are dogs. I go from you to my own people—if they be my own people. The jungle is shut to me, and I must forget your talk and your companionship. But I will be more merciful than ye are. Because I was all but your brother in blood, I promise that when I am a man among men I will not betray ye to men as ye have betrayed me." He kicked the fire with his foot, and the sparks flew up. "There shall be no war between any of us in the Pack. But here is a debt to pay before I go." He strode forward to where Shere Khan sat blinking stupidly at the flames, and caught him by the tuft on his chin. Bagheera followed in case of accidents. "Up, dog!" Mowgli cried. "Up, when a man speaks, or I will set that coat ablaze!"

Shere Khan's ears lay flat back on his head, and he shut his eyes, for the blazing branch was very near.

"This cattle-killer said he would kill me in the Council because he had not killed me when I was a cub. Thus and thus, then, do we beat dogs when we are men. Stir a whisker, Lungri, and I ram the Red Flower down thy gullet!" He beat Shere Khan over the head with the branch, and the tiger whimpered and whined in an agony of fear.

"Pah! Singed jungle cat—go now! But remember when next I come to the Council Rock, as a man should come, it will be with Shere Khan's hide on my head. For the rest, Akela goes free to live as he pleases. Ye will *not* kill him, because that is not my will. Nor do I think that ye will sit here any longer, lolling out your tongues as though ye were somebodies, instead of dogs whom I drive out—thus! Go!" The fire was burning furiously at the end of the branch, and Mowgli struck right and left round the circle, and the wolves ran howling with the sparks burning their fur. At last there were only Akela, Bagheera, and perhaps ten wolves that had taken Mowgli's part. Then something began to hurt Mowgli inside him, as he had never been hurt in his life before, and he caught his breath and sobbed, and the tears ran down his face.

"What is it? What is it?" he said. "I do not wish to leave the jungle, and I do not know what this is. Am I dying, Bagheera?"

"No, Little brother. That is only tears such as men use," said Bagheera. "Now I know thou art a man, and a man's cub no longer. The jungle is shut indeed to thee henceforward. Let them fall, Mowgli. They are only tears."

So Mowgli sat and cried as though his heart would break; and he had never cried in all his life before.

"Now," he said, "I will go to men. But first I must say farewell to my mother." And he went to the cave where she lived with Father Wolf, and he cried on her coat, while the four cubs howled miserably.

"Ye will not forget me?" said Mowgli.

"Never while we can follow a trail," said the cubs. "Come to the foot of the hill when thou art a man, and we will talk to thee; and we will come into the croplands to play with thee by night."

"Come soon!" said Father Wolf. "Oh, wise little frog, come again soon; for we be old, thy mother and I."

"Come soon," said Mother Wolf, "little naked son of mine. For, listen, child of man, I loved thee more than ever I loved my cubs."

"I will surely come," said Mowgli. "And when I come it will be to lay out Shere Khan's hide upon the Council Rock. Do not forget me! Tell them in the jungle never to forget me!"

The dawn was beginning to break when Mowgli went down the hillside alone, to meet those mysterious things that are called men.

Hunting Song of the Seeonee Pack

As the dawn was breaking the Sambhur belled
    Once, twice, and again!
And a doe leaped up, and a doe leaped up
From the pond in the wood where the wild deer
    sup.
This I, scouting alone, beheld,
    Once, twice, and again!

As the dawn was breaking the Sambhur belled
    Once, twice, and again!
And a wolf stole back, and a wolf stole back
To carry the word to the waiting pack,
And we sought and we found and we bayed on his
    track
    Once, twice, and again!

As the dawn was breaking the Wolf Pack yelled
    Once, twice, and again!
Feet in the jungle that leave no mark!
Eyes that can see in the dark—the dark!
Tongue—give tongue to it! Hark! O hark!
    Once, twice, and again!

Kaa's Hunting

His spots are the joy of the Leopard: his horns
  are the Buffalo's pride.
Be clean, for the strength of the hunter is known
  by the gloss of his hide.
If ye find that the Bullock can toss you, or the
  heavy-browed Sambhur can gore;
Ye need not stop work to inform us; we knew
  it ten seasons before.
Oppress not the cubs of the stranger, but hail
  them as Sister and Brother,
For though they are little and fubsy, it may be
  the Bear is their mother.
"There is none like to me!" says the Cub in the
  pride of his earliest kill;
But the jungle is large and the Cub he is small.
  Let him think and be still.

Maxims of Baloo

All that is told here happened some time before
Mowgli was turned out of the Seeonee Wolf Pack,
or revenged himself on Shere Khan the Tiger. It
was in the days when Baloo was teaching him the
Law of the Jungle. The big, serious, old brown

bear was delighted to have so quick a pupil, for the young wolves will only learn as much of the Law of the Jungle as applies to their own pack and tribe, and run away as soon as they can repeat the Hunting Verse—"Feet that make no noise; eyes that can see in the dark; ears that can hear the winds in their lairs, and sharp white teeth, all these things are the marks of our brothers except Tabaqui the Jackal and the Hyena whom we hate."

But Mowgli, as a man-cub, had to learn a great deal more than this. Sometimes Bagheera the Black Panther would come lounging through the jungle to see how his pet was getting on, and would purr with his head against a tree while Mowgli recited the day's lesson to Baloo. The boy could climb almost as well as he could swim, and swim almost as well as he could run. So Baloo, the Teacher of the Law, taught him the Wood and Water Laws: how to tell a rotten branch from a sound one; how to speak politely to the wild bees when he came upon a hive of them fifty feet above ground; what to say to Mang the Bat when he disturbed him in the branches at midday; and how to warn the water snakes in the pools before he splashed down among them. None of the Jungle People like being disturbed, and all are very ready to fly at an intruder.

Then, too, Mowgli was taught the Strangers'

Hunting Call, which must be repeated aloud till it is answered, whenever one of the Jungle People hunts outside his own grounds. It means, translated, "Give me leave to hunt here because I am hungry." And the answer is, "Hunt then for food, but not for pleasure."

All this will show you how much Mowgli had to learn by heart, and he grew very tired of saying the same thing over a hundred times. But, as Baloo said to Bagheera, one day when Mowgli had been cuffed and run off in a temper, "A man's cub is a man's cub, and he must learn *all* the Law of the Jungle."

"But think how small he is," said the Black Panther, who would have spoiled Mowgli if he had had his own way. "How can his little head carry all thy long talk?"

"Is there anything in the jungle too little to be killed? No. That is why I teach him these things, and that is why I hit him, very softly, when he forgets."

"Softly! What dost thou know of softness, old Iron-feet?" Bagheera grunted. "His face is bruised today by thy—softness. Ugh."

"Better he should be bruised from head to foot by me who love him than that he should come to harm through ignorance," Baloo answered very earnestly. "I am now teaching him the Master Words of the Jungle that shall protect him with the birds and the Snake People, and all that hunt on four feet, except his own pack. He can now claim protection, if he will only remember the words, from all in the jungle. Is not that worth a little beating?"

"Well, look to it then that thou dost not kill the man-cub. He is no tree trunk to sharpen thy blunt claws upon. But what are those Master Words? I am more likely to give help than to ask it"—Bagheera stretched out one paw and admired the steel-blue, ripping-chisel talons at the end of it—"still I should like to know."

"I will call Mowgli and he shall say them—if he will. Come, Little Brother!"

"My head is ringing like a bee tree," said a sullen little voice over their heads, and Mowgli slid down a tree trunk very angry and indignant, adding as he reached the ground: "I come for Bagheera and not for *thee*, fat old Baloo!"

"That is all one to me," said Baloo, though he was hurt and grieved. "Tell Bagheera, then, the Master Words of the Jungle that I have taught thee this day."

"Master Words for which people?" said Mowgli, delighted to show off. "The jungle has many tongues. *I* know them all."

"A little thou knowest, but not much. See, O Bagheera, they never thank their teacher. Not one small wolfling has ever come back to thank old

Baloo for his teachings. Say the word for the Hunting Peoples then—great scholar."

"We be of one blood, ye and I," said Mowgli, giving the words the Bear accent which all the Hunting People use.

"Good. Now for the birds."

Mowgli repeated, with the Kite's whistle at the end of the sentence.

"Now for the Snake People," said Bagheera.

The answer was a perfectly indescribable hiss, and Mowgli kicked up his feet behind, clapped his hands together to applaud himself, and jumped onto Bagheera's back, where he sat sideways, drumming with his heels on the glossy skin and making the worst faces he could think of, at Baloo.

"There—there! That was worth a little bruise," said the brown bear tenderly. "Some day thou wilt remember me." Then he turned aside to tell Bagheera how he had begged the Master Words from Hathi the Wild Elephant, who knows all about these things, and how Hathi had taken Mowgli down to a pool to get the Snake Word from a water snake, because Baloo could not pronounce it, and how Mowgli was now reasonably safe against all accidents in the jungle, because neither snake, bird, nor beast would hurt him.

"No one, then, is to be feared," Baloo wound up, patting his big furry stomach with pride.

"Except his own tribe," said Bagheera, under his breath; and then aloud to Mowgli, "Have a care for my ribs, Little Brother! What is all this dancing up and down?"

Mowgli had been trying to make himself heard by pulling at Bagheera's shoulder fur and kicking hard. When the two listened to him he was shouting at the top of his voice, "And so I shall have a tribe of my own, and lead them through the branches all day long."

"What is this new folly, little dreamer of dreams?" said Bagheera.

"Yes, and throw branches and dirt at old Baloo," Mowgli went on. "They have promised me this. Ah!"

"Whoof!" Baloo's big paw scooped Mowgli off Bagheera's back, and as the boy lay between the big forepaws he could see the Bear was angry.

"Mowgli," said Baloo, "thou hast been talking with the *Bandar-log*—the Monkey People."

Mowgli looked at Bagheera to see if the Panther was angry too, and Bagheera's eyes were as hard as jade stones.

"Thou hast been with the Monkey People—the gray apes—the people without a law—the eaters of everything. That is great shame."

"When Baloo hurt my head," said Mowgli (he was still on his back), "I went away, and the gray apes came down from the trees and had pity on me.

No one else cared." He snuffled a little.

"The pity of the Monkey People!" Baloo snorted. 'The stillness of the mountain stream! The cool of the summer sun! And then, man-cub?"

"And then, and then, they gave me nuts and pleasant things to eat, and they—they carried me in their arms up to the top of the trees and said I was their blood brother except that I had no tail, and should be their leader some day."

"They have *no* leader," said Bagheera. "They lie. They have always lied."

"They were very kind and bade me come again. Why have I never been taken among the Monkey People? They stand on their feet as I do. They do not hit me with their hard paws. They play all day. Let me get up! Bad Baloo, let me up! I will play with them again."

"Listen, man-cub," said the Bear, and his voice rumbled like thunder on a hot night. "I have taught thee all the Law of the Jungle for all the peoples of the jungle—except the Monkey Folk who live in the trees. They have no law. They are outcaste. They have no speech of their own, but use the stolen words which they overhear when they listen, and peep, and wait up above in the branches. Their way is not our way. They are without leaders. They have no remembrance. They boast and chatter and pretend that they are a great people about to do great affairs in the jungle, but the falling of a nut turns their minds to laughter and all is forgotten. We of the jungle have no dealings with them. We do not drink where the monkeys drink; we do not go where the monkeys go; we do not hunt where they hunt; we do not die where they die. Hast thou ever heard me speak of the *Bandar-log* till today?"

"No," said Mowgli in a whisper, for the forest was very still now Baloo had finished.

"The Jungle People put them out of their mouths and out of their minds. They are very many, evil, dirty, shameless, and they desire, if they have any fixed desire, to be noticed by the Jungle People. But we do *not* notice them even when they throw nuts and filth on our heads."

He had hardly spoken when a shower of nuts and twigs spattered down through the branches; and they could hear coughings and howlings and angry jumpings high up in the air among the thin branches.

"The Monkey People are forbidden," said Baloo, "forbidden to the Jungle People. Remember."

"Forbidden," said Bagheera, "but I still think Baloo should have warned thee against them."

"I—I? How was I to guess he would play with such dirt. The Monkey People! Faugh!"

A fresh shower came down on their heads and

the two trotted away, taking Mowgli with them. What Baloo had said about the monkeys was perfectly true. They belonged to the treetops, and as beasts very seldom look up, there was no occasion for the monkeys and the Jungle People to cross each other's path. But whenever they found a sick wolf, or a wounded tiger, or bear, the monkeys would torment him, and would throw sticks and nuts at any beast for fun and in the hope of being noticed. Then they would howl and shriek senseless songs, and invite the Jungle People to climb up their trees and fight them, or would start furious battles over nothing among themselves, and leave the dead monkeys where the Jungle People could see them.

They were always just going to have a leader, and laws and customs of their own, but they never did, because their memories would not hold over from day to day, and so they compromised things by making up a saying, "What the *Bandar-log* think now the jungle will think later," and that comforted them a great deal. None of the beasts could reach them, but on the other hand, none of the beasts would notice them, and that was why there were so pleased when Mowgli came to play with them, and they heard how angry Baloo was.

They never meant to do any more—the *Bandar-log* never mean anything at all. But one of them invented what seemed to him a brilliant idea, and he told all the others that Mowgli would be a useful person to keep in the tribe, because he could weave sticks together for protection from the wind; so, if they caught him, they could make him teach them. Of course Mowgli, as a woodcutter's child, inherited all sorts of instincts, and used to make little huts of fallen branches without thinking how he came to do it. The Monkey People, watching in the trees, considered his play most wonderful. This time, they said, they were really going to have a leader and become the wisest people in the jungle—so wise that everyone else would notice and envy them.

Therefore they followed Baloo and Bagheera and Mowgli through the jungle very quietly until it was time for the midday nap, and Mowgli, who was very much ashamed of himself, slept between the Panther and the Bear, resolving to have no more to do with the Monkey People.

The next thing he remembered was feeling hands on his legs and arms—hard, strong, little hands—and then a swash of branches in his face, and then he was staring down though the swaying boughs as Baloo woke the jungle with his deep cries and Bagheera bounded up the trunk with every tooth bared. The *Bandar-log* howled with triumph and scuffled away to the upper branches where Bagheera dared not follow, shouting: "He has noticed us! Bagheera has noticed us. All the

Jungle People admire us for our skill and our cunning." Then they began their flight; and the flight of the Monkey People through tree-land is one of the things nobody can describe. They have their regular roads and crossroads, up hills and down hills, all laid out from fifty to seventy or a hundred feet above ground, and by these they can travel even at night if necessary. Two of the strongest monkeys caught Mowgli under the arms and swung off with him through the treetops, twenty feet at a bound. Had they been alone they could have gone twice as fast, but the boy's weight held them back. Sick and giddy as Mowgli was he could not help enjoying the wild rush, though the glimpses of earth far down below frightened him, and the terrible check and jerk at the end of the swing over nothing but empty air brought his heart between his teeth.

His escort would rush him up a tree till he felt the thinnest topmost branches crackle and bend under them, and then with a cough and a whoop would fling themselves into the air outward and downward, and bring up, hanging by their hands or their feet to the lower limbs of the next tree. Sometimes he could see for miles and miles across the still green jungle, as a man on the top of a mast can see for miles across the sea, and then the branches and leaves would lash him across the face, and he and his two guards would be almost down to earth again. So, bounding and crashing and whooping and yelling, the whole tribe of *Bandar-log* swept along the tree-roads with Mowgli their prisoner.

For a time he was afraid of being dropped. Then he grew angry but knew better than to struggle, and then he began to think. The first thing was to send back word to Baloo and Bagheera, for, at the pace the monkeys were going, he knew his friends would be left far behind. It was useless to look down, for he could only see the topsides of the branches, so he stared upward and saw, far away in the blue, Chil the Kite balancing and wheeling as he kept watch over the jungle waiting for things to die.

Chil saw that the monkeys were carrying something, and dropped a few hundred yards to find out whether their load was good to eat. He whistled with surprise when he saw Mowgli being dragged up to a treetop and heard him give the Kite call for—"We be of one blood, thou and I." The waves of the branches closed over the boy, but Chil balanced away to the next tree in time to see the little brown face come up again. "Mark my trail!" Mowgli shouted. "Tell Baloo of the Seonee Pack and Bagheera of the Council Rock."

"In whose name, Brother?" Chil had never seen Mowgli before, though of course he had heard of him.

"Mowgli the Frog. Man-cub they call me! Mark my tra-il!"

The last words were shrieked as he was being swung through the air, but Chil nodded and rose up till he looked no bigger than a speck of dust, and there he hung, watching with his telescope eyes in the swaying of the treetops as Mowgli's escort whirled along.

"They never go far," he said with a chuckle. "They never do what they set out to do. Always pecking at new things are the *Bandar-log*. This time, if I have any eyesight, they have pecked down trouble for themselves, for Baloo is no fledgling and Bagheera can, as I know, kill more than goats."

So he rocked on his wings, his feet gathered up under him, and waited.

Meantime, Baloo and Bagheera were furious with rage and grief. Bagheera climbed as he had never climbed before, but the thin branches broke beneath his weight, and he slipped down, his claws full of bark.

"Why didst thou not warn the man-cub?" he roared to poor Baloo, who had set off at a clumsy trot in the hope of overtaking the monkeys. "What was the use of half slaying him with blows if thou didst not warn him?"

"Haste! O haste! We—we may catch them yet!" Baloo panted.

"At that speed! It would not tire a wounded cow. Teacher of the Law—cub-beater—a mile of that rolling to and fro would burst thee open. Sit still and think! Make a plan. This is no time for chasing. They may drop him if we follow too close."

"Arrula! Whoo! They may have dropped him already, being tired of carrying him. Who can trust the *Bandar-log?* Put dead bats on my head! Give me black bones to eat! Roll me into the hives of the wild bees that I may be stung to death, and bury me with the Hyena, for I am the most miserable of bears! *Arulala! Wahooa!* O Mowgli, Mowgli! Why did I not warn thee against the Monkey Folk instead of breaking thy head? Now perhaps I may have knocked the day's lesson out of his mind, and he will be alone in the jungle without the Master Words."

Baloo clasped his paws over his ears and rolled to and fro moaning.

"At least he gave me all the words correctly a little time ago," said Bagheera impatiently. "Baloo, thou hast neither memory nor respect. What would the jungle think if I, the Black Panther, curled myself up like Sahi the Porcupine and howled?"

"What do I care what the jungle thinks? He may be dead by now."

"Unless and until they drop him from the

branches in sport, or kill him out of idleness, I have no fear for the man-cub. He is wise and well taught, and above all he has the eyes that make the Jungle People afraid. But (and it is a great evil) he is in the power of the *Bandar-log*, and they, because they live in trees, have no fear of any of our people." Bagheera licked one forepaw thoughtfully.

"Fool that I am! Oh, fat, brown, root-digging fool that I am," said Baloo, uncoiling himself with a jerk, "it is true what Hathi the Wild Elephant says: *'To each his own fear'*; and they, the *Bandar-log*, fear Kaa the Rock Snake. He can climb as well as they can. He steals the young monkeys in the night. The whisper of his name makes their wicked tails cold. Let us go to Kaa."

"What will he do for us? He is not of our tribe, being footless—and with most evil eyes," said Bagheera.

"He is very old and very cunning. Above all, he is always hungry," said Baloo hopefully. "Promise him many goats."

"He sleeps for a full month after he has once eaten. He may be asleep now, and even were he awake what if he would rather kill his own goats?" Bagheera, who did not know much about Kaa, was naturally suspicious.

"Then in that case, thou and I together, old hunter, might make him see reason." Here Baloo rubbed his faded brown shoulder against the Panther, and they went off to look for Kaa the Rock Python.

They found him stretched out on a warm ledge in the afternoon sun, admiring his beautiful new coat, for he had been in retirement for the last ten days changing his skin, and now he was very splendid—darting his big blunt-nosed head along the ground, and twisting the thirty feet of his body into fantastic knots and curves, and licking his lips as he thought of his dinner to come.

"He has not eaten," said Baloo, with a grunt of relief, as soon as he saw the beautifully molted brown and yellow jacket. "Be careful, Bagheera! He is always a little blind after he has changed his skin, and very quick to strike."

Kaa was not a poison snake—in fact he rather despised the poison snakes as cowards—but his strength lay in his hug, and when he had once lapped his huge coils round anybody there was no more to be said. "Good hunting!" cried Baloo, sitting up on his haunches. Like all snakes of his breed Kaa was rather deaf, and did not hear the call at first. Then he curled up ready for any accident, his head lowered.

"Good hunting for us all," he answered. "Oho, Baloo, what dost thou do here? Good hunting, Bagheera. One of us at least needs food. Is there any news of game afoot? A doe now, or even a young buck? I am as empty as a dried well."

"We are hunting," said Baloo carelessly. He knew that you must not hurry Kaa. He is too big.

"Give me permission to come with you," said Kaa. "A blow more or less is nothing to thee, Bagheera or Baloo, but I—I have to wait and wait for days in a wood path and climb half a night on the mere chance of a young ape. Psshaw! The branches are not what they were when I was young. Rotten twigs and dry boughs are they all."

"Maybe thy great weight has something to do with the matter," said Baloo.

"I am a fair length—a fair length," said Kaa with a little pride. "But for all that, it is the fault of this new-grown timber. I came very near to falling on my last hunt—very near indeed—and the noise of my slipping, for my tail was not tight wrapped around the tree, waked the *Bandar-log,* and they called me most evil names."

"Footless, yellow earthworm," said Bagheera under his whiskers, as though he were trying to remember something.

"Sssss! Have they ever called me *that?*" said Kaa.

"Something of that kind it was that they shouted to us last moon, but we never noticed them. They will say anything—even that thou has lost all thy teeth, and wilt not face anything bigger than a kid, because (they are indeed shameless, these *Bandar-log*)—because thou art afraid of the he-goats' horns," Bagheera went on sweetly.

Now a snake, especially a wary old python like Kaa, very seldom shows that he is angry, but Baloo and Bagheera could see the big swallowing muscles on either side of Kaa's throat ripple and bulge.

"The *Bandar-log* have shifted their grounds," he said quietly. "When I came up into the sun today I heard them whooping among the treetops."

"It—it is the *Bandar-log* that we follow now," said Baloo, but the words stuck in his throat, for that was the first time in his memory that one of the Jungle People had owned to being interested in the doings of the monkeys.

"Beyond doubt then it is no small thing that takes two such hunters—leaders in their own jungle I am certain—on the trail of the *Bandar-log*," Kaa replied courteously, as he swelled with curiosity.

"Indeed," Baloo began, "I am no more than the old and sometimes very foolish Teacher of the Law to the Seeonee wolf cubs, and Bagheera here—"

"Is Bagheera," said the Black Panther, and his jaws shut with a snap, for he did not believe in being humble. "The trouble is this, Kaa. Those nut stealers and pickers of palm leaves have stolen away our man-cub of whom thou hast perhaps heard."

"I heard some news from Sahi (his quills make him presumptuous) of a man-thing that was entered into a wolf pack, but I did not believe. Sahi is full of stories half heard and very badly told."

"But it is true. He is such a man-cub as never was," said Baloo. "The best and wisest and boldest of man-cubs—my own pupil, who shall make the name of Baloo famous through all the jungles; and besides, I—we—love him, Kaa."

"Ts! Ts!" said Kaa, weaving his head to and fro. "I also have known what love is. There are tales I could tell that—"

"That need a clear night when we are all well fed to praise properly," said Bagheera quickly. "Our man-cub is in the hands of the *Bandar-log* now, and we know that of all the Jungle People they fear Kaa alone."

"They fear me alone. They have good reason," said Kaa. "Chattering, foolish, vain—vain, foolish, and chattering, are the monkeys. But a man-thing in their hands is in no good luck. They grow tired of the nuts they pick, and throw them down. They carry a branch half a day, meaning to do great things with it, and then they snap it in two. That man-thing is not to be envied. They called me also—yellow fish was it not?"

"Worm—worm—earthworm," said Bagheera, "as well as other things which I cannot now say for shame."

"We must remind them to speak well of their

master Aaa-ssp! We must help them in their wandering memories. Now, whither went they with the cub?"

"The jungle alone knows. Toward the sunset, I believe," said Baloo. "We had thought that thou wouldst know, Kaa."

"I? How? I take them when they come in my way, but I do not hunt the *Bandar-log*, or frogs— or green scum on a water hole, for that matter. Hsss!"

"Up, up! Up, up! Hillo! Illo! Illo, look up, Baloo of the Seeonee Wolf Pack!"

Baloo looked up to see where the voice came from, and there was Chil the Kite, sweeping down with the sun shining on the upturned flanges of his wings. It was near Chil's bedtime, but he had ranged all over the jungle looking for the Bear and had missed him in the thick foliage.

"What is it?" said Baloo.

"I have seen Mowgli among the *Bandar-log*. He bade me tell you. I watched. The *Bandar-log* have taken him beyond the river to the monkey city—to the Cold Lairs. They may stay there for a night, or ten nights, or an hour. I have told the bats to watch through the dark time. That is my message. Good hunting, all you below!"

"Full gorge and a deep sleep to you, Chil," cried Bagheera. "I will remember thee in my next kill, and put aside the head for thee alone—oh, best of kites!"

"It is nothing. It is nothing. The boy held the Master Word. I could have done no less," and Chil circled up again to his roost.

"He has not forgotten to use his tongue," said Baloo with a chuckle of pride. "To think of one so young remembering the Master Word for the birds too while he was being pulled across trees!"

"It was most firmly driven into him," said Baheera. "But I am proud of him, and now we must go to the Cold Lairs."

They all knew where that place was, but few of the Jungle People ever went there, because what they called the Cold Lairs was an old deserted city, lost and buried in the jungle, and beasts seldom use a place that men have once used. The wild boar will, but the hunting tribes do not. Besides, the monkeys lived there as much as they could be said to live anywhere, and no self-respecting animal would come within eyeshot of it except in times of drought, when the half-ruined tanks and reservoirs held a little water.

"It is half a night's journey—at full speed," said Bagheera, and Baloo looked very serious. "I will go as fast as I can," he said anxiously.

"We dare not wait for thee. Follow, Baloo. We must go on the quickfoot—Kaa and I."

"Feet or no feet, I can keep abreast of all thy four," said Kaa shortly. Baloo made one effort to hurry, but he had to sit down panting, and so they left him to come on later, while Bagheera hurried forward, at the quick panther-canter. Kaa said nothing, but, strive as Bagheera might, the huge Rock Python held level with him. When they came to a hill stream, Bagheera gained, because he bounded across while Kaa swam, his head and two feet of his neck clearing the water, but on level ground Kaa made up the distance.

"By the Broken Lock that freed me," said Bagheera, when twilight had fallen, "thou art no slow goer!"

"I am hungry," said Kaa. "Besides, they called me speckled frog."

"Worm—earthworm, and yellow to boot."

"All one. Let us go on," and Kaa seemed to pour himself along the ground, finding the shortest road with his steady eyes, and keeping to it.

In the Cold Lairs the Monkey People were not thinking of Mowgli's friends at all. They had brought the boy to the Lost City, and were very much pleased with themselves for the time. Mowgli had never seen an Indian city before, and though this was almost a heap of ruins it seemed very wonderful and splendid. Some king had built it long ago on a little hill. You could still trace the stone causeways that led up to the ruined gates where the last splinters of wood hung to the worn rusted hinges. Trees had grown into and out of the walls; the battlements were tumbled down and decayed, and wild creepers hung out of the windows of the towers on the walls in bushy hanging clumps.

A great roofless palace crowned the hill, and the marble of the courtyards and the fountains was split, and stained with red and green. The very cobblestones in the courtyard where the king's elephants used to live had been thrust up and apart by grasses and young trees. From the palace you could see the rows and rows of roofless houses that made up the city looking like empty honeycombs filled with blackness; the shapeless block of stone that had been an idol in the square where four roads met; the pits and dimples at street corners where the public wells once stood, and the shattered domes of temples with wild figs sprouting on their sides.

The monkeys called the place their city, and pretended to despise the Jungle People because they lived in the forest. And yet they never knew what the buildings were made for nor how to use them. They would sit in circles on the hall of the king's council chamber, and scratch for fleas and pretend to be men. Or they would run in and out of the roofless houses and collect pieces of plaster and old bricks in a corner, and forget where they had hidden them, and fight and cry in scuffling crowds, and then break off to play up and down the terraces of the king's garden, where they would shake the rose trees and the oranges in sport to see the fruit and flowers fall.

They explored all the passages and dark tunnels in the palace and the hundreds of little dark rooms, but they never remembered what they had seen and what they had not; so they drifted about in ones and twos or crowds telling each other that they were doing as men did. They drank at the tanks and made the water all muddy, and then they fought over it, and then they would all rush together in mobs and shout: "There is no one in the jungle so wise and good and clever and strong and gentle as the *Bandar-log*." Then all would begin again till they grew tired of the city and went back to the treetops, hoping the Jungle People would notice them.

Mowgli, who had been trained under the Law of the Jungle, did not like or understand this kind of life. The monkeys dragged him into the Cold Lairs late in the afternoon, and instead of going to sleep, as Mowgli would have done after a long journey, they joined hands and danced about and sang their foolish songs. One of the monkeys made a speech and told his companions that Mowgli's capture marked a new thing in the history of the *Bandar-log*, for Mowgli was going to show them how to weave sticks and canes together as a protection against the rain and cold. Mowgli picked up some creepers and began to work them in and out, and the monkeys tried to imitate; but in a very few minutes they lost interest and began to pull their friends' tails or jump up and down on all fours, coughing.

"I wish to eat," said Mowgli. "I am a stranger in this part of the jungle. Bring me food, or give me leave to hunt here."

Twenty or thirty monkeys bounded away to bring him nuts and wild papaws. But they fell to fighting on the road, and it was too much trouble to go back with what was left of the fruit. Mowgli was sore and angry as well as hungry, and he roamed through the empty city giving the Strangers' Hunting Call from time to time, but no one answered him, and Mowgli felt that he had reached a very bad place indeed. "All that Baloo has said about the *Bandar-log* is true," he thought to himself. "They have no Law, no Hunting Call, and no leaders—nothing but foolish words and little picking thievish hands. So if I am starved or killed here, it will be all my own fault. But I must try to return to my own jungle. Baloo will surely beat me, but that is better than chasing silly rose leaves with the *Bandar-log*."

No sooner had he walked to the city wall than the monkeys pulled him back, telling him that he did not know how happy he was, and pinching him to make him grateful. He set his teeth and said nothing, but went with the shouting monkeys to a terrace above the red sandstone reservoirs that were half full of rain water. There was a ruined summerhouse of white marble in the center of the terrace, built for queens dead a hundred years ago. The domed roof had half fallen in and blocked up the underground passage from the palace by which the queens used to enter. But the walls were made of screens of marble tracery—beautiful milk-white fret-work, set with agates and carnelians and jasper and lapis lazuli, and as the moon came up behind the hill it shone through the open work, casting shadows on the ground like black velvet embroidery.

Sore, sleepy and, hungry as he was, Mowgli could not help laughing when the *Bandar-log* began, twenty at a time, to tell him how great and wise and strong and gentle they were, and how foolish he was to wish to leave them.

"We are great. We are free. We are wonderful. We are the most wonderful people in all the jungle! We all say so, and so it must be true," they shouted. "Now as you are a new listener and can carry our words back to the Jungle People so that they may notice us in future, we will tell you all about our most excellent selves." Mowgli made no objection, and the monkeys gathered by hundreds and hundreds on the terrace to listen to their own speakers singing the praises of the *Bandar-log*, and whenever a speaker stopped for want of breath they would all shout together: "This is true; we all say so."

Mowgli nodded and blinked, and said "Yes" when they asked him a question, and his head spun with the noise. "Tabaqui the Jackal must have bitten all these people," he said to himself, "and now they have the madness. Certainly this is *dewanee*, the madness. Do they never go to sleep? Now there is a cloud coming to cover that moon. If it were only a big enough cloud I might try to run away in the darkness. But I am tired."

That same cloud was being watched by two good friends in the ruined ditch below the city wall, for Bangheera and Kaa, knowing well how dangerous the Monkey People were in large numbers, did not wish to run any risks. The monkeys never fight unless they are a hundred to one, and few in the jungle care for those odds.

"I will go to the west wall," Kaa whispered, "And come down swiftly with the slope of the ground in my favor. They will not throw themselves upon *my* back in their hundreds, but—"

"I know it," said Bagheera. "Would that Baloo were here, but we must do what we can. When that cloud covers the moon I shall go to the terrace. They hold some sort of council there over the boy."

"Good hunting," said Kaa grimly, and glided away to the west wall. That happened to be the least ruined of any, and the big snake was delayed awhile before he could find a way up the stones.

The cloud hid the moon, and as Mowgli wondered what would come next he heard Bagheera's light feet on the terrace. The Black Panther had raced up the slope almost without a sound and was striking—he knew better than to waste time in biting—right and left among the monkeys, who were seated round Mowgli in circles fifty and sixty deep.

There was a howl of fright and rage, and then as Bagheera tripped on the rolling kicking bodies beneath him, a monkey shouted: "There is only one here! Kill him! Kill." A scuffling mass of monkeys, biting, scratching, tearing, and pulling, closed over Bagheera, while five of six laid hold of Mowgli, dragged him up the wall of the summerhouse and pushed him through the hole of the broken dome. A man-trained boy would have been badly bruised, for the fall was a good fifteen feet, but Mowgli fell as Baloo had taught him to fall, and landed on his feet.

"Stay there," shouted the monkeys, "till we have killed thy friends, and later we will play with thee—if the Poison People leave thee alive."

"We be of one blood, ye and I," said Mowgli, quickly giving the Snake's Call. He could hear rustling and hissing in the rubbish all round him and gave the call a second time, to make sure.

"Even ssso! Down hoods all!" said half a dozen low voices (every ruin in India becomes sooner or later a dwelling place of snakes, and the old summerhouse was alive with cobras). "Stand still, Little Brother, for thy feet may do us harm."

Mowgli stood as quietly as he could, peering through the open work and listening to the furious din of the fight round the Black Panther—the yells and chatterings and scufflings, and Bagheera's deep, hoarse cough as he backed and bucked and twisted and plunged under the heaps of his enemies. For the first time since he was born, Bagheera was fighting for his life.

"Baloo must be at hand; Bagheera would not have come alone," Mowgli thought. And then he called aloud: "To the tank, Bagheera. Roll to the water tanks. Roll and plunge! Get to the water!"

Bagheera heard, and the cry that told him that Mowgli was safe gave him new courage. He worked his way desperately, inch by inch, straight for the reservoirs, halting in silence. Then from the ruined wall nearest the jungle rose up the rumbling war shout of Baloo. The old Bear had done his best, but he could not come before. "Bagheera," he shouted, "I am here. I climb! I haste! *Ahuwora!* The stones slip under my feet! Wait my coming, O most infamous *Bandar-log!*"

He panted up the terrace only to disappear to the head in a wave of monkeys, but he threw himself squarely on his haunches, and, spreading out his forepaws, hugged as many as he could hold, and then began to hit with a regular *bat-bat-bat*, like the flipping strokes of a paddle wheel. A crash and a splash told Mowgli that Bagheera had fought his way to the tank where the monkeys could not follow. The Panther lay gasping for breath, his head just out of the water, while the monkeys stood three deep on the red steps, dancing up and down with rage, ready to spring upon him from all sides if he came out to help Baloo.

It was then that Bagheera lifted up his dripping chin, and in despair gave the Snake's Call for protection—"We be of one blood, ye and I"—for he believed that Kaa had turned tail at the last minute. Even Baloo, half smothered under the monkeys on the edge of the terrace, could not help chuckling as he heard the Black Panther asking for help.

Kaa had only just worked his way over the west wall, landing with a wrench that dislodged a coping stone into the ditch. He had no intention of losing any advantage of the ground, and coiled and uncoiled himself once or twice, to be sure that every foot of his long body was in working order. All that while the fight with Baloo went on, and the monkeys yelled in the tank round Bagheera, and Mang the Bat, flying to and fro, carried the news of the great battle over the jungle, till even Hathi the Wild Elephant trumpeted, and far away, scattered bands of the Monkey Folk woke and came leaping along the tree-roads to help their comrades in the Cold Lairs, and the noise of the fight roused all the day birds for miles round.

Then Kaa came straight, quickly, and anxious to kill. The fighting strength of a python is in the driving blow of his head backed by all the strength and weight of his body. If you can imagine a lance, or a battering ram, or a hammer weighing nearly half a ton driven by a cool, quiet mind living in the handle of it you can roughly imagine what Kaa was like when he fought. A python four or five feet long can knock a man down if he hits him fairly in the chest, and Kaa was thirty feet long, as you know. His first stroke was delivered into the heart of the crowd round Baloo. It was sent home with shut mouth in silence, and there was no need of a second. The monkeys scattered with cries of—"Kaa! It is Kaa! Run! Run!"

Generations of monkeys had been scared into good behavior by the stories their elders told them of Kaa, the night thief, who could slip along the branches as quietly as moss grows, and steal away the strongest monkey that ever lived; of old Kaa, who could make himself look so like a dead branch or a rotten stump that the wisest were deceived, till the branch caught them. Kaa was everything that the monkeys feared in the jungle, for none of them knew the limits of his power, none of them could look him in the face, and none had ever come alive out of his hug. And so they ran, stammering with terror, to the walls and the roofs of the houses, and Balloo drew a deep breath of relief. His fur was much thicker than Bagheera's, but he had suffered sorely in the fight.

Then Kaa opened his mouth for the first time and spoke one long hissing word, and the faraway monkeys, hurring to the defense of the Cold Lairs, stayed where they were, cowering, till the loaded branches bent and crackled under them. The monkeys on the walls and the empty houses stopped their cries, and in the stillness that fell upon the city Mowgli heard Bagheera shaking his wet sides as he came up from the tank. Then the clamor broke out again. The monkeys leaped higher up the walls. They clung around the necks of the big stone idols and shrieked as they skipped along the battlements, while Mowgli, dancing in the summerhouse, put his eye to the screenwork and hooted owl-fashion between his front teeth, to show his derision and contempt.

"Get the man-cub out of that trap; I can do no more," Bagheera gasped. "Let us take the man-cub and go. They may attack again."

"They will not move till I order them. Stay you sssso!" Kaa hissed, and the city was silent once more. "I could not come before, Brother, but I *think* I heard thee call"—this was to Bagheera.

"I—I may have cried out in the battle,"

Bagheera answered. "Baloo, art thou hurt?"

"I am not sure that they did not pull me into a hundred little bearlings," said Baloo, gravely shaking one leg after the other. "Wow! I am sore. Kaa, we owe thee, I think our lives—Bagheera and I."

"No matter. Where is the manling?"

"Here, in a trap. I cannot climb out," cried Mowgli. The curve of the broken dome was above his head.

"Take him away. He dances like Mor the Peacock. He will crush our young," said the cobras inside.

"Hah!" said Kaa with a chuckle, "he has friends everywhere, this manling. Stand back, manling. And hide you, O Poison People. I break down the wall."

Kaa looked carefully till he found a discolored crack in the marble tracery showing a weak spot, made two or three light taps with his head to get the distance, and then lifting up six feet of his body clear of the ground, sent home half a dozen full-power smashing blows, nose first. The screenwork broke and fell away in a cloud of dust and rubbish, and Mowgli leaped through the opening and flung himself between Baloo and Bagheera—an arm around each big neck.

"Art thou hurt?" said Baloo, hugging him softly.

"I am sore, hungry, and not a little bruised. But,

oh, they have handled ye grievously, my brothers! Ye bleed."

"Others also," said Bagheera, licking his lips and looking at the monkey-dead on the terrace and round the tank.

"It is nothing, it is nothing, if thou art safe, oh, my pride of all little frogs!" whimpered Baloo.

"Of that we shall judge later," said Bagheera, in a dry voice that Mowgli did not at all like. "But here is Kaa to whom we owe the battle and thou owest thy life. Thank him according to our customs, Mowgli."

Mowgli turned and saw the great Python's head swaying a foot above his own.

"So this is the manling," said Kaa. "Very soft is his skin, and he is not unlike the *Bandar-log*. Have a care, manling, that I do not mistake thee for a monkey some twilight when I have newly changed my coat."

"We be of one blood, thou and I," Mowgli answered. "I take my life from thee tonight. My kill shall be thy kill if ever thou art hungry, O Kaa."

"All thanks, Little Brother," said Kaa, though his eyes twinkled. "And what may so bold a hunter kill? I ask that I may follow when next he goes abroad."

"I kill nothing—I am too little—but I drive goats toward such as can use them. When thou art empty come to me and see if I speak the truth. I have some skill in these"—he held out his hands—"and if ever thou art in a trap, I may pay the debt which I owe to thee, to Bagheera, and to Baloo, here. Good hunting to ye all, my masters."

"Well said," growled Baloo, for Mowgli had returned thanks very prettily. The Python dropped his head lightly for a minute on Mowgli's shoulder. "A brave heart and a courteous tongue," said he. "They shall carry thee far through the jungle, manling. But now go hence quickly with thy friends. Go and sleep, for the moon sets, and what follows is not well that thou shouldst see."

The moon was sinking behind the hills and the lines of trembling monkeys huddled together on the walls and battlements looked like ragged shaky fringes of things. Baloo went down to the tank for a drink and Bagheera began to put his fur in order, and Kaa glided out into the center of the terrace and brought his jaws together with a ringing snap that drew all the monkeys' eyes upon him.

"The moon sets," he said. "Is there yet light enough to see?"

From the walls came a moan like the wind in the treetops—"We see, O Kaa."

"Good. Begins now the dance—the Dance of the Hunger of Kaa. Sit still and watch."

He turned twice or thrice in a big circle,

weaving his head from right to left. Then he began to make loops and figures of eight with his body, and soft, oozy triangles that melted into squares and five-sided figures, and coiled mounds, never resting, never hurrying, and never stopping his low humming song. It grew darker and darker, till at last the dragging, shifting coils disappeared, but they could hear the rustle of the scales.

Baloo and Bagheera stood still as stone, growling in their throats, their neck hair bristling, and Mowgli watched and wondered.

"*Bandar-log,*" said the voice of Kaa at last, "can ye stir foot or hand without my order? Speak!"

"Without thy order we cannot stir foot or hand, O Kaa!"

"Good! Come all one pace nearer to me."

The lines of the monkeys swayed forward helplessly, and Baloo and Bagheera took one stiff step forward with them.

"Nearer!" hissed Kaa, and they all moved again.

Mowgli laid his hands on Baloo and Bagheera to get them away, and the two great beasts started as though they had been waked from a dream.

"Keep thy hand on my shoulder," Bagheera whispered. "Keep it there, or I must go back— must go back to Kaa. Aah!"

"It is only old Kaa making circles on the dust," said Mowgli. "Let us go." And the three slipped off through a gap in the walls to the jungle.

"*Whoof!*" said Baloo, when he stood under the still trees again. "Never more will I make an ally of Kaa," and he shook himself all over.

"He knows more than we," said Bagheera, trembling. "In a little time, had I stayed, I should have walked down his throat."

"Many will walk by that road before the moon rises again," said Baloo. "He will have good hunting—after his own fashion."

"But what was the meaning of it all?" said Mowgli, who did not know anything of a python's powers of fascination. "I saw no more than a big snake making foolish circles till the dark came. And his nose was all sore. Ho! Ho!"

"Mowgli," said Bagheera angrily, "his nose was sore on *thy* account, as my ears and sides and paws, and Baloo's neck and shoulders are bitten on *thy* account. Neither Baloo nor Bagheera will be able to hunt with pleasure for many days."

"It is nothing, it is nothing, if thou art safe, oh, my man-cub again."

"True, but he has cost us heavily in time which might have been spent in good hunting, in wounds, and hair—I am half plucked along my back—and last of all, in honor. For, remember, Mowgli, I, who am the Black Panther, was forced to call upon Kaa for protection, and Baloo and I were both made stupid as little birds by the Hunger Dance. All this, man-cub, came of thy playing with the *Bandar-log*."

"True, it is true," said Mowgli sorrowfully. "I am an evil man-cub, and my stomach is sad in me."

"Mf! What says the Law of the Jungle, Baloo?"

Baloo did not wish to bring Mowli into any more trouble, but he could not tamper with the Law, so he mumbled: "Sorrow never stays punishment. But remember, Bagheera, he is very little."

"I will remember. But he has done mischief, and blows must be dealt now. Mowgli, hast thou anything to say?"

"Nothing. I did wrong. Baloo and thou are wounded. It is just."

Bagheera gave him half a dozen love-taps from a panther's point of view (they would hardly have waked one of his own cubs), but for a seven-year-old boy they amounted to as severe a beating as you could wish to avoid. When it was all over Mowgli sneezed, and picked himself up without a word.

"Now," said Bagheera, "jump on my back, Little Brother, and we will go home."

One of the beauties of Jungle Law is that punishment settles all scores. There is no nagging afterward.

Mowgli laid his head down on Bagheera's back and slept so deeply that he never waked when he was put down in the home cave.

Road Song of the Bandar-Log

Here we go in a flung festoon,
Halfway up to the jealous moon!
Don't you envy our pranceful bands?
Don't you wish you had extra hands?
Wouldn't you like if your tails were—*so*—
Curved in the shape of a Cupid's bow?
    Now you're angry, but—never mind,
    Brother, thy tail hangs down behind!

Here we sit in a branchy row,
Thinking of beautiful things we know;
Dreaming of deeds that we mean to do,
All complete, in a minute or two—
Something noble and wise and good,
Done by merely wishing we could.
    We've forgotten, but—never mind.
    Brother, thy tail hangs down behind!

All the talk we ever have heard
Uttered by bat or beast or bird—
Hide or fin or scale or feather—
Jabber it quickly and all together!
Excellent! Wonderful! Once again!
Now we are talking just like men!
　　Let's pretend we are—never mind,
　　Brother, thy tail hangs down behind!
　　This is the way of the monkey-kind.

*Then join our leaping lines that scumfish
　　through the pines,*
*That rocket by where, light and high, the wild
　　grape swings.*
*By the rubbish in our wake, and the noble noise we
　　make,*
*Be sure, be sure, we're going to do some splendid
　　things!*

"Tiger! Tiger!"

What of the hunting, hunter bold?
  Brother, the watch is long and cold.
What of the quarry ye went to kill?
  Brother, he crops in the jungle still.
Where is the power that made your pride?
  Brother, it ebbs from my flank and side.
Where is the haste that ye hurry by?
  Brother, I go to my lair to die.

When Mowgli left the wolf's cave after the fight with the Pack at the Council Rock, he went down to the plowed lands where the villagers lived, but he would not stop there because it was too near to the jungle, and he knew that he had made at least one bad enemy at the Council. So he hurried on, keeping on the rough road that ran down the valley, and followed it at a steady job trot for nearly twenty miles, till he came to a country that he did not know. The valley opened out into a great plain dotted over with rocks and cut up by ravines. At one end stood a little village, and at the other the thick jungle came down in a sweep to the grazing grounds, and stopped there as though it had been cut off with a hoe. All over the plain, cattle and buffaloes were grazing, and when the little boys in charge of the herds saw Mowgli they shouted and ran away, and the yellow pariah dogs that hang about every Indian village barked. Mowgli walked on, for he was feeling hungry, and when he came to the village gate he saw the big thornbush that was drawn up before the gate at twilight, pushed to one side.

"Umph!" he said, for he had come across more than one such barricade in his night rambles after things to eat. "So men are afraid of the People of the Jungle here also."

He sat down by the gate, and when a man came out he stood up, opened his mouth, and pointed down it to show that he wanted food. The man stared, and ran back up the one street of the village shouting for the priest, who was a big, fat man dressed in white, with a red and yellow mark on his forehead. The priest came to the gate, and with him at least a hundred people, who stared and talked and shouted and pointed at Mowgli.

"They have no manners, these Men Folk," said Mowgli to himself. "Only the gray ape would behave as they do." So he threw back his long hair and frowned at the crowd.

"What is there to be afraid of?" said the priest. "Look at the marks on his arms and legs. They are the bites of wolves. He is but a wolf-child run away from the jungle."

Of course, in playing together, the cubs had often nipped Mowgli harder than they intended, and there were white scars all over his arms and legs. But he would have been the last person in the world to call these bites, for he knew what real biting meant.

"*Arré! Arré!*" said two or three women together. "To be bitten by wolves, poor child ! He is a handsome boy. He has eyes like red fire. By my honor, Messua, he is not unlike thy boy that was taken by the tiger."

"Let me look," said a woman with heavy copper rings on her wrists and ankles, and she peered at Mowgli under the palm of her hand. "Indeed he is not. He is thinner, but he has the very look of my boy."

The priest was a very clever man, and he knew that Messua was wife to the richest villager in the place. So he looked up at the sky for a minute and said solemnly: "What the jungle has taken the jungle has restored. Take the boy into thy house, my sister, and forget not to honor the priest who sees so far into the lives of men."

"By the Bull that bought me," said Mowgli to himself, "but all this talking is like another looking over by the Pack! Well, if I am a man, a man I must be."

The crowd parted as the woman beckoned

Mowgli to her hut, where there was a red-lacquered bedstead, a great earthen grain chest with funny raised patterns on it, half a dozen copper cooking pots, an image of a Hindu god in a little alcove, and on the wall a real looking glass, such as they sell at the country fairs for eight cents.

She gave him a long drink of milk and some bread, and then she laid her hand on his head and looked into his eyes; for she thought perhaps that he might be her real son come back from the jungle where the tiger had taken him. So she said, "Nathoo, O Nathoo!" Mowgli did not show that he knew the name. "Dost thou not remember the day when I gave thee new shoes?" She touched his foot, and it was almost as hard as a horn. "No," she said sorrowfully, "those feet have never worn shoes, but thou art very like my Nathoo, and thou shalt be my son."

Mowgli was uneasy, because he had never been under a roof before. But as he looked at the thatch, he saw that he could tear it out any time if he wanted to get away, and that the window had no fastenings. "What is the good of a man," he said to himself at last, "if he does not understand man's talk? Now I am as silly and dumb as a man would be with us in the jungle. I must speak their talk."

He had not learned while he was with the wolves to imitate the challenge of bucks in the jungle and the grunt of the little wild pig for fun.

So, as soon as Messua pronounced a word Mowgli would imitate it almost perfectly, and before dark he had learned the names of many things in the hut.

There was a difficulty at bedtime, because Mowgli would not sleep under anything that looked so like a panther trap as that hut, and when they shut the door he went through the window.

"Give him his will," said Messua's husband. "Remember he can never till now have slept on a bed. If he is indeed sent in the place of our son he will not run away."

So Mowgli stretched himself in some long, clean grass at the edge of the field, but before he had closed his eyes a soft gray nose poked him under the chin.

"Phew!" said Gray Brother (he was the eldest of Mother Wolf's cubs). "This is a poor reward for following thee twenty miles. Thou smellest of wood smoke and cattle—altogether like a man already. Wake, Little Brother; I bring news."

"Are all well in the jungle?" said Mowgli, hugging him.

"All except the wolves that were burned with the Red Flower. Now, listen. Shere Khan has gone away to hunt far off till his coat grows again, for he is badly singed. When he returns he swears that he will lay thy bones in the Waingunga."

"There are two words to that. I also have made a

little promise. But news is always good. I am tired tonight—very tired with new things, Gray Brother—but bring me the news always."

"Thou wilt not forget that thou art a wolf? Men will not make thee forget?" said Gray Brother anxiously.

"Never. I will always remember that I love thee and all in our cave. But also I will always remember that I have been cast out of the Pack."

"And that thou mayest be cast out of another pack. Men are only men, Little Brother, and their talk is like the talk of frogs in a pond. When I come down here again, I will wait for thee in the bamboos at the edge of the grazing ground."

For three months after that night Mowgli hardly ever left the village gate, he was so busy learning the ways and customs of men. First he had to wear a cloth round him, which annoyed him horribly; and then he had to learn about money, which he did not in the least understand, and about plowing, of which he did not see the use. Then the little children in the village made him very angry. Luckily, the Law of the Jungle had taught him to keep his temper, for in the jungle life and food depend on keeping your temper.

But when they made fun of him because he would not play games or fly kites, or because he mispronounced some word, only the knowledge that it was unsportsmanlike to kill little naked cubs kept him from picking them up and breaking them in two. He did not know his own strength in the least. In the jungle he knew he was weak compared with the beasts, but in the village people said that he was as strong as a bull. He certainly had no notion of what fear was, for when the village priest told him that the god in the temple would be angry with him if he ate the priest's mangoes, he picked up the image, brought it over to the priest's house, and asked the priest to make the god angry and he would be happy to fight him. It was a horrible scandal, but the priest hushed it up, and Messua's husband paid much good silver to comfort the god.

And Mowgli had not the faintest idea of the difference that caste makes between man and man. When the potter's donkey slipped in the clay pit, Mowgli hauled it out by the tail, and helped to stack the pots for their journey to the market at Khanhiwara. That was very shocking, too, for the potter is a low-caste man, and his donkey is worse. When the priest scolded him, Mowgli threatened to put him on the donkey too, and the priest told Messua's husband that Mowgli had better be set to work as soon as possible. So the village headman told Mowgli that he would have to go out with the buffaloes next day, and herd them while they grazed.

No one was more pleased than Mowgli; and that night, because he had been appointed a servant of the village, as it were, he went off to a circle that met every evening on a masonry platform under a great fig tree. It was the village club, and the headman and the watchman and the barber, who knew all the gossip of the village, and old Buldeo, the village hunter, who had a Tower musket, met and smoked. The monkeys sat and talked in the upper branches, and there was a hole under the platform where a cobra lived, and he had his little platter of milk every night because he was sacred.

The old men sat around the tree and talked, and pulled at the big *hugas* (the water pipes) till far into the night. They told wonderful tales of gods and men and ghosts; and Buldeo told even more wonderful ones of the ways of beasts in the jungle, till the eyes of the children sitting outside the circle bulged out of their heads. Most of the tales were about animals, for the jungle was always at their door. The deer and the wild pig grubbed up their crops, and now and again the tiger carried off a man at twilight, within sight of the village gates.

Mowgli, who naturally knew something about what they were talking of, had to cover his face not to show that he was laughing, while Buldeo, the Tower musket across his knees, climbed on from one wonderful story to another, and Mowgli's shoulders shook.

Buldeo was explaining how the tiger that had

carried away Messua's son was a ghost-tiger, and his body was inhabited by the ghost of a wicked old moneylender, who had died some years ago. "And I know that this is true," he said, "because Purun Dass always limped from the blow that he got in a riot when his account books were burned, and the tiger that I speak of *he* limps, too, for the tracks of his pads are unequal."

"True, true, that must be the truth," said the graybeards, nodding together.

"Are all these tales such cobwebs and moon talk?" said Mowgli. "That tiger limps because he was born lame, as everyone knows. To talk of the soul of a moneylender in a beast that never had the courage of a jackal is child's talk."

Buldeo was speechless with surprise for a moment, and the headman stared.

"Oho! It is the jungle brat, is it?" said Buldeo. "If thou art so wise, better bring his hide to Khanhiwara, for the Government has set a hundred rupees on his life. Better still, talk not when thy elders speak."

Mowgli rose to go. "All the evening I have lain here listening," he called back over his shoulder, "and, except once or twice, Buldeo has not said one word of truth concerning the jungle, which is at his very doors. How, then, shall I believe the tales of ghosts and gods and goblins which he says he has seen?"

"It is full time that boy went to herding," said

the headman, while Buldeo puffed and snorted at Mowgli's impertinence.

The custom of most Indian villages is for a few boys to take the cattle and buffaloes out to graze in the early morning, and bring them back at night. The very cattle that would trample a white man to death allow themselves to be banged and bullied and shouted at by children that hardly come up to their noses. So long as the boys keep with the herds they are safe, for not even the tiger will charge a mob of cattle. But if they straggle to pick flowers or hunt lizards, they are sometimes carried off.

Mowgli went through the village street in the dawn, sitting on the back of Rama, the great herd bull. The slaty-blue buffaloes, with their long, backward-sweeping horns and savage eyes, rose out of their byres, one by one, and followed him, and Mowgli made it very clear to the children with him that he was the master. He beat the buffaloes with a long, polished bamboo, and told Kamya, one of the boys, to graze the cattle by themselves, while he went on with the buffaloes, and to be very careful not to stray away from the herd.

An Indian grazing ground is all rocks and scrubs and tussocks and little ravines, among which the herds scatter and disappear. The buffaloes generally keep to the pools and muddy places, where they lie wallowing or basking in the warm mud for hours. Mowgli drove them on to the edge of the plain where the Waingunga came out of the jungle; then he dropped from Rama's neck, trotted off to a bamboo clump, and found Gray Brother.

"Ah," said Gray Brother, "I have waited here very many days. What is the meaning of this cattle-herding work?"

"It is an order," said Mowgli. "I am a village herder for a while. What news of Shere Khan?"

"He has come back to this country, and has waited here a long time for thee. Now he has gone off again, for the game is scarce. But he means to kill thee."

"Very good," said Mowgli. "So long as he is away do thou or one of the four brothers sit on that rock, so that I can see thee as I come out of the village. When he comes back wait for me in the ravine by the *dhâk* tree in the center of the plain. We need not walk into Shere Khan's mouth."

Then Mowgli picked out a shady place, and lay down and slept while the buffaloes grazed round him. Herding in India is one of the laziest things in the world. The cattle move and crunch, and lie down, and move on again, and they do not even low. They only grunt, and the buffaloes very seldom say anything, but get down into the muddy pools one after another, and work their way into the mud till only their noses and staring china-blue eyes show above the surface, and then they lie like logs.

The sun makes the rocks dance in the heat, and

the herd children hear one kite (never any more) whistling almost out of sight overhead, and they know that if they died, or a cow died, that kite would sweep down, and the next kite miles away would see him drop and follow, and the next, and the next, and almost before they were dead there would be a score of hungry kites come out of nowhere.

Then they sleep and wake and sleep again, and weave little baskets of dried grass and put grasshoppers in them; or catch two praying mantises and make them fight; or string a necklace of red and black jungle nuts; or watch a lizard basking on a rock, or a snake hunting a frog near the wallows. Then they sing long, long songs with odd native quavers at the end of them, and the day seems longer than most people's whole lives, and perhaps they make a mud castle with mud figures of men and horses and buffaloes, and put reeds into the men's hands, and pretend that they are kings and the figures are their armies, or that they are gods to be worshiped.

Then evening comes and the children call, and the buffaloes lumber up out of the sticky mud with noises like gunshots going off one after the other, and they all string across the gray plain back to the twinkling village lights.

Day after day Mowgli would lead the buffaloes out to their wallows, and day after day he would see Gray Brother's back a mile and a half away across the plain (so he knew that Shere Khan had not come back), and day after day he would lie on the grass listening to the noises round him, and dreaming of old days in the jungle. If Shere Khan had made a false step with his lame paw up in the jungles by the Waingunga, Mowgli would have heard him in those long, still mornings.

At last a day came when he did not see Gray Brother at the signal place, and he laughed and headed the buffaloes for the ravine by the *dhâk* tree, which was all covered with golden-red flowers. There sat Gray Brother, every bristle on his back lifted.

"He has hidden for a month to throw thee off thy guard. He crossed the ranges last night with Tabaqui, hotfoot on thy trail," said the Wolf, panting.

Mowgli frowned. "I am not afraid of Shere Khan, but Tabaqui is very cunning."

"Have no fear," said Gray Brother, licking his lips a little. "I met Tabaqui in the dawn. Now he is telling all his wisdom to the kites, but he told *me* everything before I broke his back. Shere Khan's plan is to wait for thee at the village gate this evening—for thee and for no one else. He is lying up now, in the big dry ravine of the Waingunga."

"Has he eaten today, or does he hunt empty?" said Mowgli, for the answer meant life and death to him.

"He killed at dawn—a pig—and he has drunk

too. Remember, Shere Khan could never fast, even for the sake of revenge."

"Oh! Fool, fool! What a cub's cub it is! Eaten and drunk too, and he thinks that I shall wait till he has slept! Now, where does he lie up? If there were but ten of us we might pull him down as he lies. These buffaloes will not charge unless they wind him, and I cannot speak their language. Can we get behind his track so that they may smell it?"

"He swam far down the Waingunga to cut that off," said Gray Brother.

"Tabaqui told him that, I know. He would never have thought of it alone." Mowgli stood with his finger in his mouth, thinking. "The big ravine of the Waingunga. That opens out on the plain not half a mile from here. I can take the herd round through the jungle to the head of the ravine and then sweep down—but he would slink out at the foot. We must block that end. Gray Brother, canst thou cut the herd in two for me?"

"Not I, perhaps—but I have brought a wise helper." Gray Brother trotted off and dropped into a hole. Then there lifted up a huge gray head that Mowgli knew well, and the hot air was filled with the most desolate cry of all the jungle—the hunting howl of a wolf at midday.

"Akela! Akela!" said Mowgli, clapping his hands. "I might have known that thou wouldst not forget me. We have a big work in hand. Cut the herd in two, Akela. Keep the cows and calves together, and the bulls and the plow buffaloes by themselves."

The two wolves ran, ladies'-chain fashion, in and out of the herd, which snorted and threw up its head, and separated into two clumps. In one, the cow-buffaloes stood with their calves in the center, and glared and pawed, ready, if a wolf would only stay still, to charge down and trample the life out of him. In the other, the bulls and the young bulls snorted and stamped, but though they looked more imposing they were much less dangerous, for they had no calves to protect. No six men could have divided the herd so neatly.

"What orders!" panted Akela. "They are trying to join again."

Mowgli slipped on to Rama's back. "Drive the bulls away to the left, Akela. Gray Brother, when we are gone, hold the cows together, and drive them into the foot of the ravine."

"How far?" said Gray Brother, panting and snapping.

"Till the sides are higher than Shere Khan can jump," shouted Mowgli. "Keep them there till we come down." The bulls swept off as Akela bayed, and Gray Brother stopped in front of the cows. They charged down on him, and he ran just before them to the foot of the ravine, as Akela drove the bulls far to the left.

"Well done! Another charge and they are fairly started. Careful, now—careful, Akela. A snap too much and the bulls will charge. *Hujah!* This is wilder work than driving black buck. Didst thou think these creatures could move so swiftly?" Mowgli called.

"I have—have hunted these too in my time," gasped Akela in the dust. "Shall I turn them into the jungle?"

"Ay! Turn. Swiftly turn them! Rama is mad with rage. Oh, if I could only tell him what I need of him today."

The bulls were turned, to the right this time, and crashed into the standing thicket. The other herd children, watching with the cattle half a mile away, hurried to the village as fast as their legs could carry them, crying that the buffaloes had gone mad and run away. But Mowgli's plan was simple enough. All he wanted to do was to make a big circle uphill and get at the head of the ravine, and then take the bulls down it and catch Shere Khan between the bulls and the cows; for he knew that after a meal and a full drink Shere Khan would not be in any condition to fight or to clamber up the sides of the ravine.

He was soothing the buffaloes now by voice, and Akela had dropped far to the rear, only whimpering once or twice to hurry the rear guard. It was a long, long circle, for they did not wish to get too near the ravine and give Shere Khan warning. At last Mowgli rounded up the bewildered herd at the head of the ravine on a grassy patch that sloped steeply down to the ravine itself. From that height you could see across the tops of the trees down to the plain below; but what Mowgli looked at was the sides of the ravine, and he saw with a great deal of satisfaction that they ran nearly straight up and down, while the vines and creepers that hung over them would give no foothold to a tiger who wanted to get out.

"Let them breathe, Akela," he said, holding up his hand. "They have not winded him yet. Let them breathe. I must tell Shere Khan who comes. We have him in the trap."

He put his hands to his mouth and shouted down the ravine—it was almost like shouting down a tunnel—and the echoes jumped from rock to rock.

After a long time there came back the drawling, sleepy snarl of a full-fed tiger just wakened.

"Who calls?" said Shere Khan, and a splendid peacock fluttered up out of the ravine screeching.

"I, Mowgli. Cattle thief, it is time to come to the Council Rock! Down—hurry them down, Akela! Down, Rama, down!"

The herd paused for an instant at the edge of the slope, but Akela gave tongue in the full hunting yell, and they pitched over one after the other, just as steamers shoot rapids, the sand and stones spurting up round them. Once started, there was no chance of stopping, and before they were fairly in the bed of the ravine Rama winded Shere Khan and bellowed.

"Ha! Ha!" said Mowgli, on his back. "Now thou knowest!" and the torrent of black horns, foaming muzzles, and staring eyes whirled down the ravine just as boulders go down in floodtime; the weaker buffaloes being shouldered out to the sides of the ravine where they tore through the creepers. They knew what the business was before them—the terrible charge of the buffalo herd against which no tiger can hope to stand. Shere Khan heard the thunder of their hoofs, picked himself up, and lumbered down the ravine, looking from side to side for some way of escape, but the walls of the ravine were straight and he had to hold on, heavy with his dinner and his drink, willing to do anything rather than fight.

The herd splashed through the pool he had just left, bellowing till the narrow cut rang. Mowgli heard an answering bellow from the foot of the ravine, saw Shere Khan turn (the tiger knew if the worst came to the worst it was better to meet the bulls than the cows with their calves), and then Rama tripped, stumbled, and went on again over something soft, and, with the bulls at his heels, crashed full into the other herd, while the weaker buffaloes were lifted clean off their feet by the shock of the meeting. That charge carried both herds out into the plain, goring and stamping and snorting. Mowgli watched his time, and slipped off Rama's neck, laying about him right and left with his stick.

"Quick, Akela! Break them up. Scatter them, or they will be fighting one another. Drive them away, Akela. *Hai*, Rama! *Hai, hai, hai!* my children. Softly now, softly! It is all over."

Akela and Gray Brother ran to and fro nipping the buffaloes' legs, and though the herd wheeled once to charge up the ravine again, Mowgli managed to turn Rama, and the others followed him to the wallows.

Shere Khan needed no more trampling. He was dead, and the kites were coming for him already.

"Brothers, that was a dog's death," said Mowgli, feeling for the knife he always carried in a sheath round his neck now that he lived with men. "But he would never have shown fight. *Wallah!* His hide will look well on the Council Rock. We must get to work swiftly."

A boy trained among men would never have dreamed of skinning a ten-foot tiger alone, but Mowgli knew better than anyone else how an animal's skin is fitted on, and how it can be taken off. But it was hard work, and Mowgli slashed and tore and grunted for an hour, while the wolves lolled out their tongues, or came forward and tugged as he ordered them. Presently a hand fell on his shoulder, and looking up he saw Buldeo with the Tower musket. The children had told the village about the buffalo stampede, and Buldeo went out angrily, only too anxious to correct Mowgli for not taking better care of the herd. The wolves dropped out of sight as soon as they saw the man coming.

"What is this folly?" said Buldeo angrily. "To think that thou canst skin a tiger! Where did the buffaloes kill him? It is the Lame Tiger too, and there is a hundred rupees on his head. Well, well, we will overlook thy letting the herd run off, and perhaps I will give thee one of the rupees of the reward when I have taken the skin to Khanhiwara." He fumbled in his waist cloth for flint and steel, and stooped down to singe Shere Khan's whiskers. Most native hunters always singe a tiger's whiskers to prevent his ghost from haunting them.

"Hum!" said Mowgli, half to himself as he ripped back the skin of a forepaw. "So thou wilt take the hide to Khanhiwara for the reward, and perhaps give me one rupee? Now it is in my mind that I need the skin for my own use. Heh! Old man, take away that fire!"

"What talk is this to the chief hunter of the village? Thy luck and the stupidity of thy buffaloes have helped thee to this kill. The tiger has just fed, or he would have gone twenty miles by this time. Thou canst not even skin him properly, little beggar brat, and forsooth I, Buldeo, must be told not to singe his whiskers. Mowgli, I will not give thee one anna of the reward, but only a very big beating. Leave the carcass!"

"By the Bull that bought me," said Mowgli, who was trying to get at the shoulder, "must I stay babbling to an old ape all noon? Here, Akela, this man plagues me."

Buldeo, who was still stooping over Shere Khan's head, found himself sprawling on the grass, with a gray wolf standing over him, while Mowgli went on skinning as though he were alone in all India.

"Ye-es," he said, between his teeth. "Thou art altogether right, Buldeo. Thou wilt never give me one anna of the reward. There is an old war between this lame tiger and myself—a very old war, and—I have won."

To do Buldeo justice, if he had been ten years younger he would have taken his chance with Akela had he met the wolf in the woods, but a wolf who obeyed the orders of this boy who had private wars with man-eating tigers was not a common animal. It was sorcery, magic of the worst kind, thought Buldeo, and he wondered whether the amulet round his neck would protect him. He lay as still as still, expecting every minute to see Mowgli turn into a tiger too.

"Maharaj! Great King," he said at last in a husky whisper.

"Yes," said Mowgli, without turning his head, chuckling a little.

"I am an old man. I did not know that thou wast anything more than a herdsboy. May I rise up and go away, or will thy servant tear me to pieces?"

"Go, and peace go with thee. Only, another time do not meddle with my game. Let him go, Akela."

Buldeo hobbled away to the village as fast as he could, looking back over his shoulder in case Mowgli should change into something terrible. When he got to the village he told a tale of magic and enchantment and sorcery that made the priest look very grave.

Mowgli went on with his work, but it was nearly twilight before he and the wolves had drawn the great gay skin clear of the body.

"Now we must hide this and take the buffaloes home! Help me to herd them, Akela."

The herd rounded up in the misty twilight, and when they got near the village Mowgli saw lights, and heard the conches and bells in the temple blowing and banging. Half the village seemed to be waiting for him by the gate. "That is because I have killed Shere Khan," he said to himself. But a shower of stones whistled about his ears, and the villagers shouted: "Sorcerer! Wolf's brat! Jungle demon! Go away! Get hence quickly or the priest will turn thee into a wolf again. Shoot, Buldeo, shoot!"

The old Tower musket went off with a bang, and a young buffalo bellowed in pain.

"More sorcery!" shouted the villagers. "He can turn bullets. Buldeo, that was *thy* buffalo."

"Now what is this?" said Mowgli, bewildered, as the stones flew thicker.

"They are not unlike the Pack, these brothers of thine," said Akela, sitting down composedly. "It is in my head that, if bullets mean anything, they would cast thee out."

"Wolf! Wolf's cub! Go away!" shouted the priest, waving a sprig of the sacred *tulsi* plant.

"Again? Last time it was because I was a man. This time it is because I am a wolf. Let us go, Akela."

A woman—it was Messua—ran across to the herd, and cried: "Oh, my son, my son! They say thou art a sorcerer who can turn himself into a beast at will. I do not believe, but go away or they will kill thee. Buldeo says thou art a wizard, but I know thou hast avenged Nathoo's death."

"Come back, Messua!" shouted the crowd. "Come back, or we will stone thee."

Mowgli laughed a little short ugly laugh, for a stone had hit him in the mouth. "Run back, Messua. This is one of the foolish tales they tell under the big tree at dusk. I have at least paid for thy son's life. Farewell; and run quickly, for I shall send the herd in more swiftly than their brickbats. I am no wizard, Messua. Farewell!"

"Now, once more, Akela," he cried. "Bring the herd in."

The buffaloes were anxious enough to get to the village. They hardly needed Akela's yell, but charged through the gate like a whirlwind, scattering the crowd right and left.

"Keep count!" shouted Mowgli scornfully. "It may be that I have stolen one of them. Keep count, for I will do your herding no more. Fare you well, children of men, and thank Messua that I do not come in with my wolves and hunt you up and down your street."

He turned on his heel and walked away with the Lone Wolf, and as he looked up at the stars he felt happy. "No more sleeping in traps for me, Akela. Let us get Shere Khan's skin and go away. No, we will not hurt the village, for Messua was kind to me."

When the moon rose over the plain, making it look all milky, the horrified villagers saw Mowgli, with two wolves at his heels and a bundle on his head, trotting across at the steady wolf's trot that eats up the long miles like fire. Then they banged the temple bells and blew the conches louder than ever. And Messua cried, and Buldeo embroidered the story of his adventures in the jungle, till he ended by saying that Akela stood up on his hind legs and talked like a man.

The moon was just going down when Mowgli and the two wolves came to the hill of the Council Rock, and they stopped at Mother Wolf's cave.

"They have cast me out from the Man Pack, Mother," shouted Mowgli, "but I come with the hide of Shere Khan to keep my word."

Mother Wolf walked stiffly from the cave with the cubs behind her, and her eyes glowed as she saw the skin.

"I told him on that day, when he crammed his head and shoulders in this cave, hunting for thy life, Little Frog—I told him that the hunter would be the hunted. It is well done."

"Little Brother, it is well done," said a deep voice in the thicket. "We were lonely in the jungle without thee," and Bagheera came running to Mowgli's bare feet. They clambered up the Council Rock together, and Mowgli spread the skin out on the flat stone where Akela used to sit, and pegged it down with four slivers of bamboo, and Akela lay down upon it, and called the old call to the Council, "Look, look well, O Wolves," exactly as he had called when Mowgli was first brought there.

Ever since Akela had been deposed, the Pack had been without a leader, hunting and fighting at their own pleasure. But they answered the call from habit; and some of them were lame from the traps they had fallen into, and some limped from shot wounds, and some were mangy from eating bad food, and many were missing. But they came to the Council Rock, all that were left of them, and saw Shere Khan's striped hide on the rock, and the huge claws dangling at the end of the empty dangling feet.

"Look well, O Wolves. Have I kept my word?" said Mowgli. And the wolves bayed Yes, and one tattered wolf howled:

"Lead us again, O Akela. Lead us again, O man-cub, for we be sick of this lawlessness, and we would be the Free People once more."

"Nay," purred Bagheera, "that may not be. When ye are full-fed, the madness may come upon you again. Not for nothing are ye called the Free People. Ye fought for freedom, and it is yours. Eat it, O Wolves."

"Man Pack and Wolf Pack have cast me out," said Mowgli. "Now I will hunt alone in the jungle."

"And we will hunt with thee," said the four cubs.

So Mowgli went away and hunted with the four cubs in the jungle from that day on. But he was not always alone, because, years afterward, he became a man and married.

But that is a story for grownups.

Mowgli's Song

The Song of Mowgli—I, Mowgli, am singing. Let
the jungle listen to the things I have done.

Shere Khan said he would kill—would kill! At the
gates in the twilight he would kill Mowgli
the Frog!

He ate and he drank. Drink deep, Shere Khan, for
when wilt thou drink again? Sleep and dream
of the kill.

I am alone on the grazing grounds. Gray Brother,
come to me! Come to me, Lone Wolf, for there
is big game afoot!

Bring up the great bull buffaloes, the blue-
skinned herd bulls with the angry eyes. Drive
them to and fro as I order.

Sleepest thou still, Shere Khan? Wake, Oh, wake!
Here come I, and the bulls are behind.

Rama the King of the Buffaloes stamped with his
foot. Waters of the Waingunga, whither went
Shere Khan?

He is not Sahi to dig holes, nor Mor the Peacock
that he should fly. He is not Mang the Bat, to
hang in the branches. Little bamboos that
creak together, tell me where he ran?

Ow! He is there. *Ahoo!* He is there. Under the feet
of Rama lies the Lame One! Up, Shere
Khan! Up and kill! Here is meat; break the
necks of the bulls!

Hsh! He is asleep. We will not wake him, for his
strength is very great. The kites have come
down to see it. The black ants have come up to
know it. There is a great assembly in his
honor.

Alala! I have no cloth to wrap me. The kites will
see that I am naked. I am ashamed to meet
all these people.

Lend me thy coat, Shere Khan. Lend me thy gay
striped coat that I may go to the Council
Rock.

By the Bull that bought me I made a promise—a
little promise. Only thy coat is lacking
before I keep my word.

With the knife, with the knife that men use, with
the knife of the hunter, I will stoop down
for my gift.

Waters of the Waingunga, Shere Khan gives me
his coat for the love that he bears me. Pull,
Gray Brother! Pull, Akela! Heavy is the hide
of Shere Khan.

The Man Pack are angry. They throw stones and talk child's talk. My mouth is bleeding. Let me run away.

Through the night, through the hot night, run swiftly with me, my brothers. We will leave the lights of the village and go to the low moon.

Waters of the Waingunga, the Man Pack have cast me out. I did them no harm, but they were afraid of me. Why?

Wolf Pack, ye have cast me out too. The jungle is shut to me and the village gates are shut. Why?

As Mang flies between the beasts and birds, so fly I between the village and the jungle. Why?

I dance on the hide of Shere Khan, but my heart is very heavy. My mouth is cut and wounded with the stones from the village, but my heart is very light, because I have come back to the jungle. Why?

These two things fight together in me as the snakes fight in the spring. The water comes out of my eyes; yet I laugh while it falls. Why?

I am two Mowglis, but the hide of Shere Khan is under my feet.

All the jungle knows that I have killed Shere Khan. Look, look well, O Wolves!

Ahae! My heart is heavy with the things that I do not understand.

The White Seal

Oh! hush thee, my baby, the night is behind us,
    And black are the waters that sparkled so green.
The moon, o'er the combers, looks downward to find us
    At rest in the hollows that rustle between.
Where billow meets billow, then soft be thy pillow,
    Ah, weary wee flipperling, curl at thy ease!
The storm shall not wake thee, nor shark overtake thee,
    Asleep in the arms of the slow-swinging seas!

Seal Lullaby

All these things happened several years ago at a place call Novastoshnah, or North East Point, on the Island of St. Paul, away and away in the Bering Sea. Limmershin, the Winter Wren, told me the tale when he was blown on to the rigging of a steamer going to Japan, and I took him down into my cabin and warmed and fed him for a couple of days till he was fit to fly back to St. Paul's again. Limmershin is a very quaint little bird, but he knows how to tell the truth.

Nobody comes to Novastoshnah except on business, and the only people who have regular business there are the seals. They come in the summer months by hundreds and hundreds of thousands out of the cold gray sea. For Novastoshnah Beach has the finest accommodation for seals of any place in all the world.

Sea Catch knew that, and every spring would swim from whatever place he happened to be in—would swim like a torpedo boat straight for Novastoshnah and spend a month fighting with his companions for a good place on the rocks, as close to the sea as possible. Sea Catch was fifteen years old, a huge gray fur seal with almost a mane on his shoulders, and long, wicked dog teeth. When he heaved himself up on his front flippers he stood more than four feet clear of the ground, and his weight, if anyone had been bold enough to weigh him, was nearly seven hundred pounds.

He was scarred all over with the marks of savage fights, but he was always ready for just one fight more. He would put his head on one side, as though he were afraid to look his enemy in the face; then he would shoot it out like lightning, and when the big teeth were firmly fixed on the other seal's neck, the other seal might get away if he could, but Sea Catch would not help him. Yet Sea Catch never chased a beaten seal, for that was against the Rules of the Beach. He only wanted room by the sea for his nursery. But as there were forty or fifty thousand other seals hunting for the same thing each spring, the whistling, bellowing, roaring, and blowing on the beach was something frightful.

From a little hill called Hutchinson's Hill, you could look over three and a half miles of ground covered with fighting seals; and the surf was dotted all over with the heads of seals hurrying to land and begin their share of the fighting. They fought in the breakers, they fought in the sand, and they fought on the smooth-worn basalt rocks of the nurseries, for they were just as stupid and unaccommodating as men.

Their wives never came to the island until late in May or early in June, for they did not care to be torn to pieces; and the young two-, three-, and four-year-old seals who had not begun housekeeping went inland about half a mile through the ranks of the fighters and played about on the sand dunes in droves and legions, and rubbed off every single green thing that grew. They were called the holluschickie—the bachelors—and there were perhaps two or three hundred thousand of them at Novastoshnah alone.

Sea Catch had just finished his forty-fifth fight one spring when Matkah, his soft, sleek, gentle-eyed wife, came up out of the sea, and he caught her by the scruff of the neck and dumped her down on his reservation, saying gruffly: "Late as usual. Where *have* you been?"

It was not the fashion for Sea Catch to eat

anything during the four months he stayed on the beaches, and so his temper was generally bad. Matkah knew better than to answer back. She looked round and cooed: "How thoughtful of you. You've taken the old place again."

"I should think I had," said Sea Catch. "Look at me!"

He was scratched and bleeding in twenty places; one eye was almost out, and his sides were torn to ribbons.

"Oh, you men, you men!" Matkah said, fanning herself with her hind flipper. "Why can't you be sensible and settle your places quietly? You look as though you had been fighting with the Killer Whale."

"I haven't been doing anything *but* fight since the middle of May. The beach is disgracefully crowded this season. I've met at least a hundred seals from Lukannon Beach, house hunting. Why can't people stay where they belong?"

"I've often thought we should be much happier if we hauled out at Otter Island instead of this crowded place," said Matkah.

"Bah! Only the holluschickie go to Otter Island. If we went there they would say we were afraid. We must preserve appearances, my dear."

Sea Catch sunk his head proudly between his fat shoulders and pretended to go to sleep for a few minutes, but all the time he was keeping a sharp lookout for a fight. Now that all the seals and their wives were on the land, you could hear their clamor miles out to sea above the loudest gales. At the lowest counting there were over a million seals on the beach—old seals, mother seals, tiny babies, and holluschickie, fighting, scuffling, bleating, crawling, and playing together—going down to the sea and coming up from it in gangs and regiments, lying over every foot of ground as far as the eye could reach, and skirmishing about in brigades through the fog. It is nearly always foggy at Novastoshnah, except when the sun comes out and makes everything look all pearly and rainbow-colored for a little while.

Kotick, Matkah's baby, was born in the middle of that confusion, and he was all head and shoulders, with pale, watery blue eyes, as tiny seals must be, but there was something about his coat that made his mother look at him very closely.

"Sea Catch," she said, at last, "our baby's going to be white!"

"Empty clamshells and dry seaweed!" snorted Sea Catch. "There never has been such a thing in the world as a white seal."

"I can't help that," said Matkah; "there's going to be now." And she sang the low, crooning seal song that all mother seals sing to their babies:

You mustn't swim till you're six weeks old,
　Or your head will be sunk by your heels;
And summer gales and Killer Whales
　Are bad for baby seals.

Are bad for baby seals, dear rat,
　As bad as bad can be;
But splash and grow strong,
And you can't be wrong.
　Child of the Open sea!

Of course the little fellow did not understand the words at first. He paddled and scrambled about by his mother's side, and learned to scuffle out of the way when his father was fighting with another seal, and the two rolled and roared up and down the slippery rocks. Matkah used to go to sea to get things to eat, and the baby was fed only once in two days, but then he ate all he could and throve upon it.

The first thing he did was to crawl inland, and there he met tens of thousands of babies of his own age, and they played together like puppies, went to sleep on the clean sand, and played again.

The old people in the nurseries took no notice of them, and the holluschickie kept to their own grounds, and the babies had a beautiful playtime. When Matkah came back from her deep-sea fishing she would go straight to their playground and call as a sheep calls for a lamb, and wait until she heard Kotick bleat. Then she would take the straightest of straight lines in his direction, striking out with her foreflippers and knocking the youngsters head over heels right and left. There were always a few hundred mothers hunting for their children through the playgrounds, and the babies were kept lively. But, as Matkah told Kotick, "So long as you don't lie in muddy water and get mange, or rub the hard sand into a cut or scratch, and so long as you never go swimming when there is a heavy sea, nothing will hurt you here."

Little seals can no more swim than little children, but they are unhappy till they learn. The first time that Kotick went down to the sea a wave carried him out beyond his depth, and his big head sank and his little hind flippers flew up exactly as his mother had told him in the song, and if the next wave had not thrown him back again he would have drowned. After that, he learned to lie in a beach pool and let the wash of the waves just cover him and lift him up while he paddled, but he always kept his eye open for big waves that might hurt.

He was two weeks learning to use his flippers; and all that while he floundered in and out of the water, and coughed and grunted and crawled up the beach and took catnaps on the sand, and went back again, until at last he found that he truly belonged to the water. Then you can imagine the times that he had with his companions, ducking under the rollers; or coming in on top of a comber and landing with a swash and a splutter as the big wave went whirling far up the beach; or standing up on his tail and scratching his head as the old people did; or playing "I'm the King of the Castle" on slippery, weedy rocks that just stuck out of the wash.

Now and then he would see a thin fin, like a big shark's fin, drifting along close to shore, and he knew that that was the Killer Whale, the Grampus, who eats young seals when he can get them; and Kotick would head for the beach like an arrow, and the fin would jig off slowly, as if it were looking for nothing at all.

Late in October the seals began to leave St. Paul's for the deep sea, by families and tribes, and there was no more fighting over the nurseries, and the holluschickie played anywhere they liked. "Next year," said Matkah to Kotick, "you will be a holluschickie; but this year you must learn how to catch fish."

They set out together across the Pacific, and Matkah showed Kotick how to sleep on his back with his flippers tucked down by his side and his little nose just out of the water. No cradle is so comfortable as the long, rocking swell of the Pacific. When Kotick felt his skin tingle all over, Matkah told him he was learning the "feel of the water," and that tingly, prickly feelings meant bad weather coming, and he must swim hard and get away.

"In a little time," she said, "you'll know where to swim to, but just now we'll follow Sea Pig, for he is very wise." A school of porpoises were ducking and tearing through the water, and little Kotick followed them as fast as he could. "How do you know where to go to?" he panted. The leader of the school rolled his white eye and ducked under. "My tail tingles, youngster," he said. "That means there's a gale behind me. Come along! When you're south of the Sticky Water [he meant the Equator] and your tail tingles, that means there's a gale in front of you and you must head north. Come along. The water feels bad here."

This was one of very many things that Kotick learned, and he was always learning. Matkah taught him to follow the cod and the halibut along the undersea banks and wrench the rockling out of his hole among the weeds; how to skirt the wrecks lying a hundred fathoms below water and dart like a rifle bullet in at one porthole and out at another as the fishes ran; how to dance on the top of the waves when the lightning was racing all over the sky, and wave his flipper politely to the stumpy-tailed albatross and the man-of-war hawk as they went down the wind; how to jump three or four feet clear of the water like a dolphin, flippers close to the side and tail curved; to leave the flying fish alone because they are all bony; to take the shoulder piece out of a cod at full speed ten fathoms deep, and never to stop and look at a boat or a ship, but particularly a rowboat. At the end of six months what Kotick did not know about deep-sea fishing was not worth the knowing. And all that time he never set flipper on dry ground.

One day, however, as he was lying half asleep in the warm water somewhere off the Island of Juan Fernández, he felt faint and lazy all over, just as human people do when the Spring is in their legs, and he remembered the good firm beaches of Novastoshnah seven thousand miles away, the games his companions played, the smell of the seaweed, the seal roar, and the fighting. That very minute he turned north, swimming steadily, and as he went on he met scores of his mates, all bound for the same place, and they said: "Greeting, Kotick! This year we are all holluschickie, and we can dance the Fire Dance in the breakers off Lukannon and play on the new grass. But where did you get that coat?"

Kotick's fur was almost pure white now, and though he felt very proud of it, he only said,

"Swim quickly! My bones are aching for the land." And so they all came to the beaches where they had been born, and heard the old seals, their fathers, fighting in the rolling mist.

That night Kotick danced the Fire Dance with the yearling seals. The sea is full of fire on summer nights all the way down from Novastoshnah to Lukannon, and each seal leaves a wake like burning oil behind him and a flaming flash when he jumps, and the waves break in great phosphorescent streaks and swirls.

Then they went inland to the holluschickie grounds and rolled up and down in the new wild wheat and told stories of what they had done while they had been at sea. They talked about the Pacific as boys would talk about a wood that they had been nutting in, and if anyone had understood them he could have gone away and made such a chart of that ocean as never was. The three- and four-year-old holluschickie romped down from Hutchinson's Hill crying: "Out of the way, youngsters! The sea is deep and you don't know all that's in it yet. Wait till you've rounded the Horn. Hi, you yearling, where did you get that white coat?"

"I didn't get it," said Kotick. "It grew." And just as he was going to roll the speaker over, a couple of black-haired men with flat red faces came from behind a sand dune, and Kotick, who had never seen a man before, coughed and lowered his head. The holluschickie just bundled off a few yards and sat staring stupidly. The men were no less than Kerick Booterin, the chief of the seal hunters on the island, and Patalamon, his son. They came from the little village not half a mile from the seal nurseries, and they were deciding what seals they would drive up to the killing pens—for the seals were driven just like sheep—to be turned into seal-skin jackets later on.

"Ho!" said Patalamon. "Look! There's a white seal!"

Kerick Booterin turned nearly white under his oil and smoke, for he was an Aleut, and Aleuts are not clean people. Then he began to mutter a prayer. "Don't touch him, Patalamon. There has never been a white seal since—since I was born. Perhaps it is old Zaharrof's ghost. He was lost last year in the big gale."

"I'm not going near him," said Patalamon. "He's unlucky. Do you really think he is old Zaharrof come back? I owe him for some gulls' eggs."

"Don't look at him," said Kerick. "Head off that drove of four-year-olds. The men ought to skin two hundred today, but it's the beginning of the season and they are new to the work. A hundred will do. Quick!"

Patalamon rattled a pair of seal's shoulder

bones in front of a heard of holluschickie and they stopped dead, puffing and blowing. Then he stepped near and the seals began to move, and Kerick headed them inland, and they never tried to get back to their companions. Hundreds and hundreds of thousands of seals watched them being driven, but they went on playing just the same. Kotick was the only one who asked questions, and none of his companions could tell him anything, except that the men always drove seals in that way for six weeks or two months of every year.

"I am going to follow," he said and his eyes nearly popped out of his head as he shuffled along in the wake of the herd.

"The white seal is coming after us," cried Patalamon. "That's the first time a seal has ever come to the killing grounds alone."

"Hsh! Don't look behind you," said Kerick. "It *is* Zaharrof's ghost! I must speak to the priest about this."

The distance to the killing grounds was only half a mile, but it took an hour to cover, because if the seals went too fast Kerick knew that they would get heated and then their fur would come off in patches when they were skinned. So they went on very slowly, past Sea Lion's Neck, past Webster House, till they came to the Salt House just beyond the sight of the seals on the beach.

Kotick followed, panting and wondering. He thought that he was at the world's end, but the roar of the seal nurseries behind him sounded as loud as the roar of a train in a tunnel.

Then Kerick sat down on the moss and pulled out a heavy pewter watch and let the drove cool off for thirty minutes, and Kotick could hear the fog dew dripping off the brim of his cap. Then ten or twelve men, each with an ironbound club three or four feet long, came up, and Kerick pointed out one or two of the drove that were bitten by their companions or too hot, and the men kicked those aside with their heavy boots made of the skin of a walrus's throat, and then Kerick said, "Let go!" and then the men clubbed the seals on the head as fast as they could.

Ten minutes later little Kotick did not recognize his friends any more, for their skins were ripped off from the nose to the hind flippers, whipped off and thrown down on the ground in a pile. That was enough for Kotick. He turned and galloped (a seal can gallop very swiftly for a short time) back to the sea; his little new mustache bristling with horror. At Sea Lion's Neck, where the great sea lions sit on the edge of the surf, he flung himself flipper-overhead into the cool water and rocked there, gasping miserably.

"What's here?" said a sea lion gruffly, for as a rule the sea lions keep themselves to themselves.

"Scoochnie! Ochen scoochnie!" ("I'm lonesome, very lonesome!") said Kotick. "They're killing *all* the holluschickie on *all* the beaches!"

The Sea Lion turned his head inshore. "Nonsense!" he said. "Your friends are making as much noise as ever. You must have seen old Kerick polishing off a drove. He's done that for thirty years."

"It's horrible," said Kotick, backing water as a wave went over him, and steadying himself with a screw stroke of his flippers that brought him all standing within three inches of a jagged edge of rock.

"Well done for a yearling!" said the Sea Lion, who could appreciate good swimming. "I suppose it *is* rather awful from your way of looking at it, but if you seals will come here year after year, of course the men get to know of it, and unless you can find an island where no men ever come you will always be driven."

"Isn't there any such island?" began Kotick.

"I've followed the *poltoos* [the halibut] for twenty years, and I can't say I've found it yet. But look here—you seem to have a fondness for talking to your betters—suppose you go to Walrus Islet and talk to Sea Vitch. He may know something. Don't flounce off like that. It's a six-mile swim, and if I were you I should haul out and take a nap first, little one."

Kotick thought that that was good advice, so he swam round to his own beach, hauled out, and slept for half an hour, twitching all over, as seals will. Then he headed straight for Walrus Islet, a little low sheet of rocky island almost due northeast from Novastoshnah, all ledges of rock and gulls' nests, where the walrus herded by themselves.

He landed close to old Sea Vitch—the big, ugly, bloated, pimpled, fat-necked, long-tusked walrus of the North Pacific, who has no manners except when he is asleep—as he was then—with his hind flippers half in and half out of the surf.

"Wake up!" barked Kotick, for the gulls were making a great noise.

"Hah! Ho! Hmph! What's that?" said Sea Vitch, and he struck the next walrus a blow with his tusks and waked him up, and the next struck the next, and so on till they were all awake and staring in every direction but the right one.

"Hi! It's me," said Kotick, bobbing in the surf and looking like a little white slug.

"Well! May I be—skinned!" said Sea Vitch, and they all looked at Kotick as you can fancy a club full of drowsy old gentlemen would look at a little boy.

Kotick did not care to hear any more about skinning just then; he had seen enough of it. So he called out: "Isn't there any place for seals to go where men don't ever come?"

"Go and find out," said Sea Vitch, shutting his eyes. "Run away. We're busy here."

"Kotick made his dolphin-jump in the air and shouted as loud as he could: "Clam-eater! Clam-eater!" He knew that Sea Vitch never caught a fish in his life but always rooted for clams and seaweed; though he pretended to be a very terrible person. Naturally the Chickies and the Goo-verooskies and the Epatkas—the Burgomaster gulls and the Kittiwakes and the Puffins, who are always looking for a chance to be rude, took up the cry, and—so Limmershin told me—for nearly five minutes you could not have heard a gun fired on Walrus Islet. All the population was yelling and screaming "Clam-eater! *Stareek* [old man]!" while Sea Vitch rolled from side to side grunting and coughing.

"*Now* will you tell?" said Kotick, all out of breath.

"Go and ask Sea Cow," said Sea Vitch. "If he is living still, he'll be able to tell you."

"How shall I know Sea Cow when I meet him?" said Kotick, sheering off.

"He's the only thing in the sea uglier than Sea Vitch," screamed a Burgomaster gull, wheeling under Sea Vitch's nose. "Uglier, and with worse manners! *Stareek!*"

Kotick swam back to Novastoshnah, leaving the

gulls to scream. There he found that no one sympathized with him in his little attempt to discover a quiet place for the seals. They told him that men had always driven the holluschickie—it was part of the day's work—and that if he did not like to see ugly things he should not have gone to the killing grounds. But none of the other seals had seen the killing, and that made the difference between him and his friends. Besides, Kotick was a white seal.

"What you must do," said old Sea Catch, after he had heard his son's adventures, "is to grow up and be a big seal like your father, and have a nursery on the beach, and then they will leave you alone. In another five years you ought to be able to fight for yourself." Even gentle Matkah, his mother, said: "You will never be able to stop the killing. Go and play in the sea, Kotick." And Kotick went off and danced the Fire Dance with a very heavy little heart.

That autumn he left the beach as soon as he could, and set off alone because of a notion in his bullethead. He was going to find Sea Cow, if there was such a person in the sea, and he was going to find a quiet island with good firm beaches for seals to live on, where men could not get at them. So he explored and explored by himself from the North to the South Pacific, swimming as much as three hundred miles in a day and a night.

He met with more adventures than can be told,

and narrowly escaped being caught by the Basking shark, and the Spotted shark, and the Hammerhead, and he met all the untrustworthy ruffians that loaf up and down the seas, and the heavy polite fish, and the scarlet spotted scallops that are moored in one place for hundreds of years, and grow very proud of it; but he never met Sea Cow, and he never found an island that he could fancy. If the beach was good and hard, with a slope behind it for seals to play on, there was always the smoke of a whaler on the horizon, boiling down blubber, and Kotick knew what *that* meant. Or else he could see that seals had once visited the island and been killed off, and Kotick knew that where men had come once they would come again.

He picked up with an old stumpy-tailed albatross, who told him that Kerguelen Island was the very place for peace and quiet, and when Kotick went down there he was all but smashed to pieces against some wicked black cliffs in a heavy sleet storm with lightning and thunder. Yet as he pulled out against the gale he could see that even there had once been a seal nursery. And it was so in all the other islands that he visited.

Limmershin gave a long list of them, for he said that Kotick spent five seasons exploring, with a four months' rest each year at Novastoshnah, when the holluschickie used to make fun of him and his imaginary islands. He went to the Galapagos, a horrid dry place on the Equator, where he was nearly baked to death; he went to the Georgia Islands, the Orkneys, Emerald Island, Little Nightingale Island, Gough's Island, Bouvet's Island, the Crossets, and even to a little speck of an island south of the Cape of Good Hope.

But everywhere the People of the Sea told him the same things. Seals had come to those islands once upon a time, but men had killed them all off. Even when he swam thousands of miles out of the Pacific and got to a place called Cape Corientes (that was when he was coming back from Gough's Island) he found a few hundred mangy seals on a rock and they told him that men came there too. That nearly broke his heart, and he headed round the Horn back to his own beaches; and on his way north he hauled out on an island full of green trees, where he found an old, old seal who was dying, and Kotick caught fish for him and told him all his failures.

"Now," said Kotick, "I am going back to Novastoshnah, and if I am driven to the killing pens with the holluschickie I shall not care."

The old seal said, "Try once more. I am the last of the Lost Rookery of Masafuera, and in the days when men killed us by the hundred thousand there was a story on the beaches that some day a white seal would come out of the North and lead the seal people to a quiet place. I am old, and I shall never live to see that day, but others will. Try once more."

And Kotick curled up his mustache (it was a beauty) and said, "I am the only white seal that has ever been born on the beaches, and I am the only seal, black or white, who ever thought of looking for new islands."

This cheered him immensely; and when he came back to Novastoshnah that summer, Matkah, his mother, begged him to marry and settle down, for he was no longer a holluschick but a full-grown sea catch, with a curly white mane on his shoulders, as heavy, as big, and as fierce as his father.

"Give me another season," he said. "Remember, Mother, it is always the seventh wave that goes farthest up the beach."

Curiously enough, there was another seal who thought that she would put off marrying till the next year, and Kotick danced the Fire Dance with her all down Lukannon Beach the night before he set off on his last exploration. This time he went westward, because he had fallen on the trail of a great shoal of halibut, and he needed at least one hundred pounds of fish a day to keep him in good condition. He chased them till he was tired, and then he curled himself up and went to sleep on the hollows of the ground swell that sets in to Cooper Island. He knew the coast perfectly well, so about midnight, when he felt himself gently bumped on a weed bed, he said, "Hm, tide's running strong tonight," and turning over under water opened his eyes slowly and stretched. Then he jumped like a cat, for he saw huge things nosing about in the shoal water and browsing on the heavy fringes of the weeds.

"By the Great Combers of Magellan!" he said, beneath his mustache. "Who in the Deep Sea are these people?"

They were like not walrus, sea lion, seal, bear, whale, shark, fish, squid, or scallop that Kotick had ever seen before. They were between twenty and thirty feet long, and they had no hind flippers, but a shovel-like tail that looked as if it had been whittled out of wet leather. Their heads were the most foolish-looking things you ever saw, and they balanced on the ends of their tails in deep water when they weren't grazing, bowing solemnly to each other and waving their front flippers as a fat man waves his arm.

"Ahem!" said Kotick. "Good sport, gentlemen?"

The big things answered by bowing and waving their flippers like the Frog Footman. When they began feeding again Kotick saw that their upper lip was split into two pieces that they could twitch apart about a foot and bring together again with a whole bushel of seaweed between the splits. They tucked the stuff into their mouths and chumped solemnly.

"Messy style of feeding, that," said Kotick. They

bowed again, and Kotick began to lose his temper. "Very good," he said. "If you *do* happen to have an extra joint in your front flipper you needn't show off so. I see you bow gracefully, but I should like to know your names."

The split lips moved and twitched; and the glassy green eyes stared, but they did not speak.

"Well!" said Kotick. "You're the only people I've ever met uglier than Sea Vitch—and with worse manners."

Then he remembered in a flash what the Burgomaster gull had screamed to him when he was a little yearling at Walrus Islet, and he tumbled backward in the water, for he knew that he had found Sea Cow at last! The sea cows went on schlooping and grazing and chumping in the weed, and Kotick asked them questions in every language that he had picked up in his travels; and the Sea People talk nearly as many languages as human beings. But the sea cows did not answer, because Sea Cow cannot talk. He has only six bones in his neck where he ought to have seven, and they say under the sea that that prevents him from speaking even to his companions. But, as you know, he has an extra joint in his foreflipper, and by waving it up and down and about he makes what answers to a sort of clumsy telegraphic code.

By daylight Kotick's mane was standing on end and his temper was gone where the dead crabs go.

Then the Sea Cow began to travel northward very slowly, stopping to hold absurd bowing councils from time to time, and Kotick followed them, saying to himself, "People who are such idiots as these are would have been killed long ago if they hadn't found out some safe island. And what is good enough for the Sea Cow is good enough for the Sea Catch. All the same, I wish they'd hurry."

It was weary work for Kotick. The sea cows' herd never went more than forty or fifty miles a day, and stopped to feed at night, and kept close to the shore all the time. Kotick swam round them, and over them, and under them, but he could not hurry them up one mile. As they went farther north they held a bowing council every few hours, and Kotick nearly bit off his mustache with impatience till he saw that they were following up a warm current of water, and then he respected them more.

One night they sank through the shiny water—sank like stones—and for the first time since he had known them began to swim quickly. Kotick followed, and the pace astonished him, for he never dreamed that Sea Cow was anything of a swimmer. They headed for a cliff by the shore, a cliff that ran down into deep water, and plunged into a dark hole at the foot of it, twenty fathoms under the sea. It was a long, long swim, and Kotick badly wanted fresh air before he was out of the dark tunnel they led him through.

"My wig!" he said, when he rose, gasping and puffing, into open water at the farther end. "It was a long dive, but it was worth it."

The sea cows had separated and were browsing lazily along the edges of the finest beaches that Kotick had ever seen. They were long stretches of smooth-worn rock running for miles, exactly fitted to make seal nurseries, and there were playgrounds of hard sand sloping inland behind them, and there were rollers for seals to dance in, and long grass to roll in, and sand dunes to climb up and down, and best of all, Kotick knew by the feel of the water, which never deceives a true sea catch, that no men had ever come there.

The first thing he did was to assure himself that the fishing was good, and then he swam along the beaches and counted up the delightful low sandy islands half hidden in the beautiful rolling fog. Away to the northward, out to sea, ran a line of bars and shoals and rocks that would never let a ship come within six miles of the beach, and between the islands and the mainland was a stretch of deep water that ran up to the perpendicular cliffs, and somewhere below the cliffs was the mouth of the tunnel.

"It's Novastoshnah over again, but ten times better," said Kotick. "Sea Cow must be wiser than I thought. Men can't come down the cliffs, even if there were any men; and the shoals to seaward would knock a ship to splinters. If any place in the sea is safe, this is it."

He began to think of the seal he had left behind him, but though he was in a hurry to go back to Novastoshnah, he thoroughly explored the new country, so that the would be able to answer all questions.

Then he dived and made sure of the mouth of the tunnel, and raced through to the southward. No one but a sea cow or a seal would have dreamed of there being such a place, and when he looked back at the cliffs even Kotick could hardly believe that he had been there.

He was ten days going home, though he was not swimming slowly; and when he hauled out just above Sea Lion's Neck the first person he met was the seal who had been waiting for him, and she saw by the look in his eyes that he had found his island at last.

But the holluschickie and Sea Catch, his father, and all the other seals laughed at him when he told them what he had discovered, and a young seal about his own age said, "This is all very well, Kotick, but you can't come from no one knows where and order us off like this. Remember *we*'ve been fighting for our nurseries, and that's a thing you never did. You preferred prowling about in the sea." The other seals laughed at this, and the young seal began twisting his head from side to side. He had just married that year, and was making a great fuss about it.

"I've no nursery to fight for," said Kotick. "I only want to show you all a place where you will be safe. What's the use of fighting?"

"Oh, if you're trying to back out, of course I've no more to say," said the young seal with an ugly chuckle.

"Will you come with me if I win?" said Kotick. And a green light came into his eye, for he was very angry at having to fight at all.

"Very good," said the young seal carelessly. "*If* you win, I'll come."

He had no time to change his mind, for Kotick's head was out and his teeth sunk in the blubber of the young seal's neck. Then he threw himself back on his haunches and hauled his enemy down the beach, shook him, and knocked him over. Then Kotick roared to the seals: "I've done my best for you these five seasons past. I've found you the island where you'll be safe, but unless your heads are dragged off your silly necks you won't believe. I'm going to teach you now. Look out for yourselves!"

Limmershin told me that never in his life—and Limmershin sees ten thousand big seals fighting every year—never in all his little life did he see anything like Kotick's charge into the nurseries. He flung himself at the biggest sea catch he could find, caught him by the throat, choked him and bumped him and banged him till he grunted for mercy, and then threw him aside and attacked the next. You see, Kotick had never fasted for four months as the big seals did every year, and his deep-sea swimming trips kept him in perfect condition, and, best of all, he had never fought before.

His curly white mane stood up with rage, and his eyes flamed, and his big dog teeth glistened, and he was splendid to look at. Old Sea Catch, his father, saw him tearing past, hauling the grizzled old seals about as though they had been halibut, and upsetting the young bachelors in all directions; and Sea Catch gave a roar and shouted:

"He may be a fool, but he is the best fighter on the beaches! Don't tackle your father, my son! He's with you!"

Kotick roared in answer, and old Sea Catch waddled in with his mustache on end, blowing like a locomotive, while Matkah and the seal that was going to marry Kotick cowered down and admired their menfolk. It was a gorgeous fight, for the two fought as long as there was a seal that dared lift up his head, and when there were none they paraded grandly up and down the beach side by side, bellowing.

At night, just as the Northern Lights were winking and flashing through the fog, Kotick climbed a bare rock and looked down on the scattered nurseries and the torn and bleeding seals. "Now," he said, "I've taught you your lesson."

"My wig!" said Sea Catch, boosting himself up stiffly, for he was fearfully mauled. "The Killer Whale himself could not have cut them up worse. Son, I'm proud of you, and what's more, *I'll* come with you to your island—if there is such a place."

"Hear you, fat pigs of the sea. Who comes with me to the Sea Cow's tunnel? Answer, or I shall teach you again," roared Kotick.

There was a murmur like the ripple of the tide all up and down the beaches. "We will come," said thousands of tired voices. "We will follow Kotick, the White Seal."

Then Kotick dropped his head between his shoulders and shut his eyes proudly. He was not a white seal any more, but red from head to tail. All the same he would have scorned to look at or touch one of his wounds.

A week later he and his army (nearly ten thousand holluschickie and old seals) went away north to the Sea Cow's tunnel, Kotick leading them, and the seals that stayed at Novastoshnah called them idiots. But next spring, when they all met off the fishing banks of the Pacific, Kotick's seals told such tales of the new beaches beyond Sea Cow's tunnel that more and more seals left Novastoshnah. Of course it was not all done at once, for the seals are not very clever, and they need a long time to turn things over in their minds, but year after year more seals went away from Novastoshnah, and Lukannon, and the other nurseries, to the quiet, sheltered beaches where Kotick sits all the summer through, getting bigger and fatter and stronger each year, while the holluschickie played around him, in that sea where no man comes.

Lukannon

THIS IS A SORT OF SAD SEAL NATIONAL ANTHEM

I met my mates in the morning (and, oh, but I am
old!)
Where roaring on the ledges the summer ground
swell rolled.
I heard them lift the chorus that drowned the
breakers' song—
The Beaches of Lukannon—two million voices
strong.

*The song of pleasant stations beside the salt
lagoons,*
*The song of blowing squadrons that shuffled
down the dunes,*
*The song of midnight dances that churned the sea
to flame—*
*The Beaches of Lukannon—before the sealers
came!*

I met my mates in the morning (I'll never meet
    them more!).
They came and went in legions that darkened all
    the shore.
And o'er the foam-flecked offing as far as voice
    could reach
We hailed the landing parties and we sang them
    up the beach.

*The Beaches of Lukannon—the winter wheat so
    tall,*
*The dripping, crinkled lichens, and the sea fog
    drenching all!*
*The platforms of our playground, all shining
    smooth and worn!*
*The Beaches of Lukannon—the home where we
    were born!*

I met my mates in the morning, a broken, scattered
    band,
Men shoot us in the water and club us on the land;
Men drive us to the Salt House like silly sheep and
    tame,
And still we sing Lukannon—before the sealers
    came.

*Wheel down, wheel down to southward—O
    Gooverooska, go!*

And tell the Deep Sea Viceroys the story of our woe.
Ere, empty as the shark's egg the tempest flings ashore,
The Beaches of Lukannon shall know their sons no more!

"Rikki-Tikki-Tavi"

At the hole where he went in
Red Eye called to Wrinkle Skin.
Hear what little Red Eye saith:
"Nag, come up and dance with death!"

Eye to eye and head to head
    (*Keep the measure, Nag*).
This shall end when one is dead
    (*At thy pleasure, Nag*).
Turn for turn and twist for twist
    (*Run and hide thee, Nag*).
Hah! The hooded Death has missed!
    (*Woe betide thee, Nag!*)

This is the story of the great war that Rikki-tikki-tavi fought single-handed, through the bathrooms of the big bungalow in Segowlee cantonment. Darzee the Tailorbird helped him, and Chuchundra the Muskrat, who never comes out into the middle of the floor, but always creeps round by the wall, gave him advice, but Rikki-tikki did the real fighting.

He was a mongoose, rather like a little cat in his fur and his tail, but quite like a weasel in his head and his habits. His eyes and the end of his restless nose were pink. He could scratch himself anywhere he pleased with any leg, front or back, that he chose to use. He could fluff up his tail till it looked like a bottle brush, and his war cry as he scuttled through the long grass was: *Rikk-tikk-tikki-tikki-tchk!*

One day, a high summer flood washed him out of the burrow where he lived with his father and mother, and carried him, kicking and clucking, down a roadside ditch. He found a little wisp of grass floating there, and clung to it till he lost his senses. When he revived, he was lying in the hot sun on the middle of a garden path, very draggled indeed, and a small boy was saying, "Here's a dead mongoose. Let's have a funeral."

"No," said his mother, "let's take him in and dry him. Perhaps he isn't really dead."

They took him into the house, and a big man picked him up between his finger and thumb and said he was not dead but half choked. So they wrapped him in cotton wool, and warmed him over a little fire, and he opened his eyes and sneezed.

"Now," said the big man (he was an Englishman who had just moved into the bungalow), "don't frighten him, and we'll see what he'll do."

It is the hardest thing in the world to frighten a mongoose, because he is eaten up from nose to tail with curiosity. The motto of all the mongoose family is "Run and find out," and Rikki-tikki was a true mongoose. He looked at the cotton wool, decided that it was not good to eat, ran all round the table, sat up and put his fur in order, scratched himself, and jumped on the small boy's shoulder.

"Don't be frightened, Teddy," said his father. "That's his way of making friends."

"Ouch! He's tickling under my chin," said Teddy.

Rikki-tikki looked down between the boy's collar and neck, snuffed at his ear, and climbed down to the floor where he sat rubbing his nose.

"Good gracious," said Teddy's mother, "and that's a wild creature! I suppose he's so tame because we've been kind to him."

"All mongooses are like that," said her husband. "If Teddy doesn't pick him up by the tail, or try to put him in a cage, he'll run in and out of the house all day long. Let's give him something to eat."

They gave him a little piece of raw meat. Rikki-tikki liked it immensely, and when it was finished he went out into the veranda and sat in the sunshine and fluffed up his fur to make it dry to the roots. Then he felt better.

"There are more things to find out about in this

house," he said to himself, "than all my family could find out in all their lives. I shall certainly stay and find out."

He spent all that day roaming over the house. He nearly drowned himself in the bathtubs, put his nose into the ink on a writing table, and burned it on the end of the big man's cigar, for he climbed up in the big man's lap to see how writing was done. At nightfall he ran into Teddy's nursery to watch how kerosene lamps were lighted, and when Teddy went to bed Rikki-tikki climbed up too. But he was a restless companion, because he had to get up and attend to every noise all through the night, and find out what made it. Teddy's mother and father came in, the last thing, to look at their boy, and Rikki-tikki was awake on the pillow. "I don't like that," said Teddy's mother. "He may bite the child." "He'll do no such thing," said the father. "Teddy's safer with that little beast than if he had a bloodhound to watch him. If a snake came into the nursery now—"

But Teddy's mother wouldn't think of anything so awful.

Early in the morning Rikki-tikki came to early breakfast in the veranda riding on Teddy's shoulder, and they gave him banana and some boiled egg. He sat on all their laps one after the other, because every well-brought-up mongoose always hopes to be a house mongoose some day and have rooms to run about in; and Rikki-tikki's mother (she used to live in the general's house at Segowlee) had carefully told Rikki what to do if ever he came across white men.

Then Rikki-tikki went out into the garden to see what was to be seen. It was a large garden, only half cultivated, with bushes, as big as summerhouses, of Marshal Niel roses, lime and orange trees, clumps of bamboos, and thickets of high grass. Rikki-tikki licked his lips. "This is a splendid hunting ground," he said, and his tail grew bottle-brushy at the thought of it, and he scuttled up and down the garden, snuffing here and there till he heard very sorrowful voices in a thornbush. It was Darzee the Tailorbird and his wife. They had made a beautiful nest by pulling two big leaves together and stitching them up the edges with fibers, and had filled the hollow with cotton and downy fluff. The nest swayed to and fro, as they sat on the rim and cried.

"What is the matter?" said Rikki-tikki.

"We are very miserable," said Darzee. "One of our babies fell out of the nest yesterday and Nag ate him."

"H'm!" said Rikki-tikki, "that is very sad—but I am a stranger here. Who is Nag?"

Darzee and his wife only cowered down in the nest without answering, for from the thick grass at the foot of the bush there came a low hiss—a horrible cold sound that made Rikki-tikki jump back two clear feet. Then inch by inch out of the grass rose up the head and spread hood of Nag, the big black cobra, and he was five feet long from tongue to tail. When he had lifted one-third of himself clear of the ground, he stayed balancing to and fro exactly as a dandelion tuft balances in the wind, and he looked at Rikki-tikki with the wicked snake's eyes that never change their expression, whatever the snake may be thinking of.

"Who is Nag?" said he. "*I* am Nag. The great God Brahm put his mark upon all our people, when the first cobra spread his hood to keep the sun off Brahm as he slept. Look, and be afraid!"

He spread out his hood more than ever, and Rikki-tikki saw the spectacle mark on the back of it that looks exactly like the eye part of a hook-and-eye fastening. He was afraid for a minute, but it is impossible for a mongoose to stay frightened for any length of time, and though Rikki-tikki had never met a live cobra before, his mother had fed him on dead ones, and he knew that all a grown mongoose's business in life was to fight and eat snakes. Nag knew that too and, at the bottom of his cold heart, he was afraid.

"Well," said Rikki-tikki, and his tail began to fluff up again, "marks or no marks, do you think it is right for you to eat fledglings out of a nest?"

Nag was thinking to himself, and watching the least little movement in the grass behind Rikki-tikki. He knew that mongooses in the garden meant death sooner or later for him and his family, but he wanted to get Rikki-tikki off his guard. So he dropped his head a little, and put it on one side.

"Let us talk," he said. "You eat eggs. Why should not I eat birds?"

"Behind you! Look behind you!" sang Darzee.

Rikki-tikki knew better than to waste time in staring. He jumped up in the air as high as he could go, and just under him whizzed by the head of Nagaina, Nag's wicked wife. She had crept up behind him as he was talking, to make an end of him. He heard her savage hiss as the stroke missed. He came down almost across her back, and if he had been an old mongoose he would have known that then was the time to break her back with one bite; but he was afraid of the terrible lashing return stroke of the cobra. He bit, indeed, but did not bite long enough, and he jumped clear of the whisking tail, leaving Nagaina torn and angry.

"Wicked, wicked Darzee!" said Nag, lashing up as high as he could reach toward the nest in the thornbush. But Darzee had built it out of reach of snakes, and it only swayed to and fro.

Rikki-tikki felt his eyes growing red and hot (when a mongoose's eyes grow red, he is angry), and he sat back on his tail and hind legs like a little kangaroo, and looked all round him, and chattered with rage. But Nag and Nagaina had disappeared into the grass. When a snake misses its stroke, it never says anything or gives any sign of what it means to do next. Rikki-tikki did not care to follow them, for he did not feel sure that he could manage two snakes at once. So he trotted off to the gravel path near the house, and sat down to think. It was a serious matter for him.

If you read the old books of natural history, you will find they say that when the mongoose fights the snake and happens to get bitten, he runs off and eats some herb that cures him. That is not true. The victory is only a matter of quickness of eye and quickness of foot—snake's blow against mongoose's jump—and as no eye can follow the motion of a snake's head when it strikes, this makes things much more wonderful than any magic herb. Rikki-tikki knew he was a young mongoose, and it made him all the more pleased to think that he had managed to escape a blow from behind.

It gave him confidence in himself, and when Teddy came running down the path, Rikki-tikki was ready to be petted. But just as Teddy was stooping, something wriggled a little in the dust, and in a tiny voice said: "Be careful. I am Death!" It was Karait, the dusty brown snakeling that lies for choice on the dusty earth; and his bite is as dangerous as the cobra's. But he is so small that nobody thinks of him, and so he does the more harm to people.

Rikki-tikki's eyes grew red again, and he danced up to Karait with the peculiar rocking, swaying motion that he had inherited from his family. It looks very funny, but it is so perfectly balanced a gait that you can fly off from it at any angle you please, and in dealing with snakes this is an advantage.

If Rikki-tikki had only known he was doing a much more dangerous thing than fighting Nag, for Karait is so small, and can turn so quickly, that unless Rikki bit him close to the back of the head, he would get the return stroke in his eye or his lip. But Rikki did not know. His eyes were all red, and he rocked back and forth, looking for a good place to hold. Karait struck out. Rikki jumped sideways and tried to run in, but the wicked little dusty gray head lashed within a fraction of his shoulder, and he had to jump over the body, and the head followed his heels close.

Teddy shouted to the house: "Oh, look here! Our mongoose is killing a snake." And Rikki-tikki heard a scream from Teddy's mother. His father ran out with a stick, but by the time he came up, Karait had lunged out once too far, and Rikki-tikki had sprung, jumped on the snake's back, dropped his head far between his forelegs, bitten as high up the back as he could get hold, and rolled away.

That bite paralyzed Karait, and Rikki-tikki was just going to eat him up from the tail, after the custom of his family at dinner, when he remembered that a full meal makes a slow mongoose, and if he wanted all his strength and quickness ready, he must keep himself thin. He went away for a dust bath under the castor-oil bushes, while Teddy's father beat the dead Karait.

"What is the use of that?" thought Rikki-tikki. "I have settled it all."

And then Teddy's mother picked him up from the dust and hugged him, crying that he had saved Teddy from death, and Teddy's father said that he was a providence, and Teddy looked on with big scared eyes. Rikki-tikki was rather amused at all the fuss, which, of course, he did not understand. Teddy's mother might just as well have petted Teddy for playing in the dust. Rikki was thoroughly enjoying himself.

That night at dinner, walking to and fro among the wineglasses on the table, he might have stuffed himself three times over with nice things. But he remembered Nag and Nagaina, and though it was very pleasant to be patted and petted by Teddy's mother, and to sit on Teddy's shoulder, his eyes would get red from time to time, and he would go off into his long war cry of *"Rikk-tikk-tikki-tikki-tchk!"*

Teddy carried him off to bed, and insisted on Rikki-tikki sleeping under his chin. Rikki-tikki was too well bred to bite or scratch, but as soon as Teddy was asleep he went off for his nightly walk round the house, and in the dark he ran up against Chuchundra the Muskrat creeping around by the wall. Chuchundra is a broken-hearted little beast. He whimpers and cheeps all the night, trying to make up his mind to run into the middle of the room. But he never gets there.

"Don't kill me," said Chuchundra, almost weeping. "Rikki-tikki, don't kill me!"

"Do you think a snake-killer kills muskrats?" said Rikki-tikki scornfully.

"Those who kill snakes get killed by snakes," said Chuchundra, more sorrowfully than ever. "And how am I to be sure that Nag won't mistake me for you some dark night?"

"There's not the least danger," said Rikki-tikki. "But Nag is in the garden, and I know you don't go there."

"My cousin Chua the Rat told me—" said Chuchundra, and then he stopped.

"Told you what?"

"H'sh! Nag is everywhere, Rikki-tikki. You should have talked to Chua in the garden."

"I didn't—so you must tell me. Quick, Chuchundra, or I'll bite you!"

Chuchundra sat down and cried till the tears rolled off his whiskers. "I am a very poor man," he sobbed. "I never had spirit enough to run out into the middle of the room. H'sh! I mustn't tell you anything. Can't you *hear*, Rikki-tikki?"

Rikki-tikki listened. The house was as still as still, but he thought he could just catch the faintest *scratch-scratch* in the world—a noise as faint as that of a wasp walking on a window-pane—the dry scratch of a snake's scales on brickwork.

"That's Nag or Nagaina," he said to himself, "and he is crawling into the bathroom sluice. You're right, Chuchundra; I should have talked to Chua."

He stole off to Teddy's bathroom, but there was nothing there, and then to Teddy's mother's bathroom. At the bottom of the smooth plaster wall there was a brick pulled out to make a sluice for the bath water, and as Rikki-tikki stole in by the masonry curb where the bath is put, he heard Nag and Nagaina whispering together outside in the moonlight.

"When the house is emptied of people," said Nagaina to her husband, "*he* will have to go away, and then the garden will be our own again. Go in quietly, and remember that the big man who killed Karait is the first one to bite. Then come out and tell me, and we will hunt for Rikki-tikki together."

"But are you sure that there is anything to be gained by killing the people?" said Nag.

"Everything. When there were no people in the bungalow, did we have any mongoose in the garden? So long as the bungalow is empty, we are king and queen of the garden; and remember that as soon as our eggs in the melon bed hatch (as they may tomorrow), our children will need room and quiet."

"I had not thought of that," said Nag. "I will go, but there is no need that we should hunt for Rikki-tikki afterward. I will kill the big man and his wife, and the child if I can, and come away quietly. Then the bungalow will be empty, and Rikki-tikki will go."

Rikki-tikki tingled all over with rage and hatred at this, and then Nag's head came through the sluice, and his five feet of cold body followed it. Angry as he was, Rikki-tikki was very frightened as he saw the size of the big cobra. Nag coiled himself up, raised his head, and looked into the bathroom in the dark, and Rikki could see his eyes glitter.

"Now, if I kill him here, Nagaina will know; and if I fight him on the open floor, the odds are in his favor. What am I to do?" said Rikki-tikki-tavi.

Nag waved to and fro, and then Rikki-tikki heard him drinking from the biggest water jar that was used to fill the bath. "That is good," said the snake. "Now, when Karait was killed, the big man had a stick. He may have that stick still, but when he comes in to bathe in the morning he will not have a stick. I shall wait here till he comes. Nagaina—do you hear me?—I shall wait here in the cool till daytime."

There was no answer from outside, so Rikki-tikki knew Nagaina had gone away. Nag coiled himself down, coil by coil, round the bulge at the bottom of the water jar, and Rikki-tikki stayed still as death. After an hour he began to move, muscle by muscle, toward the jar. Nag was asleep, and Rikki-tikki looked at his big back, wondering which would be the best place for a good hold. "If I don't break his back at the first jump," said Rikki, "he can still fight. And if he fights—O Rikki!" He looked at the thickness of the neck below the hood, but that was too much for him; and a bite near the tail would only make Nag savage.

"It must be the head," he said at last; "the head above the hood. And, when I am once there, I must not let go."

Then he jumped. The head was lying a little clear of the water jar, under the curve of it; and, as his teeth met, Rikki braced his back against the bulge of the red earthenware to hold down the head. This gave him just one second's purchase, and he made the most of it. Then he was battered to and fro as a rat is shaken by a dog—to and fro on the floor, up and down, and around in great circles, but his eyes were red and he held on as the body cart-whipped over the floor, upsetting the tin dipper and the soap dish and the flesh brush, and banged against the tin side of the bath.

As he held he closed his jaws tighter and tighter, for he made sure he would be banged to death, and, for the honor of his family, he preferred to be found with his teeth locked. He was dizzy, aching, and felt shaken to pieces when something went off like a thunderclap just behind him. A hot wind knocked him senseless and red fire singed his fur. The big man had been wakened by the noise, and had fired both barrels of a shotgun into Nag just behind the hood.

Rikki-tikki held on with his eyes shut, for now he was quite sure he was dead. But the head did not move, and the big man picked him up and said, "It's the mongoose again, Alice. The little chap has saved *our* lives now."

Then Teddy's mother came in with a very white face, and saw what was left of Nag, and Rikki-tikki dragged himself to Teddy's bedroom and spent half the rest of the night shaking himself tenderly to find out whether he really was broken into forty pieces, as he fancied.

When morning came he was very stiff, but well pleased with his doings. "Now I have Nagaina to settle with, and she will be worse than five Nags, and there's no knowing when the eggs she spoke of will hatch. Goodness! I must go and see Darzee," he said.

Without waiting for breakfast, Rikki-tikki ran to the thornbush where Darzee was singing a song of triumph at the top of his voice. The news of Nag's death was all over the garden, for the sweeper had thrown the body on the rubbish heap.

"Oh, you stupid tuft of feathers!" said Rikki-tikki angrily. "Is this the time to sing?"

"Nag is dead—is dead—is dead!" sang Darzee. "The valiant Rikki-tikki caught him by the head and held fast. The big man brought the bang stick, and Nag fell in two pieces! He will never eat my babies again."

"All that's true enough. But where's Nagaina?" said Rikki-tikki, looking carefully round him.

"Nagaina came to the bathroom sluice and called for Nag," Darzee went on, "and Nag came out on the end of a stick—the sweeper picked him up on the end of a stick and threw him upon the rubbish heap. Let us sing about the great, the red-eyed Rikki-tikki!" And Darzee filled his throat and sang.

"If I could get up to your nest, I'd roll your babies out!" said Rikki-tikki. "You don't know when to do the right thing at the right time. You're safe enough in your nest there, but it's war for me down here. Stop singing a minute, Darzee."

"For the great, the beautiful Rikki-tikki's sake I will stop," said Darzee. "What is it, O Killer of the terrible Nag?"

"Where is Nagaina, for the third time?"

"On the rubbish heap by the stables, mourning for Nag. Great is Rikki-tikki with the white teeth."

"Bother my white teeth! Have you ever heard where she keeps her eggs?"

"In the melon bed, on the end nearest the wall, where the sun strikes nearly all day. She hid them there weeks ago."

"And you never thought it worthwhile to tell me? The end nearest the wall, you said?"

"Rikki-tikki, you are not going to eat her eggs?"

"Not eat exactly, no. Darzee, if you have a grain of sense you will fly off to the stables and pretend that your wing is broken, and let Nagaina chase you away to this bush. I must get to the melon bed, and if I went there now she'd see me."

Darzee was a feather-brained little fellow who could never hold more than one idea at a time in his head. And just because he knew that Nagaina's children were born in eggs like his own, he didn't think at first that it was fair to kill them. But his wife was a sensible bird, and she knew that cobra's eggs meant young cobras later on. So she flew off from the nest, and left Darzee to keep the babies warm, and continue his song about the death of Nag. Darzee was very like a man in some ways.

She fluttered in front of Nagaina by the rubbish heap and cried out, "Oh, my wing is broken! The boy in the house threw a stone at me and broke it." Then she fluttered more desperately than ever.

Nagaina lifted up her head and hissed, "You warned Rikki-tikki when I would have killed him. Indeed and truly, you've chosen a bad place to be lame in." And she moved toward Darzee's wife, slipping along over the dust.

"The boy broke it with a stone!" shrieked Darzee's wife.

"Well! It may be some consolation to you when you're dead to know that I shall settle accounts with the boy. My husband lies on the rubbish heap this morning, but before night the boy in the house will lie very still. What is the use of running away? I am sure to catch you. Little fool, look at me!"

Darzee's wife knew better than to do *that*, for a bird who looks at a snake's eyes gets so frightened that she cannot move. Darzee's wife fluttered on, piping sorrowfully, and never leaving the ground, and Nagaina quickened her pace.

Rikki-tikki heard them going up the path from the stables, and he raced for the end of the melon patch near the wall. There, in the warm litter above the melons, very cunningly hidden, he found twenty-five eggs, about the size of a bantam's eggs, but with whitish skins instead of shells.

"I was not a day too soon," he said, for he could see the baby cobras curled up inside the skin, and he knew that the minute they were hatched they could each kill a man or a mongoose. He bit off the tops of the eggs as fast as he could, taking care to crush the young cobras, and turned over the litter from time to time to see whether he had missed any. At last there were only three eggs left, and Rikki-tikki began to chuckle to himself, when he heard Darzee's wife screaming:

"Rikki-tikki, I led Nagaina toward the house, and she has gone into the veranda, and—oh, come quickly—she means killing!"

Rikki-tikki smashed two eggs, and tumbled backward down the melon bed with the third egg in his mouth, and scuttled to the veranda as hard as he could put foot to the ground. Teddy and his mother and father were there at early breakfast, but Rikki-tikki saw that they were not eating anything. They sat stone-still, and their faces were white. Nagaina was coiled up on the matting by Teddy's chair, within easy striking distance of Teddy's bare leg, and she was swaying to and fro, singing a song of triumph.

"Son of the big man that killed Nag," she hissed, "stay still. I am not ready yet. Wait a little. Keep very still, all you three! If you move I strike, and if you do not move I strike. Oh, foolish people, who killed my Nag!"

Teddy's eyes were fixed on his father, and all his father could do was to whisper, "Sit still, Teddy. You mustn't move. Teddy, keep still."

Then Rikki-tikki came up and cried, "Turn around, Nagaina. Turn and fight!"

"All in good time," said she, without moving her eyes. "I will settle my account with *you* presently. Look at your friends, Rikki-tikki. They are still and white. They are afraid. They dare not move, and if you come a step nearer I strike."

"Look at your eggs," said Rikki-tikki, "in the melon bed near the wall. Go and look, Nagaina!"

The big snake turned half around, and saw the egg on the veranda. "Ah-h! Give it to me," she said.

Rikki-tikki put his paws one on each side of the egg, and his eyes were blood-red. "What price for a snake's egg? For a young cobra? For a young king cobra? For the last—the very last of the brood? The ants are eating all the others down by the melon bed."

Nagaina spun clear round, forgetting everything for the sake of the one egg. Rikki-tikki saw Teddy's father shoot out a big hand, catch Teddy by the shoulder, and drag him across the little table with the teacups, safe and out of reach of Nagaina.

"Tricked! Tricked! Tricked! *Rikk-tck-tck!*"

155

chuckled Rikki-tikki. "The boy is safe, and it was I—I—I that caught Nag by the hood last night in the bathroom." Then he began to jump up and down, all four feet together, his head close to the floor. "He threw me to and fro, but he could not shake me off. He was dead before the big man blew him in two. I did it! *Rikki-tikki-tck-tck!* Come then, Nagaina. Come and fight with me. You shall not be a widow long."

Nagaina saw that she had lost her chance of killing Teddy, and the egg lay between Rikki-tikki's paws. "Give me the egg, Rikki-tikki. Give me the last of my eggs, and I will go away and never come back," she said, lowering her hood.

"Yes, you will go away, and you will never come back. For you will go to the rubbish heap with Nag. Fight, widow! The big man has gone for his gun! Fight!"

Rikki-tikki was bounding all round Nagaina, keeping just out of reach of her stroke, his little eyes like hot coals. Nagaina gathered herself together and flung out at him. Rikki-tikki jumped up and backward. Again and again and again she struck, and each time her head came with a whack on the matting of the veranda and she gathered herself together like a watch spring. Then Rikki-tikki danced in a circle to get behind her, and Nagaina spun round to keep her head to his head, so that the rustle of her tail on the matting sounded like dry leaves blown along by the wind.

He had forgotten the egg. It still lay on the veranda, and Nagaina came nearer and nearer to it, till at last, while Rikki-tikki was drawing breath, she caught it in her mouth, turned to the veranda steps, and flew like an arrow down the path, with Rikki-tikki behind her. When the cobra runs for her life, she goes like a whiplash flicked across a horse's neck. Rikki-tikki knew that he must catch her, or all the trouble would begin again.

She headed straight for the long grass by the thornbush, and as he was running Rikki-tikki heard Darzee still singing his foolish little song of triumph. But Darzee's wife was wiser. She flew off her nest as Nagaina came alone, and flapped her wings about Nagaina's head. If Darzee had helped they might have turned her, but Nagaina only lowered her hood and went on. Still, the instant's delay brought Rikki-tikki up to her, and as she plunged into the rathole where she and Nag used to live, his little white teeth were clenched on her tail, and he went down with her—and very few mongooses, however wise and old they may be, care to follow a cobra into its hole.

It was dark in the hole; and Rikki-tikki never knew when it might open out and give Nagaina room to turn and strike at him. He held on savagely, and stuck out his feet to act as brakes on the dark slope of the hot, moist earth.

Then the grass by the mouth of the hole stopped waving, and Darzee said, "It is all over with Rikki-tikki! We must sing his death song. Valiant Rikki-tikki is dead! For Nagaina will surely kill him underground."

So he sang a very mournful song that he made up on the spur of the minute, and just as he got to the most touching part, the grass quivered again, and Rikki-tikki, covered with dirt, dragged himself out of the hole leg by leg, licking his whiskers. Darzee stopped with a little shout. Rikki-tikki shook some of the dust out of his fur and sneezed. "It is all over," he said. "The widow will never come out again." And the red ants that live between the grass stems heard him, and began to troop down one after the other to see if he had spoken the truth.

Rikki-tikki curled himself up in the grass and slept where he was—slept and slept till it was late in the afternoon, for he had done a hard day's work.

"Now," he said, when he awoke, "I will go back to the house. Tell the Coppersmith, Darzee, and he will tell the garden that Nagaina is dead."

The Coppersmith is a bird who makes a noise exactly like the beating of a little hammer on a copper pot. The reason he is always making it is because he is the town crier to every Indian garden, and tells all the news to everybody who cares to listen. As Rikki-tikki went up the path, he heard his "attention" notes like a tiny dinner gong, and then the steady *"Ding-dong-tock!* Nag is dead— *dong!* Nagaina is dead! *Ding-dong-tock!"* That set all the birds in the garden singing, and the frogs croaking, for Nag and Nagaina used to eat frogs as well as little birds.

When Rikki got to the house, Teddy and Teddy's mother (she looked very white still, for she had been fainting) and Teddy's father came out and almost cried over him; and that night he ate all that was given him till he could eat no more, and went to bed on Teddy's shoulder, where Teddy's mother saw him when she came to look late at night.

"He saved our lives and Teddy's life," she said to her husband. "Just think, he saved all our lives."

Rikki-tikki woke up with a jump, for the mongooses are light sleepers.

"Oh, it's you," said he. "What are you bothering for? All the cobras are dead. And if they weren't, I'm here."

Rikki-tikki had a right to be proud of himself. But he did not grow too proud, and he kept that garden as a mongoose should keep it, with tooth and jump and spring and bite, till never a cobra dared show its head inside the walls.

Darzee's Chant

SUNG IN HONOR OF RIKKI-TIKKI-TAVI

Singer and tailor am I—
    Doubled the joys that I know—
Proud of my lilt to the sky,
    Proud of the house that I sew.
Over and under, so weave I my music—so weave I
    the house that I sew.

Sing to your fledglings again,
    Mother, O lift up your head!
Evil that plagued us is slain,
    Death in the garden lies dead.
Terror that hid in the roses is impotent—flung on
    the dunghill and dead!

Who has delivered us, who?
    Tell me his nest and his name.
Rikki, the valiant, the true,
    Tikki, with eyeballs of flame,
Rikki-tikki-tikki, the ivory-fanged, the hunter with
    eyeballs of flame!

Give him the Thanks of the Birds,
   Bowing with tail feathers spread.
Praise him with nightingale words—
   Nay, I will praise him instead.
Hear! I will sing you the praise of the bottle-tailed
   Rikki, with eyeballs of red!

*(Here Rikki-tikki interrupted, so the rest of the song
is lost.)*

Toomai of the Elephants

I will remember what I was. I am sick of rope and chain.
　I will remember my old strength and all my forest affairs.
I will not sell my back to man for a bundle of sugar cane:
　I will go out to my own kind, and the wood folk in their lairs.

I will go out until the day, until the morning break—
　Out to the wind's untainted kiss, the water's clean caress—
I will forget my ankle ring and snap my picket stake.
　I will revisit my lost loves, and playmates masterless!

Kala Nag, which means Black Snake, had served the Indian Government in every way that an elephant could serve it for forty-seven years, and as he was fully twenty years old when he was caught, that makes him nearly seventy—a ripe age for an elephant.

He remembered pushing, with a big leather pad on his forehead, at a gun stuck in deep mud, and that was before the Afghan War of 1842, and he had not then come to his full strength. His mother Radha Pyari—Radha the Darling—who had been

162

caught in the same drive with Kala Nag, told him, before his little milk tusks had dropped out, that elephants who were afraid always got hurt. Kala Nag knew that that advice was good, for the first time that he saw a shell burst he backed, screaming, into a stand of piled rifles, and the bayonets pricked him in all his softest places. So, before he was twenty-five, he gave up being afraid, and so he was the best-loved and the best-looked-after elephant in the service of the Government of India.

He had carried tents, twelve hundred pounds' weight of tents, on the march in Upper India. He had been hoisted into a ship at the end of a steam crane and taken for days across the water, and made to carry a mortar on his back in a strange and rocky country very far from India, and had seen the Emperor Theodore lying dead in Magdala, and had come back again in the steamer entitled, so the soldiers said, to the Abyssinian War medal.

He had seen his fellow elephants die of cold and epilepsy and starvation and sunstroke up at a place called Ali Musjid, ten years later; and afterward he had been sent down thousands of miles south to haul and pile big balks of teak in the timberyards at Moulmein. There he had half killed an insubordinate young elephant who was shirking his fair share of work.

After that he was taken off timber-hauling, and

employed, with a few score other elephants who were trained to the business, in helping to catch wild elephants among the Garo hills. Elephants are very strictly preserved by the Indian Government. There is one whole department which does nothing else but hunt them, and catch them, and break them in, and send them up and down the country as they are needed for work.

Kala Nag stood ten fair feet at the shoulders, and his tusks had been cut off short at five feet, and bound round the ends, to prevent them splitting, with bands of copper; but he could do more with those stumps than any untrained elephant could do with the real sharpened ones. When, after weeks and weeks of cautious driving of scattered elephants across the hills, the forty or fifty wild monsters were driven into the last stockade, and the big drop gate, made of tree trunks lashed together, jarred down behind them, Kala Nag, at the word of command, would go into that flaring, trumpeting pandemonium (generally at night, when the flicker of the torches made it difficult to judge distances), and, picking out the biggest and wildest tusker of the mob, would hammer him and hustle him into quiet while the men on the backs of the other elephants roped and tied the smaller ones.

There was nothing in the way of fighting that Kala Nag, the old wise Black Snake, did not know, for he had stood up more than once in his time to the charge of the wounded tiger, and, curling up his soft trunk to be out of harm's way, had knocked the springing brute sideways in mid-air with a quick sickle cut of his head, that he had invented all by himself; had knocked him over, and kneeled upon him with his huge knees till the life went out with a gasp and a howl, and there was only a fluffy striped thing on the ground for Kala Nag to pull by the tail.

"Yes," said Big Toomai, his driver, the son of Black Toomai who had taken him to Abyssinia, and grandson of Toomai of the Elephants who had seen him caught, "there is nothing that the Black Snake fears except me. He has seen three generations of us feed him and groom him, and he will live to see four."

"He is afraid of *me* also," said Little Toomai, standing up to his full height of four feet, with only one rag upon him. He was ten years old, the eldest son of Big Toomai, and, according to custom, he would take his father's place on Kala Nag's neck when he grew up, and would handle the heavy iron *ankus*, the elephant goad, that had been worn smooth by his father, and his grandfather, and his great-grandfather.

He knew what he was talking of; for he had been born under Kala Nag's shadow, had played with the end of his trunk before he could walk, had taken him down to water as soon as he could walk, and Kala Nag would no more have dreamed of disobeying his shrill little orders than he would have dreamed of killing him on that day when Big Toomai carried the little brown baby under Kala Nag's tusks, and told him to salute his master that was to be.

"Yes," said Little Toomai, "he is afraid of *me*," and he took long strides up to Kala Nag, called him a fat old pig, and made him lift up his feet one after the other.

"Wah!" said Little Toomai, "thou art a big elephant," and he wagged his fluffy head, quoting his father. "The Government may pay for elephants, but they belong to us mahouts. When thou art old, Kala Nag, there will come some rich rajah, and he will buy thee from the Government, on account of thy size and thy manners, and then thou wilt have nothing to do but to carry gold earrings in thy ears, and a gold howdah on thy back, and a red cloth covered with gold on thy sides, and walk at the head of the processions of the king. Then I shall sit on thy neck, O Kala Nag, with a silver *ankus,* and men will run before us with golden sticks, crying, 'Room for the king's elephant!' That will be good, Kala Nag, but not so good as this hunting in the jungles."

"Umph!" said Big Toomai. "Thou art a boy, and as wild as a buffalo calf. This running up and down among the hills is not the best Government service. I am getting old, and I do not love wild elephants. Give me brick elephant lines, one stall to each elephant, and big stumps to tie them to safely, and flat, broad roads to exercise upon, instead of this come-and-go camping. Aha, the Cawnpore barracks were good. There was a bazaar close by, and only three hours' work a day."

Little Toomai remembered the Cawnpore elephant lines and said nothing. He very much preferred the camp life, and hated those broad, flat roads, with the daily grubbing for grass in the forage reserve, and the long hours when there was nothing to do except to watch Kala Nag fidgeting in his pickets. What Little Toomai liked was to scramble up bridle paths that only an elephant could take; the dip in the valley below; the glimpses of the wild elephants browsing miles away; the rush of the frightened pig and peacock under Kala Nag's feet; the blinding warm rains, when all the hills and valleys smoked; the beautiful misty mornings when nobody knew where they would camp that night; the steady, cautious drive of the wild elephants, and the mad rush and blaze and hullabaloo of the last night's drive, when the elephants poured into the stockade like boulders in a landslide, found that they could not get out, and flung themselves at the heavy posts only to be driven back by yells and flaring torches and volleys of blank cartridge.

Even a little boy could be of use there, and Toomai was as useful as three boys. He would get his torch and wave it, and yell with the best. But the really good time came when the driving out began, and the Keddah, that is, the stockade, looked like a picture of the end of the world, and men had to make signs to one another, because they could not hear themselves speak. Then Little Toomai would climb up to the top of one of the quivering stockade posts, his sun-bleached brown hair flying loose all over his shoulders, and he looking like a goblin in the torchlight. And as soon as there was a lull you could hear his high-pitched yells of encouragement to Kala Nag, above the trumpeting and crashing, and snapping of ropes, and groans of the tethered elephants. *"Maîl, maîl, Kala Nag!* (Go on, go on, Black Snake!) *Dant do!* (Give him the tusk!) *Somalo! Somalo!* (Careful, careful) *Maro! Mar!* (Hit him, hit him!) Mind the post! *Arré! Arré! Hai! Yai! Kya-a-ah!"* he would shout, and the big fight between Kala Nag and the wild elephant would sway to and fro across the Keddah, and the old elephant catchers would wipe the sweat out of their eyes, and find time to nod to Little Toomai wriggling with joy on the top of the posts.

He did more than wriggle. One night he slid down from the post and slipped in between the elephants and threw up the loose end of a rope, which had dropped, to a driver who was trying to get a purchase on the leg of a kicking young calf (calves always give more trouble than full-grown animals). Kala Nag saw him, caught him in his trunk, and handed him up to Big Toomai, who slapped him then and there, and put him back on the post.

Next morning he gave him a scolding and said, "Are not good brick elephant lines and a little tent carrying enough, that thou must needs go elephant catching on thy own account, little worthless? Now those foolish hunters, whose pay is less than my pay, have spoken to Petersen Sahib of the matter."

Little Toomai was frightened. He did not know much of white men, but Petersen Sahib was the greatest white man in the world to him. He was the head of all the Keddah operations—the man who caught all the elephants for the Government of India, and who knew more about the ways of elephants than any living man.

"What—what will happen?" said Little Toomai.

"Happen! The worst that can happen. Petersen Sahib is a madman. Else why should he go hunting these wild devils? He may even require thee to be an elephant catcher, to sleep anywhere in these fever-filled jungles, and at last to be trampled to death in the Keddah. It is well that this nonsense ends safely. Next week the catching is over, and we of the plains are sent back to our stations. Then we will march on smooth roads, and forget all this hunting. But, Son, I am angry that thou shouldst meddle in the business that belongs to these dirty Assamese jungle folk. Kala Nag will obey none but me, so I must go with him into the Keddah, but he is only a fighting elephant, and he does not help to rope them. So I sit at my ease, as befits a mahout—not a mere hunter—a mahout, I say, and a man who gets a pension at the end of his service. Is the family of Toomai of the Elephants to be trodden underfoot in the dirt of a Keddah? Bad one! Wicked one! Worthless son! Go and wash Kala Nag and attend to his ears, and see that there are no thorns in his feet. Or else Petersen Sahib will surely catch thee and make thee a wild hunter—a follower of elephant's foot tracks, a jungle bear. Bah! Shame! Go!"

Little Toomai went off without saying a word, but he told Kala Nag all his grievances while he was examining his feet. "No matter," said Little Toomai, turning up the fringe of Kala Nag's huge right ear. "They have said my name to Petersen Sahib, and perhaps—and perhaps—and perhaps—who knows? Hai! That is a big thorn that I have pulled out!"

The next few days were spent in getting the elephants together, in walking the newly caught wild elephants up and down between a couple of tame ones to prevent them giving too much trouble on the downward march to the plains, and in taking stock of the blankets and ropes and things that had been worn out or lost in the forest.

Petersen Sahib came in on his clever she-elephant Pudmini. He had been paying off other camps among the hills, for the season was coming to an end, and there was a native clerk sitting at a table under a tree, to pay the drivers their wages. As each man was paid he went back to his elephant, and joined the line that stood ready to start. The catchers, and hunters, and beaters, the men of the regular Keddah, who stayed in the jungle year in and year out, sat on the backs of the elephants that belonged to Petersen Sahib's permanent force, or leaned against the trees with their guns across their arms, and made fun of the drivers who were going away, and laughed when the newly caught elephants broke the line and ran about.

Big Toomai went up to the clerk with Little Toomai behind him, and Machua Appa, the head tracker, said in an undertone to a friend of his, "There goes one piece of good elephant stuff at least. 'Tis a pity to send that young jungle cock to molt in the plains."

Now Petersen Sahib had ears all over him, as a man must have who listens to the most silent of all living things—the wild elephant. He turned where he was lying all along on Pudmini's back and said, "What is that? I did not know of a man among the plains drivers who had wit enough to rope even a dead elephant."

"This is not a man, but a boy. He went into the Keddah at the last drive, and threw Barmao there the rope, when we were trying to get that young calf with the blotch on his shoulder away from his mother."

Machua Appa pointed at Little Toomai, and Petersen Sahib looked, and Little Toomai bowed to the earth.

"He throw a rope? He is smaller than a picket pin. Little one, what is thy name?" said Petersen Sahib.

Little Toomai was too frightened to speak, but Kala Nag was behind him, and Toomai made a sign with his hand, and the elephant caught him up in his trunk and held him level with Pudmini's forehead, in front of the great Petersen Sahib. Then Little Toomai covered his face with his hands, for he was only a child, and except where elephants were concerned, he was just as bashful as a child could be.

"Oho!" said Petersen Sahib, smiling underneath his mustache, "and why didst thou teach thy elephant *that* trick? Was it to help thee steal green corn from the roofs of the houses when the ears are put out to dry?"

"Not green corn, Protector of the Poor—melons," said Little Toomai, and all the men sitting about broke into a roar of laughter. Most of them had taught their elephants that trick when they were boys. Little Toomai was hanging eight feet up in the air, and he wished very much that he were eight feet underground.

"He is Toomai, my son, Sahib," said Big Toomai, scowling. "He is a very bad boy, and he will end in a jail, Sahib."

"Of course I have my doubts," said Petersen Sahib. "A boy who can face a full Keddah at his age does not end in jails. See, little one, here are four annas to spend in sweetmeats because thou hast a little head under that great thatch of hair. In time thou mayest become a hunter too." Big Toomai scowled more than ever. "Remember, though, that Keddahs are not good for children to play in," Petersen Sahib went on.

"Must I never go there, Sahib?" said Little Toomai with a big gasp.

"Yes." Petersen Sahib smiled again. "When thou hast seen the elephants dance. That is the proper time. Come to me when thou hast seen the elephants dance, and then I will let thee go into all the Keddahs."

There was another roar of laughter, for that is an old joke among elephant catchers, and it means just never. There are great cleared flat places hidden away in the forests that are called elephants' ballrooms, but even these are only found by accident, and no man has ever seen the elephants dance. When a driver boasts of his skill and bravery the other drivers say, "And when didst *thou* see the elephants dance?"

Kala Nag put Little Toomai down, and he bowed to the earth again and went away with his father, and gave the silver four-anna piece to his mother, who was nursing his baby brother, and they all were put up on Kala Nag's back, and the line of grunting, squealing elephants rolled down the hill path to the plains. It was a very lively march on account of the new elephants, who gave trouble at every ford, and needed coaxing or beating every other minute.

Big Toomai prodded Kala Nag spitefully, for he was very angry, but Little Toomai was too happy to speak. Petersen Sahib had noticed him, and given him money, so he felt as a private soldier would feel if he had been called out of the ranks and praised by his commander-in-chief.

"What did Petersen Sahib mean by the elephant dance?" he said, at last, softly to his mother.

Big Toomai heard him and grunted. "That thou shouldst never be one of these hill buffaloes of trackers. *That* was what he meant. Oh, you in front, what is blocking the way?"

An Assamese driver, two or three elephants ahead, turned round angrily, crying: "Bring up Kala Nag, and knock this youngster of mine into good behavior. Why should Petersen Sahib have chosen *me* to go down with you donkeys of the rice fields? Lay your beast alongside, Toomai, and let him prod with his tusks. By all the Gods of the Hills, these new elephants are possessed, or else they can smell their companions in the jungle."

Kala Nag hit the new elephant in the ribs and knocked the wind out of him, as Big Toomai said, "We have swept the hills of wild elephants at the last catch. It is only your carelessness in driving. Must I keep order along the whole line?"

"Hear him!" said the other driver. "*We* have swept the hills! Ho! Ho! You are very wise, you plains people. Anyone but a mudhead who never saw the jungle would know that *they* know that the drives are ended for the season. Therefore all the wild elephants tonight will—but why should I waste wisdom on a river turtle?"

"What will they do?" Little Toomai called out.

"*Ohé*, little one. Art thou there? Well, I will tell thee, for thou hast a cool head. They will dance, and it behooves thy father, who has swept *all* the hills of *all* the elephants, to double chain his pickets tonight."

"What talk is this?" said Big Toomai. "For forty years, father and son, we have tended elephants, and we have never heard such moonshine about dances."

"Yes, but a plainsman who lives in a hut knows only the four walls of his hut. Well, leave thy elephants unshackled tonight and see what comes. As for their dancing, I have seen the place where—*Bapree bap!* How many windings has the Dihang River? Here is another ford, and we must swim the calves. Stop still, you behind there."

And in this way, talking and wrangling and splashing through the rivers, they made their first march to a sort of receiving camp for the new elephants. But they lost their tempers long before they got there.

Then the elephants were chained by their hind legs to their big stumps of pickets, and extra ropes were fitted to the new elephants, and the fodder was piled before them, and the hill drivers went back to Petersen Sahib through the afternoon light, telling the plains drivers to be extra careful that night, and laughing when the plains drivers asked the reason.

Little Toomai attended to Kala Nag's supper, and as evening fell, wandered through the camp, unspeakably happy, in search of a tom-tom. When an Indian child's heart is full, he does not run about and make a noise in an irregular fashion. He sits down to a sort of revel all by himself. And Little Toomai had been spoken to by Petersen Sahib! If he had not found what he wanted, I believe he would have been ill.

But the sweetmeat seller in the camp lent him a little tom-tom—a drum beaten with the flat of the hand—and he sat down, cross-legged, before Kala Nag as the stars began to come out, the tom-tom in his lap, and he thumped and he thumped and he thumped, and the more he thought of the great honor that had been done to him, the more he thumped, all alone among the elephant fodder. There was no tune and no words, but the thumping made him happy.

The new elephants strained at their ropes, and squealed and trumpeted from time to time, and he could hear his mother in the camp hut putting his small brother to sleep with an old, old song about the great God Shiv, who once told all the animals what they should eat. It is a very soothing lullaby, and the first verse says:

Shiv, who poured the harvest and made the winds
    to blow,
Sitting at the doorways of a day of long ago,
Gave to each his portion, food and toil and fate,
From the King upon the *guddee* to the Beggar at
    the gate.
    All things made he—Shiva the Preserver.
Mahadeo! Mahadeo! He made all—
Thorn for the camel, fodder for the kine,
And mother's heart for sleepyhead, O little son of
    mine!

Little Toomai came in with a joyous *tunk-a-tunk* at the end of each verse, till he felt sleepy and stretched himself on the fodder at Kala Nag's side. At last the elephants began to lie down one after another as is their custom, till only Kala Nag at the right of the line was left standing up; and he rocked slowly from side to side, his ears put forward to listen to the night wind as it blew very slowly across the hills. The air was full of all the night noises that, taken together, make one big silence—the click of one bamboo stem against the other, the rustle of something alive in the undergrowth, the scratch and squawk of a half-waked bird (birds are awake in the night much more often than we imagine), and the fall of water ever so far away.

Little Toomai slept for some time, and when he waked it was brilliant moonlight, and Kala Nag was still standing up with his ears cocked. Little Toomai turned, rustling in the fodder, and watched the curve of his big back against half the stars in heaven, and while he watched he heard, so far away that it sounded no more than a pinhole of noise pricked through the stillness, the "hoot-toot" of a wild elephant.

All the elephants in the lines jumped up as if they had been shot, and their grunts at last waked the sleeping mahouts, and they came out and drove in the picket pegs with big mallets, and tightened this rope and knotted that till all was quiet. One new elephant had nearly grubbed up his picket, and Big Toomai took off Kala Nag's leg chain and shackled that elephant forefoot to hindfoot, but slipped a loop of grass string round Kala Nag's leg, and told him to remember that he was tied fast. He knew that he and his father and his grandfather had done the very same thing hundreds of times before. Kala Nag did not answer to the order by gurgling, as he usually did. He stood still, looking out across the moonlight, his head a little raised and his ears spread out like fans, up to the great folds of the Garo hills.

"Tend to him if he grows restless in the night," said Big Toomai to Little Toomai, and he went into the hut and slept. Little Toomai was just going to sleep, too, when he heard the coir string snap with a little "ting," and Kala Nag rolled out of his pickets as slowly and as silently as a cloud rolls out of the mouth of a valley. Little Toomai pattered after him barefooted, down the road in the moonlight, calling under his breath, "Kala Nag! Kala Nag! Take me with you, O Kala Nag!" The elephant turned, without a sound, took three strides back to the boy in the moonlight, put down his trunk, swung him up to his neck, and almost before Little Toomai had settled his knees, slipped into the forest.

There was one blast of furious trumpeting from

the lines, and then the silence shut down on everything, and Kala Nag began to move. Sometimes a tuft of high grass washed along his sides as a wave washes along the sides of a ship, and sometimes a cluster of wild-pepper vines would scrape along his back, or a bamboo would creak where his shoulder touched it. But between those times he moved absolutely without any sound, drifting through the thick Garo forest as though it had been smoke. He was going uphill, but though Little Toomai watched the stars in the rifts of the trees, he could not tell in what direction.

Then Kala Nag reached the crest of the ascent and stopped for a minute, and Little Toomai could see the tops of the trees lying all speckled and furry under the moonlight for miles and miles, and the blue-white mist over the river in the hollow. Toomai leaned forward and looked, and he felt that the forest was awake below him— awake and alive and crowded.

A big brown fruit-eating bat brushed past his ear; a porcupine's quills rattled in the thicket; and in the darkness between the tree stems he heard a hog bear digging hard in the moist warm earth, and snuffing as it digged. Then the branches closed over his head again, and Kala Nag began to go down into the valley—not quietly this time, but as a runaway gun goes down a steep bank—in one rush. The huge limbs moved as steadily as pistons, eight feet to each stride, and the wrinkled skin of the elbow points rustled. The undergrowth on either side of him ripped with a noise like torn canvas, and the saplings that he heaved away right and left with his shoulders sprang back again and banged him on the flank, and great trails of creepers, all matted together, hung from his tusks as he threw his head from side to side and plowed out his pathway.

Then Little Toomai laid himself down close to the great neck lest a swinging bough should sweep him to the ground, and he wished that he were back in the the lines again. The grass began to get squashy, and Kala Nag's feet sucked and squelched as he put them down, and the night mist at the bottom of the valley chilled Little Toomai. There was a splash and a trample, and the rush of running water, and Kala Nag strode through the bed of a river, feeling his way at each step.

Above the noise of the water, as it swirled round the elephant's legs, Little Toomai could hear more splashing and some trumpeting both upstream and down—great grunts and angry snortings, and all the mist about him seemed to be full of rolling, wavy shadows.

"*Ai!*" he said, half aloud, his teeth chattering. "The elephant folk are out tonight. It *is* the dance, then!"

Kala Nag swashed out of the water, blew his

trunk clear, and began another climb. But this time he was not alone, and he had not to make his path. That was made already, six feet wide, in front of him, where the bent jungle grass was trying to recover itself and stand up. Many elephants must have gone that way only a few minutes before. Little Toomai looked back, and behind him a great wild tusker with his little pig's eyes glowing like hot coals was just lifting himself out of the misty river.

Then the trees closed up again, and they went on and up, with trumpetings and crashings, and the sound of breaking branches on every side of them. At last Kala Nag stood still between two tree trunks at the very top of the hill. They were part of a circle of trees that grew round an irregular space of some three or four acres, and in all that space, as Little Toomai could see, the ground had been trampled down as hard as a brick floor. Some trees grew in the center of the clearing, but their bark was rubbed away, and the white wood beneath showed all shiny and polished in the patches of moonlight. There were creepers hanging from the upper branches, and the bells of the flowers of the creepers, great waxy white things like convolvuluses, hung down fast asleep. But within the limits of the clearing there was not a single blade of green—nothing but the trampled earth.

The moonlight showed it all iron gray, except

where some elephants stood upon it, and their shadows were inky black. Little Toomai looked, holding his breath, with his eyes starting out of his head, and as he looked, more and more and more elephants swung out into the open from between the tree trunks. Little Toomai could only count up to ten, and he counted again and again on his fingers till he lost count of the tens, and his head began to swim. Outside the clearing he could hear them crashing in the undergrowth as they worked their way up the hillside, but as soon as they were within the circle of the tree trunks they moved like ghosts.

There were white-tusked wild males, with fallen leaves and nuts and twigs lying in the wrinkles of their necks and the folds of their ears; fat, slow-footed she-elephants, with restless, little pinky black calves only three or four feet high running under their stomachs; young elephants with their tusks just beginning to show, and very proud of them; lanky, scraggy old-maid elephants, with their hollow anxious faces, and trunks like rough bark; savage old bull elephants, scarred from shoulder to flank with great weals and cuts of bygone fights, and the caked dirt of their solitary mud baths dropping from their shoulders; and there was one with a broken tusk and the marks of the full-stroke, the terrible drawing scrape, of a tiger's claws on his side.

They were standing head to head, or walking to and fro across the ground in couples, or rocking and swaying all by themselves—scores and scores of elephants. Toomai knew that so long as he lay still on Kala Nag's neck nothing would happen to him, for even in the rush and scramble of a Keddah drive a wild elephant does not reach up with his trunk and drag a man off the neck of a tame elephant. And these elephants were not thinking of men that night.

Once they started and put their ears forward when they heard the chinking of a leg iron in the forest, but it was Pudmini, Petersen Sahib's pet elephant, her chain snapped short off, grunting, snuffling up the hillside. She must have broken her pickets and come straight from Petersen Sahib's camp; and Little Toomai saw another elephant, one that he did not know, with deep rope galls on his back and breast. He, too, must have run away from some camp in the hills about.

At last there was no sound of any more elephants moving in the forest, and Kala Nag rolled out from his station between the trees and went into the middle of the crowd, clucking and gurgling, and all the elephants began to talk in their own tongue, and to move about. Still lying down, Little Toomai looked down upon scores and scores of broad backs, and wagging ears, and tossing trunks, and little rolling eyes. He heard the click of tusks as they crossed other tusks by accident, and the dry rustle of trunks twined together, and the chafing of enormous sides and shoulders in the crowd, and the incessant flick and *hissh* of the great tails.

Then a cloud came over the moon, and he sat in black darkness. But the quiet, steady hustling and pushing and gurgling went on just the same. He knew that there were elephants all round Kala Nag, and that there was no chance of backing him out of the assembly; so he set his teeth and shivered. In a Keddah at least there was torchlight and shouting, but here he was all alone in the dark, and once a trunk came up and touched him on the knee. Then an elephant trumpeted, and they all took it up for five or ten terrible seconds. The dew from the trees above spattered down like rain on the unseen backs, and a dull booming noise began, not very loud at first, and Little Toomai could not tell what it was. But it grew and grew, and Kala Nag lifted up one forefoot and then the other, and brought them down on the ground—one-two, one-two, as steadily as trip hammers.

The elephants were stamping all together now, and it sounded like a war drum beaten at the mouth of a cave. The dew fell from the trees till there was no more left to fall, and the booming went on, and the ground rocked and shivered, and

Little Toomai put his hands up to his ears to shut out the sound. But it was all one gigantic jar that ran through him—this stamp of hundreds of heavy feet on the raw earth. Once or twice he could feel Kala Nag and all the others surge forward a few strides, and the thumping would change to the crushing sound of juicy green things being bruised, but in a minute or two the boom of feet on hard earth began again.

A tree was creaking and groaning somewhere near him. He put out his arm and felt the bark, but Kala Nag moved forward, still tramping, and he could not tell where he was in the clearing. There was no sound from the elephants, except once, when two or three little calves squeaked together. Then he heard a thump and a shuffle, and the booming went on. It must have lasted fully two hours, and Little Toomai ached in every nerve, but he knew by the smell of the night air that the dawn was coming.

The morning broke in one sheet of pale yellow behind the green hills, and the booming stopped with the first ray, as though the light had been an order. Before Little Toomai had got the ringing out of his head, before even he had shifted his position, there was not an elephant in sight except Kala Nag, Pudmini, and the elephant with the rope galls, and there was neither sign nor rustle nor whisper down the hillsides to show where the others had gone. Little Toomai stared again and again. The clearing, as he remembered it, had grown in the night. More trees stood in the middle of it, but the undergrowth and the jungle grass at the sides had been rolled back. Little Toomai stared once more. Now he understood the trampling. The elephants had stamped out more room—had stamped the thick grass and juicy cane to trash, the trash into slivers, the slivers into tiny fibers, and the fibers into hard earth.

"Wah!" said Little Toomai, and his eyes were very heavy. "Kala Nag, my lord, let us keep by Pudmini and go to Petersen Sahib's camp, or I shall drop from thy neck."

The third elephant watched the two go away, snorted, wheeled round, and took his own path. He may have belonged to some little native king's establishment, fifty or sixty or a hundred miles away.

Two hours later, as Petersen Sahib was eating early breakfast, his elephants, who had been double chained that night, began to trumpet, and Pudmini, mired to the shoulders, with Kala Nag, very footsore, shambled into the camp. Little Toomai's face was gray and pinched, and his hair was full of leaves and drenched with dew, but he tried to salute Petersen Sahib, and cried faintly: "The dance—the elephant dance! I have seen it, and—I die!" As Kala Nag sat down, he slid off his neck in a dead faint.

But, since native children have no nerves worth

speaking of, in two hours he was lying very contentedly in Petersen Sahib's hammock with Petersen Sahib's shooting coat under his head, and a glass of warm milk, a little brandy, with a dash of quinine, inside of him, and while the old hairy, scarred hunters of the jungles sat three deep before him, looking at him as though he were a spirit, he told his tale in short words, as a child will, and wound up with:

"Now, if I lie in one word, send men to see, and they will find that the elephant folk have trampled down more room in their dance room, and they will find ten and ten, and many times ten, tracks leading to that dance room. They made more room with their feet. I have seen it. Kala Nag took me, and I saw. Also Kala Nag is very leg weary!"

Little Toomai lay back and slept all through the long afternoon and into the twilight, and while he slept Petersen Sahib and Machua Appa followed the track of the two elephants for fifteen miles across the hills. Petersen Sahib had spent eighteen years in catching elephants, and he had only once before found such a dance place. Machua Appa had no need to look twice at the clearing to see what had been done there, or to scratch with his toe in the packed, rammed earth.

"The child speaks truth," said he. "All this was done last night, and I have counted seventy tracks crossing the river. See, Sahib, where Pudmini's leg iron cut the bark of that tree! Yes; she was there too."

They looked at one another and up and down, and they wondered. For the ways of elephants are beyond the wit of any man, black or white, to fathom.

"Forty years and five," said Machua Appa, "have I followed my lord, the elephant, but never have I heard that any child of a man had seen what this child has seen. By all the Gods of the Hills, it is—what can we say?" and he shook his head.

When they got back to camp it was time for the evening meal. Petersen Sahib ate alone in his tent, but he gave orders that the camp should have two sheep and some fowls, as well as a double ration of flour and rice and salt, for he knew that there would be a feast. Big Toomai had come up hotfoot from the camp in the plains to search for his son and his elephant, and now that he had found them he looked at them as though he were afraid of them both.

And there was a feast by the blazing campfires in front of the lines of picketed elephants, and Little Toomai was the hero of it all. And the big brown elephant catchers, and the trackers and drivers and ropers, and the men who know all the secrets of breaking the wildest elephants, passed him from one to the other, and they marked his forehead with blood from the breast of a newly killed jungle cock, to show that he was a forester, initiated and free of all the jungles.

And at last, when the flames died down, and the red light of the logs made the elephants look as though they had been dipped in blood too, Machua Appa, the head of all the drivers of all the Keddahs—Machua Appa, Petersen Sahib's other self, who had never seen a made road in forty years: Machua Appa, who was so great that he had no other name than Machua Appa—leaped to his feet, with Little Toomai held high in the air above his head, and shouted:

"Listen, my brothers. Listen, too, you my lords in the lines there, for I, Machua Appa, am speaking! This little one shall no more be called Little Toomai, but Toomai of the Elephants, as his great-grandfather was called before him. What never man has seen he has seen through the long night, and the favor of the elephant folk and of the Gods of the Jungles is with him. He shall become a great tracker. He shall become greater than I, even I, Machua Appa! He shall follow the new trail, and the stale trail, and the mixed trail, with a clear eye! He shall take no harm in the Keddah when he runs under their bellies to rope the wild tuskers; and if he slips before the feet of the charging bull elephant, the bull elephant shall know who he is and shall not crush him. *Aihai!* my lords in the chains"—he whirled up the line of pickets—"here is the little one that has seen your dances in your hidden places—the sight that never man saw! Give him honor, my lords! *Salaam karo,* my children. Make your salute to Toomai of the Elephants! Gunga Pershad, ahaa! Hira Guj, Birchi Guj, Kuttar Guj, ahaa! Pudmini—thou hast seen him at the dance, and thou too Kala Nag, my pearl among elephants!—ahaa! Together! To Toomai of the Elephants. *Barrao!*"

And at that last wild yell the whole line flung up their trunks till the tips touched their foreheads, and broke out into the full salute—the crashing trumpet peal that only the Viceroy of India hears, the Salaamut of the Keddah.

But it was all for the sake of Little Toomai, who had seen what never man had seen before—the dance of the elephants at night and alone in the heart of the Garo hills!

Shiv and the Grasshopper

THE SONG THAT TOOMAI'S MOTHER SANG
TO THE BABY

Shiv, who poured the harvest and made the winds
    to blow,
Sitting at the doorways of a day of long ago,
Gave to each his portion, food and toil and fate,
From the King upon the *guddee* to the Beggar at
    the gate.
    All things made he—Shiva the Preserver.
    Mahadeo! Mahadeo! He made all—
    Thorn for the camel, fodder for the kine,
    And mother's heart for sleepyhead, O little son of
    mine!

Wheat he gave to rich folk, millet to the poor,
Broken scraps for holy men that beg from door to
    door.
Cattle to the tiger, carrion to the kite,

And rags and bones to wicked wolves without the
    wall at night.
Naught he found too lofty, none he saw too low—
Parbati beside him watched them come and go,
Thought to cheat her husband, turning Shiv to
    jest,
Stole the little grasshopper and hid it in her breast!
  So she tricked him, Shiva the Preserver.
  Mahadeo! Mahadeo! Turn and see.
  Tall are the camels, heavy are the kine,
  But this was Least of Little Things, O little son
    of mine!

When the dole was ended, laughingly she said,
"Master of a million mouths, is not one unfed?"
Laughing, Shiv made answer, "All have had their
    part,
Even he, the little one, hidden 'neath thy heart."
From her breast she plucked it, Parbati the thief,
Saw the Least of Little Things gnawed a new-
    grown leaf.
Saw and feared and wondered, making prayer to
    Shiv,
Who hath surely given meat to all that live.
  All things made he—Shiva the Preserver.
  Mahadeo! Mahadeo! He made all—
  Thorn for the camel, fodder for the kine,
  And mother's heart for sleepyhead, O little son
    of mine!

Servants of the Queen

You can work it out by Fractions or by simple
  Rule of Three,
But the way of Tweedle-dum is not the way of
  Tweedle-dee.
You can twist it, you can turn it, you can plait it
  till you drop,
But the way of Pilly Winky's *not* the way of
  Winkie Pop!

It had been raining heavily for one whole
month—raining on a camp of thirty thousand
men and thousands of camels, elephants, horses,
bullocks, and mules all gathered together at a
place called Rawal Pindi, to be reviewed by the
Viceroy of India. He was receiving a visit from the
Amir of Afghanistan—a wild king of a very wild
country. The Amir had brought with him for a
bodyguard eight hundred men and horses who
had never seen a camp or a locomotive before in
their lives—savage men and savage horses from
somewhere at the back of Central Asia.

Every night a mob of these horses would be sure to break their heel ropes and stampede up and down the camp through the mud in the dark, or the camels would break loose and run about and fall over the ropes of the tents, and you can imagine how pleasant that was for men trying to go to sleep. My tent lay far away from the camel lines, and I thought it was safe. But one night a man popped his head in and shouted, "Get out quick! They're coming! My tent's gone!"

I knew who "they" were, so I put on my boots and waterproof and scuttled out into the slush. Little Vixen, my fox terrier, went out through the other side; and then there was a roaring and a grunting and bubbling, and I saw the tent cave in, as the pole snapped, and begin to dance about like a mad ghost. A camel had blundered into it, and wet and angry as I was, I could not help laughing. Then I ran on, because I did not know how many camels might have got loose, and before long I was out of sight of the camp, plowing my way through the mud.

At last I fell over the tail end of a gun, and by that knew I was somewhere near the artillery lines where the cannon were stacked at night. As I did not want to plouter about any more in the drizzle and the dark, I put my waterproof over the muzzle of one gun, and made a sort of wigwam with two or three rammers that I found, and lay along the tail of another gun, wondering where Vixen had got to, and where I might be. Just as I was getting ready to go to sleep I heard a jingle of harness and a grunt, and a mule passed me shaking his wet ears. He belonged to a screw-gun battery, for I could hear the rattle of the straps and rings and chains and things on his saddle pad.

The screw guns are tiny little cannon made in two pieces, that are screwed together when the time comes to use them. They are taken up mountains, anywhere that a mule can find a road, and they are very useful for fighting in rocky country.

Behind the mule there was a camel, with his big soft feet squelching and slipping in the mud, and his neck bobbing to and from like a strayed hen's. Luckily, I knew enough of beast language—not wild-beast language, but camp-beast language, of course—from the natives to know what he was saying.

He must have been the one that flopped into my tent, for he called to the mule, "What shall I do? Where shall I go? I have fought with a white Thing that waved, and it took a stick and hit me on the neck." (That was my broken tent pole, and I was very glad to know it.) "Shall we run on?"

"Oh, it was you," said the mule, "you and your friends, that have been disturbing the camp? All right. You'll be beaten for this in the morning. But

I may as well give you something on account now."

I heard the harness jingle as the mule backed and caught the camel two kicks in the ribs that rang like a drum. "Another time," he said, "you'll know better than to run through a mule battery at night, shouting 'Thieves and fire!' Sit down, and keep your silly neck quiet."

The camel doubled up camel-fashion, like a two-foot rule, and sat down whimpering. There was a regular beat of hoofs in the darkness, and a big troop horse cantered up as steadily as though he were on parade, jumped a gun tail, and landed close to the mule.

"It's disgraceful," he said, blowing out his nostrils. "Those camels have racketed through our lines again—the third time this week. How's a horse to keep his condition if he isn't allowed to sleep. Who's here?"

"I'm the breech-piece mule of number two gun of the First Screw Battery," said the mule, "and the other's one of your friends. He's waked me up too. Who are you?"

"Number Fifteen, E troop, Ninth Lancers—Dick Cunliffe's horse. Stand over a little, there."

"Oh, beg your pardon," said the mule. "It's too dark to see much. Aren't these camels too sickening for anything? I walked out of my lines to get a little peace and quiet here."

"My lords," said the camel humbly, "we dreamed bad dreams in the night, and we were very much afraid. I am only a baggage camel of the 39th Native Infantry, and I am not as brave as you are, my lords."

"Then why didn't you stay and carry baggage for the 39th Native Infantry, instead of running all round the camp?" said the mule.

"They were such very bad dreams," said the camel. "I am sorry. Listen! What is that? Shall we run on again?"

"Sit down," said the mule, "or you'll snap your long stick-legs between the guns."He cocked one ear and listened. "Bullocks!" he said. "Gun bullocks. On my word, you and your friends have waked the camp very thoroughly. It takes a good deal of prodding to put up a gun bullock."

I heard a chain dragging along the ground, and a yoke of the great sulky white bullocks that drag the heavy siege guns when the elephants won't go any nearer to the firing, came shouldering along together. And almost stepping on the chain was another battery mule, calling wildly for "Billy."

"That's one of our recruits," said the old mule to the troop horse. "He's calling for me. Here, youngster, stop squealing. The dark never hurt anybody yet."

The gun bullocks lay down together and began chewing the cud, but the young mule huddled close to Billy.

"Things!" he said. "Fearful and horrible Things, Billy! They came into our lines while we were asleep. D'you think they'll kill us?"

"I've a very great mind to give you a number one kicking," said Billy. "The idea of a fourteen-hand mule with your training disgracing the battery before this gentleman!"

"Gently, gently!" said the troop horse. "Remember they are always like this to begin with. The first time I ever saw a man (it was in Australia when I was a three-year-old) I ran for half a day, and if I'd seen a camel, I should have been running still."

Nearly all our horses for the English cavalry are brought to India from Australia, and are broken in by the troopers themselves.

"True enough," said Billy. "Stop shaking, youngster. The first time they put the full harness with all its chains on my back I stood on my forelegs and kicked every bit of it off. I hadn't learned the *real* science of kicking then, but the battery said they had never seen anything like it."

"But this wasn't harness or anything that jingled," said the young mule. "You know I don't mind that now, Billy. It was Things like trees, and they fell up and down the lines and bubbled. And my head rope broke, and I couldn't find my driver, and I couldn't find you, Billy, so I ran off with—with these gentlemen."

"H'm!" said Billy. "As soon as I heard the

camels were loose I came away on my own account. When a battery—a screw gun—mule calls gun bullocks gentlemen, he must be very badly shaken up. Who are you fellows on the ground there?"

The gun bullocks rolled their cuds, and answered both together: "The seventh yoke of the first gun of the Big Gun Battery. We were asleep when the camels came, but when we were trampled on we got up and walked away. It is better to lie quiet in the mud than to be disturbed on good bedding. We told your friend here that there was nothing to be afraid of, but he knew so much that he thought otherwise. Wah!"

They went on chewing.

"That comes of being afraid," said Billy. "You get laughed at by gun bullocks. I hope you like it young'un."

The young mule's teeth snapped, and I heard him say something about not being afraid of any beefy old bullock in the world. But the bullocks only clicked their horns together and went on chewing.

"Now, don't be angry after you've been afraid. That's the worst kind of cowardice," said the troop horse. "Anybody can be forgiven for being scared in the night, *I* think, if they see things they don't understand. We've broken out of our pickets, again and again, four hundred and fifty of us, just because a new recruit got to telling tales of whip snakes at home in Australia till we were scared to death of the loose ends of our head ropes."

"That's all very well in camp," said Billy. "I'm not above stampeding myself, for the fun of the thing, when I haven't been out for a day or two. But what do you do on active service?"

"Oh, that's quite another set of new shoes," said the troop horse. "Dick Cunliffe's on my back then, and drives his knees into me, and all I have to do is to watch where I am putting my feet, and to keep my hind legs well under me, and be bridlewise."

"What's bridlewise?" said the young mule.

"By the Blue Gums of the Back Blocks," snorted the troop horse, "do you mean to say that you aren't taught to be bridlewise in your business? How can you do anything, unless you can spin round at once when the rein is pressed on your neck? It means life or death to your man, and of course that's life and death to you. Get round with your hind legs under you the instant you feel the rein on your neck. If you haven't room to swing round, rear up a little and come round on your hind legs. That's being bridlewise."

"We aren't taught that way," said Billy the Mule stiffly. "We're taught to obey the man at our head: step off when he says so, and step in when he says so. I suppose it comes to the same thing. Now, with all this fine fancy business and rearing, which must be very bad for your hocks, what do you *do*?"

"That depends," said the troop horse. "Generally I have to go in among a lot of yelling, hairy men with knives—long shiny knives, worse than the farrier's knives—and I have to take care that Dick's boot is just touching the next man's boot without crushing it. I can see Dick's lance to the right of my right eye, and I know I'm safe. I shouldn't care to be the man or horse that stood up to Dick and me when we're in a hurry."

"Don't the knives hurt?" said the young mule.

"Well, I got one across the chest once, but that wasn't Dick's fault—"

"A lot I should have cared whose fault it was, if it hurt!" said the young mule.

"You must," said the troop horse. "If you don't trust your man, you may as well run away at once. That's what some of our horses do, and I don't blame them. As I was saying, it wasn't Dick's fault. The man was lying on the ground, and I stretched myself not to tread on him, and he slashed up at me. Next time I have to go over a man lying down I shall step on him—hard."

"H'm!" said Billy. "It sounds very foolish. Knives are dirty things at any time. The proper thing to do is to climb up a mountain with a well-balanced saddle, hang on by all four feet and your ears too, and creep and crawl and wriggle along, till you come out hundreds of feet above anyone else on a ledge where there's just room enough for your hoofs. Then you stand still and keep quiet— never ask a man to hold your head, young'un— keep quiet while the guns are being put together, and then you watch the little poppy shells drop down into the treetops ever so far below."

"Don't you ever trip?" said the troop horse.

"They say that when a mule trips you can split a hen's ear," said Billy. "Now and again *per-haps* a badly packed saddle will upset a mule, but it's very seldom. I wish I could show you our business. It's beautiful. Why, it took me three years to find out what the men were driving at. The science of the thing is never to show up against the skyline, because, if you do, you may get fired at. Remember that, young'un. Always keep hidden as much as possible, even if you have to go a mile out of your way. I lead the battery when it comes to that sort of climbing."

"Fired at without the chance of running into the people who are firing!" said the troop horse, thinking hard. "I couldn't stand that. I should want to charge—with Dick."

"Oh, no, you wouldn't. You know that as soon as the guns are in position *they'll* do all the charging. That's scientific and neat. But knives— pah!"

The baggage camel had been bobbing his head to and fro for some time past, anxious to get a word in edgewise. Then I heard him say, as he cleared his throat, nervously:

"I—I—I have fought a little, but not in that climbing way or that running way."

"No. Now you mention it," said Billy, "you don't look as though you were made for climbing or running—much. Well, how was it, old Haybale?"

"The proper way," said the camel. "We all sat down—"

"Oh, my crupper and breastplate!" said the troop horse under his breath. "Sat down!"

"We sat down—a hundred of us," the camel went on, "in a big square, and the men piled our *kajawahs*, our packs and saddles, outside the square, and they fired over our backs, the men did, on all sides of the square."

"What sort of men? Any men that came along?" said the troop horse. "They teach us in riding school to lie down and let our masters fire across us, but Dick Cunliffe is the only man I'd trust to do that. It tickles my girths, and, besides, I can't see with my head on the ground."

"What does it matter who fires across you?" said the camel. "There are plenty of men and plenty of other camels close by, and a great many clouds of smoke. I am not frightened then. I sit still and wait."

"And yet," said Billy, "you dream bad dreams and upset the camp at night. Well, well! Before I'd lie down, not to speak of sitting down, and let a man fire across me, my heels and his head would have something to say to each other. Did you ever hear anything so awful as that?"

There was a long silence, and then one of the gun bullocks lifted up his big head and said, "This is very foolish indeed. There is only one way of fighting."

"Oh, go on," said Billy. "*Please* don't mind me. I suppose you fellows fight standing on your tails?"

"Only one way," said the two together. (They must have been twins.) "This is that way. To put all twenty yoke of us to the big gun as soon as Two Tails trumpets." ("Two Tails" is camp slang for the elephant.)

"What does Two Tails trumpet for?" said the young mule.

"To show that he is not going any nearer to the smoke on the other side. Two Tails is a great coward. Then we tug the big gun all together— *Heya—Hullah! Heeyah! Hullah!* We do not climb like cats nor run like calves. We go across the level plain, twenty yoke of us, till we are unyoked again, and we graze while the big guns talk across the plain to some town with mud walls, and pieces of the wall fall out, and the dust goes up as though many cattle were coming home '

"Oh! And you choose that time for grazing?" said the young mule.

"That time or any other. Eating is always good. We eat till we are yoked up again and tug the gun back to where Two Tails is waiting for it. Sometimes there are big guns in the city that speak back, and some of us are killed, and then there is all the more grazing for those that are left. This is Fate—nothing but Fate. Nonetheless, Two Tails is a great coward. That is the proper way to fight. We are brothers from Hapur. Our father was a sacred bull of Shiva. We have spoken."

"Well, I've certainly learned something tonight," said the troop horse. "Do you gentlemen of the screw-gun battery feel inclined to eat when you are being fired at with big guns, and Two Tails is behind you?"

"About as much as we feel inclined to sit down and let men sprawl all over us, or run into people with knives. I never heard such stuff. A mountain ledge, a well-balanced load, a driver you can trust to let you pick your own way, and I'm your mule. But—the other things—No!" said Billy, with a stamp of his foot.

"Of course," said the troop horse, "everyone is not made in the same way, and I can quite see that your family, on your father's side, would fail to understand a great many things."

"Never you mind my family on my father's

side," said Billy angrily, for every mule hates to be reminded that his father was a donkey. "My father was a Southern gentleman, and he could pull down and bite and kick into rags every horse he came across. Remember that, you big brown Brumby!"

Brumby means wild horse without any breeding. Imagine the feelings of Ormonde if a 'bus horse called him a cocktail, and you can imagine how the Australian horse felt. I saw the white of his eye glitter in the dark.

"See here, you son of an imported Malaga jackass," he said between his teeth, "I'd have you know that I'm related on my mother's side to Carbine, winner of the Melbourne Cup, and where I come from we aren't accustomed to being ridden over roughshod by any parrot-mouthed, pig-headed mule in a popgun pea-shooter battery. Are you ready?"

"On your hind legs!" squealed Billy. They both reared up facing each other, and I was expecting a furious fight, when a gurgly, rumbly voice, called out of the darkness to the right—"Children, what are you fighting about there? Be quiet."

Both beasts dropped down with a snort of disgust, for neither horse nor mule can bear to listen to an elephant's voice.

"It's Two Tails!" said the troop horse. "I can't stand him. A tail at each end isn't fair!"

"My feelings exactly," said Billy, crowding into the troop horse for company. "We're very alike in some things."

"I suppose we've inherited them from our mothers," said the troop horse. "It's not worth quarreling about. Hi! Two Tails, are your tied up?"

"Yes," said Two Tails, with a laugh all up his trunk. "I'm picketed for the night. I've heard what you fellows have been saying. But don't be afraid. I'm not coming over."

The bullocks and the camel said, half aloud, "Afraid of Two Tails—what nonsense!" And the bullocks went on, "We are sorry that you heard, but it is true. Two Tails, why are you afraid of the guns when they fire?"

"Well," said Two Tails, rubbing one hind leg against the other, exactly like a little boy saying a poem, "I don't quite know whether you'd understand."

"We don't, but we have to pull the guns," said the bullocks.

"I know it, and I know you are a good deal braver than you think you are. But it's different with me. My battery captain called me a Pachydermatous Anachronism the other day."

"That's another way of fighting, I suppose?" said Billy, who was recovering his spirits.

"*You* don't know what that means, of course,

but I do. It means betwixt and between, and that is just where I am. I can see inside my head what will happen when a shell bursts, and you bullocks can't."

"I can," said the troop horse. "At least a little bit. I try not to think about it."

"I can see more than you, and I *do* think about it. I know there's a great deal of me to take care of, and I know that nobody knows how to cure me when I'm sick. All they can do is to stop my driver's pay till I get well, and I can't trust my driver."

"Ah!" said the troop horse. "That explains it. I can trust Dick."

"You can put a whole regiment of Dicks on my back without making me feel any better. I know just enough to be uncomfortable, and not enough to go on in spite of it."

"We do not understand," said the bullocks.

"I know you don't. I'm not talking to you. You don't know what blood is."

"We do," said the bullocks. "It is red stuff that soaks into the ground and smells."

The troop horse gave a kick and a bound and a snort.

"Don't talk of it," he said. "I can smell it now, just thinking of it. It makes me want to run—when I haven't Dick on my back."

"But it is not here," said the camel and the

bullocks. "Why are you so stupid?"

"It's vile stuff," said Billy. "I don't want to run, but I don't want to talk about it."

"There you are!" said Two Tails, waving his tail to explain.

"Surely. Yes, we have been here all night," said the bullocks.

Two Tails stamped his foot till the iron ring on it jingled. "Oh, I'm not talking to *you*. You can't see inside your heads."

"No. We see out of our four eyes," said the bullocks. "We see straight in front of us."

"If I could do *that* and nothing else, you wouldn't be needed to pull the big guns at all. If I was like my captain—he can see things inside his head before the firing begins, and he shakes all over, but he knows too much to run away—if I was like him I could pull the guns. But if I were wise as all that I should never be here. I should be a king in the forest, as I used to be, sleeping half the day and bathing when I liked. I haven't had a good bath for a month."

"That's all very fine," said Billy. "But giving a thing a long name doesn't make it any better."

"H'sh!" said the troop horse. "I think I understand what Two Tails means."

"You'll understand better in a minute," said Two Tails angrily. "Now you just explain to me why you don't like this!"

He began trumpeting furiously at the top of his trumpet.

"Stop that!" said Billy and the troop horse together, and I could hear them stamp and shiver. An elephant's trumpeting is always nasty, especially on a dark night.

"I shan't stop," said Two Tails. "Won't you explain that, please? *Hhrrmph! Rrrt! Rrrmph! Rrrhha!*" Then he stopped suddenly, and I heard a little whimper in the dark and knew that Vixen had found me at last. She knew as well as I did that if there is one thing in the world the elephant is more afraid of than another it is a little barking dog. So she stopped to bully Two Tails in his pickets, and yapped round his big feet. Two Tails shuffled and squeaked. "Go away, little dog!" he said. "Don't snuff at my ankles, or I'll kick at you. Good little dog—nice little doggie, then! Go home, you yelping little beast! Oh, why doesn't someone take her away? She'll bite me in a minute."

"Seems to me," said Billy to the troop horse, "that our friend Two Tails is afraid of most things. Now, if I had a full meal for every dog I've kicked across the parade ground I should be as fat as Two Tails nearly."

I whistled, and Vixen ran up to me, muddy all over, and licked my nose, and told me a long tale about hunting for me all through the camp. I never let her know that I understood beast talk, or she would have taken all sorts of liberties. So I buttoned her into the breast of my overcoat, and Two Tails shuffled and stamped and growled to himself.

"Extraordinary! Most extraordinary!" he said. "It runs in our family. Now, where has that nasty little beast gone to?"

I heard him feeling about with his trunk.

"We all seem to be affected in various ways," he went on, blowing his nose. "Now, you gentlemen were alarmed, I believe, when I trumpeted."

"Not alarmed, exactly," said the troop horse, "but it made me feel as though I had hornets where my saddle ought to be. Don't begin again."

"I'm frightened of a little dog, and the camel here is frightened by bad dreams in the night."

"It is very lucky for us that we haven't all got to fight in the same way," said the troop horse.

"What I want to know," said the young mule, who had been quiet for a long time—"what *I* want to know is, why we have to fight at all."

"Because we're told to," said the troop horse, with a snort of contempt.

"Orders," said Billy the Mule, and his teeth snapped.

"*Hukm hai!*" (It is an order!), said the camel with a gurgle, and Two Tails and the bullocks repeated, *"Hukm hai!"*

"Yes, but who gives the orders?" said the recruit mule.

"The man who walks at your head—or sits on your back—or holds the nose rope—or twists your tail," said Billy and the troop horse and the camel and the bullocks one after the other.

"But who gives them the orders?"

"Now you want to know too much, young'un," said Billy, "and that is one way of getting kicked. All you have to do is obey the man at your head and ask no questions."

"He's quite right," said Two Tails. "I can't always obey, because I'm betwixt and between. But Billy's right. Obey the man next to you who gives the order, or you'll stop all the battery, besides getting a thrashing."

The gun bullocks got up to go. "Morning is coming," they said. "We will go back to our lines. It is true that we only see out of our eyes, and we are not very clever. But still, we are the only people tonight who have not been afraid. Good night, you brave people."

Nobody answered, and the troop horse said, to change the conversation, "Where's that little dog? A dog means a man somewhere about."

"Here I am," yapped Vixen, "under the gun tail with my man. You big, blundering beast of a camel you, you upset our tent. My man's very angry."

"Phew!" said the bullocks. "He must be English!"

"Of course he is," said Vixen.

"*Huah! Ouach! Ugh!*" said the bullocks. "Let us get away quickly."

They plunged forward in the mud, and managed somehow to run their yoke on the pole of an ammunition wagon, where it jammed.

"Now you *have* done it," said Billy calmly. "Don't struggle. You're hung up till daylight. What on earth's the matter?"

The bullocks went off into the long hissing snorts that Indian cattle give, and pushed and crowded and slued and stamped and slipped and nearly fell down in the mud, grunting savagely.

"You'll break your necks in a minute," said the troop horse. "What's the matter with Englishmen? I live with 'em."

"They—eat—us! Pull!" said the near bullock. The yoke snapped with a twang, and they lumbered off together.

I never knew before what made Indian cattle so scared of Englishmen. We eat beef—a thing that no cattle driver touches—and of course the cattle do not like it.

"May I be flogged with my own pad chains! Who'd have thought of two big lumps like those losing their heads?" said Billy.

"Never mind. I'm going to look at this man.

Most of the men, I know, have things in their pockets," said the troop horse.

"I'll leave you, then. I can't say I'm overfond of 'em myself. Besides, some men who haven't a place to sleep in are more than likely to be thieves, and I've a good deal of Government property on my back. Come along, young'un, and we'll go back to our lines. Good night, Australia! See you on the parade tomorrow, I suppose. Good night, old Haybale!—try to control your feelings, won't you? Good night, Two Tails! If you pass us on the ground tomorrow, don't trumpet. It spoils our formation."

Billy the Mule stumped off with the swaggering limp of an old campaigner, as the troop horse's head came nuzzling into my breast, and I gave him biscuits, while Vixen, who is a most conceited little dog, told him fibs about the scores of horses that she and I kept.

"I'm coming to the parade tomorrow in my dogcart," she said. "Where will you be?"

"On the left hand of the second squadron. I set the time for all my troop, little lady," he said politely. "Now I must go back to Dick. My tail's all muddy, and he'll have two hours' hard work dressing me for parade."

The big parade of all the thirty thousand men was held that afternoon, and Vixen and I had a good place close to the Viceroy and the Amir of

Afghanistan, with his high, big black hat of astrakhan wool and the great diamond star in the center. The first part of the review was all sunshine, and the regiments went by in wave upon wave of legs all moving together, and guns all in a line, till our eyes grew dizzy. Then the cavalry came up, to the beautiful cavalry canter of "Bonnie Dundee," and Vixen cocked her ear where she sat on the dogcart. The second squadron of the Lancers shot by, and there was the troop horse, with his tail like spun silk, his head pulled into his breast, one ear forward and one back, setting the time for all his squadron, his legs going as smoothly as waltz music.

Then the big guns came by, and I saw Two Tails and two other elephants harnessed in line to a forty-pounder siege gun, while twenty yoke of oxen walked behind. The seventh pair had a new yoke, and they looked rather stiff and tired. Last came the screw guns, and Billy the Mule carried himself as though he commanded all the troops, and his harness was oiled and polished till it winked. I gave a cheer all by myself for Billy the Mule, but he never looked right or left.

The rain began to fall again, and for a while it was too misty to see what the troops were doing. They had made a big half circle across the plain, and were spreading out into a line. That line grew and grew and grew till it was three-quarters of a mile long from wing to wing—one solid wall of men, horses, and guns. Then it came on straight toward the Viceroy and the Amir, and as it got nearer the ground began to shake, like the deck of a steamer when the engines are going fast.

Unless you have been there you cannot imagine what a frightening effect this steady comedown of troops has on the spectators, even when they know it is only a review. I looked up at the Amir. Up till then he had not shown the shadow of a sign of astonishment or anything else. But now his eyes began to get bigger and bigger, and he picked up the reins on his horse's neck and looked behind him. For a minute it seemed as though he were going to draw his sword and slash his way out through the English men and women in the carriages at the back. Then the advance stopped dead, the ground stood still, the whole line saluted, and thirty bands began to play all together. That was the end of the review, and the regiments went off to their camps in the rain, and an infantry band struck up with—

> The animals went in two by two,
> Hurrah!
> The animals went in two by two,
> The elephant and the battery mul',
> and they all got into the Ark
> For to get out of the rain!

Then I heard an old grizzled, long-haired Central Asian chief, who had come down with the Amir, asking questions of a native officer.

"Now," said he, "in what manner was this wonderful thing done?"

And the officer answered, "An order was given, and they obeyed."

"But are the beasts as wise as the men?" said the chief.

"They obey, as the men do. Mule, horse, elephant, or bullock, he obeys his driver, and the driver his sergeant, and the sergeant his lieutenant, and the lieutenant his captain, and the captain his major, and the major his colonel, and the colonel his brigadier commanding three regiments, and the brigadier the general, who obeys the Viceroy, who is the servant of the Empress. Thus it is done."

"Would it were so in Afghanistan!" said the chief, "for there we obey only our own wills."

"And for that reason," said the native officer, twirling his mustache, "your Amir whom you do not obey must come here and take orders from our Viceroy."

Parade Song of the Camp Animals

ELEPHANTS OF THE GUN TEAMS

We lent to Alexander the strength of Hercules,
The wisdom of our foreheads, the cunning of our knees;
We bowed our necks to service: they ne'er were
    loosed again—
Make way there—way for the ten-foot teams
    Of the Forty-Pounder train!

GUN BULLOCKS

Those heroes in their harness avoid a cannon ball,
And what they know of powder upsets them one
    and all;
Then *we* come into action and tug the guns
    again—
Make way there—way for the twenty yoke
    Of the Forty-Pounder train!

CAVALRY HORSES

By the brand on my shoulder, the finest of tunes
Is played by the Lancers, Hussars, and Dragoons,
And it's sweeter than "Stables" or "Water" to
    me—
The Cavalry Center of "Bonnie Dundee!"

Then feed us and break us and handle and groom,
And give us good riders and plenty of room,
And launch us in column of squadron and see
The way of the war horse to "Bonnie Dundee!"

SCREW-GUN MULES

As me and my companions were scrambling up a
    hill,
The path was lost in rolling stones but we went
    forward still,
For we can wriggle and climb, my lads, and turn
    up everywhere,
Oh, it's our delight on a mountain height, with a
    leg or two to spare!

Good luck to every sergeant, then, that lets us pick
    our road;
Bad luck to all the driver-men that cannot pack a
    load;
For we can wriggle and climb, my lads, and turn
    up everywhere,

Oh, it's our delight on a mountain height, with a
    leg or two to spare!

COMMISSARIAT CAMELS

We haven't a camelty tune of our own
To help us trollop along,
But every neck is hair trombone
(*Rtt-ta-ta-ta!* is a hair trombone!)
And this is our marching-song:
Can't! Don't! Shan't! Won't!
Pass it along the line!
Somebody's pack has slid from his back,
Wish it were only mine!
Somebody's load has tipped off in the road—
Cheer for a halt and a row!
Urrr! Yarrh! Grr! Arrh!
Somebody's catching it now!

ALL THE BEASTS TOGETHER

Children of the Camp are we,
Serving each in his degree;
Children of the yoke and goad,
Pack and harness, pad and load.
See our line across the plain,
Like a heel rope bent again,
Reaching, writhing, rolling far,
Sweeping all away to war·

While the men that walk beside,
Dusty, silent, heavy-eyed,
Cannot tell why we or they
March and suffer day by day.
    Children of the Camp are we,
    Serving each in his degree;
    Children of the yoke and goad,
    Pack and harness, pad and load!

About the author:
Rudyard Kipling

In 1865, Rudyard Kipling was born in India to British parents. At the age of six, Kipling was sent to England to be educated. He returned to India when he was seventeen years old, and began working for a newspaper in Lahore.

With the publication of JUST SO STORIES and THE JUNGLE BOOKS, Kipling attracted a large, international audience. These famous children's stories imaginatively describe the jungle and the animal world. Kipling also wrote KIM and "CAPTAINS COURAGEOUS," two adventure stories that are still widely read and enjoyed. Rudyard Kipling was awarded the Nobel prize for literature in 1907.